AN IMPROPER CORRESPONDENCE

JAYNE DAVIS

Verbena Books

Copyediting: Sue Davison

Cover Design: P Johnson

AI: AI has not been used in writing this book or producing the cover.

ACKNOWLEDGEMENTS

Thanks to my critique partners of Scribophile for comments and suggestions: Leslie, Jim, Allison, Royaline and Erin.

Thanks also to my alpha readers Tina, Helen, Georgianna and Kristen, and beta readers Gail, Barbara, Carole, Cilla, Corinne, Dawn, Diane, Doris, Frances, Julie, Karen. Leigh, Lis, Margaret, Mary M, Melanie, Nicky, Safina, Sarah D, Sarah M, and Sue. Particular thanks to Julie for helping me with the French phrases used in the story.

CHAPTER 1

elden Court, Hampshire, August 1812

Joanna Stretton reached for her pencil before recalling that this was Uncle Henry's newspaper she was reading, not Papa's. No matter—she would make a note of the new manufactory proposal in Lancashire and look into the details when they returned to London; it might be a project that Papa would allow her to invest in.

"You should not spend so much time reading the newspapers, Jo," Mama said from her place by the fire. "You are already twenty, and taking an interest in men's things is likely to discourage young men from courting you."

"There's no one to see me here, Mama." And besides, Lord and Lady Yelden—Uncle Henry and Aunt Sarah—already knew she took an interest in Papa's business. But Jo set the paper aside anyway; she was here to keep Mama company. "Shall I read to you for a while?" Mama would probably fall into a doze when Jo was part way through the chapter and she would have to read it to her again next time, but she didn't mind. She could do little else for Mama while she was unwell.

"Sarah tells me she expects George to come down from London

today," Mama said. "Or tomorrow at the latest. I do wish you would try to befriend him while he is here."

This again. "We are already friends, Mama. Besides, Cousin George spends most of his time riding, and I am not a good enough horse-woman to keep up."

Mama sighed. "You would enjoy riding more, I think, had you more practice." She glanced out of the window at the rolling grass and scattered trees of the parkland surrounding Yelden Court. "I do miss having a place in the country, and I used to enjoy house parties so much before I married."

"Papa would have bought a property had you really wished for it." Although it would not have been as grand as Kenton Priory, where Mama and Aunt Sarah had grown up.

"Your father would rarely be at a country estate, so what use would it be? If I were not so unwell, I would be with him now." Mama adjusted her shawl around her shoulders. "Marriage to George might get you the invitations that have been denied to me. There is nothing wrong with first cousins marrying, you know."

"There is, if they think of each other as brother and sister. Besides, he's younger than me, and—"

"He's only younger by a few months, Jo. That does not signify."

It did to Jo; George still had a boyish enthusiasm for sports, and life in general. It was endearing in its way, but not what she wanted in a husband. However, it was no use saying that to Mama. "George has no more wish to marry me than I have to marry him. Mama, why are you so set on him?" Jo waved a hand towards the park beyond the window. "You know Papa will settle enough on me to buy something like this if I do not marry a landed gentleman."

Mama leaned her head against the high back of the chair. "Don't be silly, dear; of course it's not that. But you do not meet any other suit-able young men."

"I have met several very pleasant young men over the last two years, Mama. And all more interested in my future inheritance than in me." Her parents had wanted more children, but over the years several babies had come too far before their time; Mama had never properly

2

recovered from her last disastrous pregnancy. It was now all but certain that Jo would be Papa's sole heiress.

She regretted her sharp tone when she noticed that Mama was suddenly looking more wan than usual, a crease forming between her brows. Then Mama's gaze slid sideways. "Is that someone arriving?"

Walking over to the windows, Jo saw two riders approaching the stables. Her cousin, riding next to a man in a scarlet uniform.

"George has brought a friend." The riders passed out of sight and she turned back to Mama. "I will do my best to spend some time with George while we are here; I cannot promise more than that."

"Thank you, Jo."

"Now, shall I help you to your room? If we are to meet a new acquaintance at dinner, you will need to be well rested."

"That's a good idea. I will feel better when I have had some of my tonic."

Once Mama was settled in her room, Jo read to her until she drifted into a doze, then returned to the parlour to continue her perusal of the newspaper. She enjoyed her visits to Yelden Court but, unlike Mama, did not pine for a country estate—life in Town was much more interesting.

Mama was right about her not meeting many suitable young men, although their ideas of 'suitable' differed. Mama wanted her to marry someone who could give her the entrée into the *ton* that Mama had lost by following her heart rather than family obligations when she married.

Years ago, Papa had visited Kenton Priory to advise the Earl of Kenton on investing some of his considerable wealth, and had been there often enough for him and Lady Frances to fall in love. But the earl did not consider Nathaniel Stretton a suitable son-in-law, as although Papa's grandfather had been a baron, there were no other members of the aristocracy in his family tree. It was only Mama's determination in refusing all her other suitors over four years that had finally made the earl agree to their marriage—although he did not go so far as to welcome Papa and Jo to Kenton Priory.

Mama had become more set on the idea of Jo finding a husband in the ranks of the aristocracy since she became unwell over a year ago, but Jo could not understand why she thought it so important. Jo was in no hurry to wed, but when she did, she wanted it to be a love match like her parents'.

From Mama's stories of her seasons in Town before her marriage, Jo thought that the men she was likely to meet from aristocratic families seemed a frippery lot, devoting their time to gambling or sporting activities. She would prefer a man like Papa. His own investments had made their family wealthy, and those investments also allowed other men to improve their lands, increase their business, or develop inventions. But his activities were too close to being in trade for most of the people of Mama's class. The young men Jo did sometimes encounter who were in Papa's line of business were too busy to spend time at assemblies or soirées. However, spending time with Cousin George, if he were also willing, would be no hardship, as long as it did not lead Mama to hope for a union that would not happen.

She glanced at the clock quietly ticking on the mantelpiece. Aunt Sarah would be taking tea in the drawing room soon; Jo would join her once she had returned the newspaper to Uncle Henry's study. Male voices sounded from above as Jo crossed the entrance hall.

"Jo! Mama said you were still here." George clattered down the stairs, no longer in riding dress, and a wide smile on his face.

His friend followed more slowly behind. The newcomer was taller than George, and broader at the shoulders, with blond hair waving gently above a square-jawed, lightly tanned face. He was older than George, she thought, but only by a couple of years. His eyes met Jo's, and his smile made her breath catch.

"Jo, this is Captain Alfred Bengrove. He has come to stay for a week or so on his way to Portsmouth." George turned to the captain. "Bengrove, my cousin, Miss Stretton."

Captain Bengrove bowed. "I am pleased to make your acquaintance, Miss Stretton." His eyes slid downwards, and she thought a crease briefly formed between his brows. But that impression vanished as he spoke again. "I see you keep up with events in the Peninsula. Most admirable."

Jo was puzzled as she made her curtsey, then dragged her mind away from his blue eyes to the newspaper in her hand; the item on the front page concerned the Marquess of Wellington's activities in Spain. "I'm pleased to meet any friend of George."

George's voice broke the spell of the captain's mesmerising gaze. "Come on, Bengrove. You said you fancied a game of billiards."

Jo blinked as her cousin's guest bowed again and followed George towards the back of the house. She sighed, feeling sadly flat, and headed for the drawing room.

"I met Cousin George's friend earlier," Jo said later, in Mama's room. Halsey, the maid who'd been with Mama since she first went into Society, was pinning a lacy cap over Mama's freshly combed hair. "Captain Bengrove."

Mama's tired expression sharpened. "Bengrove... The name is familiar." She closed her eyes for a moment. "Ah, yes. There is a Viscount Bengrove in the next county to Kenton Priory. He could be some relation."

"He didn't say."

"All finished, ma'am." Halsey stepped back, regarding her mistress critically, then nodded her head.

"Thank you. I will ring when I need you after dinner."

The maid curtseyed and left. Mama turned on the stool. "Run down and fetch a peerage from the library, will you?"

"You could just ask about his family at dinner, Mama," Jo protested.

"You know I try not to do that, dear."

Jo sighed, but did as Mama requested. Such an enquiry often resulted in the same questions being asked of Mama, and there had been several occasions when the answer resulted in a friendly conversation turning into one of brittle and forced politeness when it became clear that Mama had married someone her companions regarded as beneath her.

"Here you are, Mama." Jo turned to the correct page as she reentered her mother's bedroom. "'Viscount Bengrove, of Bengrove Hall in Staffordshire.' You were right about it being in the next county. 'Married 1785…. issue Edmond, born 1787, Alfred, born 1790.'" She closed the book with a snap. "Cousin George introduced him as Alfred."

"A second son," Mama said, as if to herself. "I suppose that would do."

"Now, Mama, do not think to push me at him." Even as Jo protested, she recalled the effect of the captain's smile and thought that she might not mind at least getting to know him better.

"I still think George would be more suitable, dear. He will have a title, after all. But if you insist he will not do, you should not let this opportunity slip."

"No, Mama. Are you ready for dinner?"

Dinner was more lively than usual that evening. Aunt Sarah had invited the local squire and his lady, and Captain Bengrove's presence helped the conversation along. Understandably, he was the centre of attention, and replied to questions about his exploits in the Peninsula with good humour. George and Lydia, the only other of Aunt Sarah's children old enough to dine with them, were enthralled by his tales. George had always said he wished he could buy a commission, but Lord Yelden would not use his influence to get him a place in a good regiment, nor give him the funds required. Jo wondered if the captain's arrival might have the opposite effect to the one Mama wanted; if George spent all his time here with his new friend, Jo would not see much of either of them.

Jo awoke to a sunny morning and went down early to breakfast, as was her habit. Only George and the captain were in the breakfast parlour. They stood as she entered, and the captain drew out a chair for her as the footman poured coffee and served her buttered eggs and toast. Jo had not seen either of them after dinner the previous evening; she had accompanied Mama to her room when the ladies withdrew, and by the time Jo came downstairs after seeing her settled, the gentlemen had retired to the billiards room.

"Yelden promised to show me around the estate," the captain said, when Jo had finished eating. "Would you care to join us, Miss Stretton?"

"Good heavens, no!" George said, before Jo could answer. "She sits on a horse like—" He pressed his lips together.

"A sack of turnips?" Jo asked, managing a smile. "Potatoes?" She'd heard George's opinion of her riding before, and usually wasn't at all offended, as it had some truth in it. But it felt different now he had said it in front of Captain Bengrove.

"Sorry, Jo." He looked shamefaced.

Jo turned to Captain Bengrove. "I *can* ride, Captain, but I am no horsewoman and would only slow you down."

"I would not mind," the captain said with a smile. "I had your cousin's company all the way from London; a prettier companion would be a pleasure."

Jo felt a blush warming her cheeks.

"Oh, very well," George said. "But I warn you, Bengrove, the animal Jo usually uses here is a slug. There's no other word for it."

Jo could think of several: gentle, well mannered, comfortable. But she wasn't going to argue the point with his friend listening. "What time do you set off?"

"Half an hour," George said.

"Whenever you are ready, Miss Stretton. We are not in a hurry." The captain spoke at the same time.

"I will not keep you waiting too long, gentlemen."

Jo rang for her maid, and had already laid her habit out on the bed when Martha arrived. The maid's brows rose. "You're going riding, miss?" Then she gave a happy smile. "That captain is ever so good looking, isn't he?"

Jo felt her cheeks warming again, glad that Martha had gone to fetch her half boots from the closet and could not see her pink cheeks. The captain was indeed handsome, and she found herself taking more care than usual over her appearance. The deep burgundy of the habit and matching hat set off her grey eyes and black hair nicely. If only her hair didn't curl so much, Martha might be able to create more elegant styles.

Martha handed Jo her whip. "You look very fine, miss," she said, with a knowing look in her eyes.

"Thank you." As she descended the stairs, Jo wondered why she'd never seen that expression on Martha's face before. Was it because this was the first time *she* had felt this odd feeling inside—a kind of fluttering in her stomach? The two men awaited her at the foot of the stairs, and the flutterings increased as the captain greeted her with a smile.

Captain Bengrove sat his horse well. Jo admired his figure from behind as George monopolised his attention, pointing out features of the park and parts of the more distant views. The countryside was open here, with gently rolling hills and areas of open land where those inclined could gallop without harming crops. And gallop they did, leaving Jo cantering along behind. But they waited for her at the top of the rise, and she couldn't begrudge them their exhilaration. Perhaps she *should* try to improve her riding.

"My apologies, Miss Stretton," Captain Bengrove said as she reached them, with the same intimate smile that he had bestowed on her yesterday. It had a similar effect now.

"It is no matter, Captain."

"Is this countryside like your home?" he asked, waving a hand at the view before them. "Lead on, George, if you will. I will talk to Miss Stretton for a while."

George shrugged and urged his horse into motion. Jo and the captain followed suit, and the three proceeded together at a leisurely walk.

"You do not live permanently at Yelden Court, I think?" the captain went on.

"No, we live in London. We do not have a country home."

His brows rose a little. "That is a pity. There is so much enjoyment to be had on days like this."

"There is also much of interest in Town." Jo hesitated, but then decided to speak. Better to find out now if Captain Bengrove took the same view as Mama's family of men like her father. "Papa has business interests there. Investments, and the like."

To her relief, he nodded, his expression thoughtful rather than disapproving. "Investors are as necessary as those who get their income from the land. And you, Miss Stretton? What do you enjoy in Town?"

"There are so many things to see and do, Captain. The theatre, museums…" Some of Mama's warnings came back to her—it might be better not to tell him that Papa had recently allowed her to decide on some investments of her own. "And the circulating libraries and shops, of course," she added. "Tell me about your family's home."

"Bengrove Hall is near Cannock Chase, in Staffordshire. There was a Tudor mansion there, but my grandfather tore it down. He built a new house in the Neoclassical style, with columns and entablature in marble from Italy, and had the grounds laid out by Capability Brown." He broke off and laughed. "I sound like a guidebook! I wouldn't know a Neoclassical design from a Palladian, but I can recall my father saying that many times to guests."

His amusement warmed her to him further; she did like people who could laugh at themselves. "Did you not wish to see your family while you were on leave? They must be in the country at this time of year."

He paused briefly before replying. "I saw them while I was in London."

"That was fortunate for you," George put in. "Saved you going all the way to Staffordshire." He turned to Jo. "Bengrove regrets that he missed the battle at Salamanca."

"Indeed. My mother had been unwell, and Father wrote to summon me home. Fortunately, she had recovered by the time I arrived."

"I suppose you will be keen to get back, Captain," Jo said, although she could not understand why men should wish to spend their lives fighting. It seemed an unfortunate necessity to her, rather than something to be desired. "When does your ship sail?"

"In eight days, weather permitting."

"I've invited him to stay the week," George said. "Portsmouth is less than a day away by post chaise."

"I had been in two minds whether to accept." Captain Bengrove turned that devastating smile on Jo again. "But now, I will gladly stay."

Never before had Jo looked forward quite so much to the days ahead.

CHAPTER 2

ne week later
     For Jo, Captain Bengrove's stay had passed too quickly. They had ridden out or taken an excursion every day, as part of a party, or with only a groom for propriety's sake. Jo knew she would remember certain things for a long time: the way he handed her in and out of the carriage on their trips to Winchester and Salisbury, as if she were made of delicate porcelain; his strong fingers weaving a garland of poppies and buttercups for her when they rested their horses at the edge of a wheat field; his smile of sympathy when she made a careless discard at whist, which only served to distract her even more than his presence at the table. He had joined in games of battledore and shuttlecock on the lawn that turned into romps with the younger Yelden children, and even sat with Mama sometimes to keep her company when the others were playing cards.

Now, it was his last day, and the sun was shining. Before she went down to breakfast, Jo tapped on Mama's door and entered when she heard a response. Mama was already sitting up in bed, drinking a cup of tea.

"How are you feeling this morning, Mama?"

"I am feeling well, thank you. Such a pity that the dear captain cannot stay longer."

"The ship will not wait for him, Mama, although I wish it could."

"He seems to like you, Jo. When he has sat with me in the parlour, he talks about how your riding has improved and how much he enjoys your company."

"Yes, Mama." She felt more than liking for him—was this what it felt like to be in love? A kind of breathless excitement when she was with him; looking for him across a room full of people and feeling happy when their eyes met and they shared a smile.

"Your father will wish to check that he is not merely a fortune hunter before your acquaintance goes much further," Mama warned. "However, he seems such an open and honest young man to me; I cannot believe he could be."

Jo felt a sudden doubt; could she have been mistaken in him? "I'm sure he isn't. He has not mentioned Papa's business at all since the first morning, nor said anything that might make me think he is."

"That's all right, then, dear. I will breakfast here, and spend the morning with Sarah. Do not feel you need to keep me company on such a lovely day. Perhaps you should take the opportunity for some more riding practice before the captain leaves?"

"What a subtle hint, Mama! But unnecessary—we will have a last ride around the park with George this afternoon."

On her way downstairs, Jo thought that Papa would want more reassurance than her feeling that the captain was not a fortune hunter. Seeing George about to enter the breakfast parlour ahead of her, she called and drew him aside. "George, what did you tell Captain Bengrove about my family before you came here?"

George's brows rose. "Not much. I might have mentioned that your uncle is an earl, but that's all. Why?"

"Mama said my father will want to be sure he isn't a fortune hunter."

"Not a bit of it! I didn't say a word about that." He clapped her on the shoulder. "Don't worry on that score, Jo."

Relieved, she followed him in to breakfast.

. . .

When the time came for their ride, only Captain Bengrove and a groom were at the stables waiting for her, George having sent apologies just beforehand. The groom mounted a third horse himself, dropping behind as they rode through the park and up to a low hill that provided a view across the green valley beyond. Captain Bengrove turned and gestured to the groom, who stopped while they rode on a little further. Then the captain dismounted, and Jo slid off her own horse.

He stepped closer to her, his gaze intent, and she suddenly found it hard to breathe. "Miss Stretton... may I call you Joanna?"

Her heart racing, she nodded.

"The days I spent here have been some of the most enjoyable in my life."

The feeling in his voice did strange things to her stomach. "I... I have enjoyed the time, too."

"I wish... I..." He cleared his throat. "Will you wait for me, Joanna? This war cannot last forever." He took her hands and gripped them gently. "I never thought I would find a woman with whom I would be happy to spend the rest of my life, not until I met you."

She wanted to reply, but she could only nod again. She had known he liked her, but not that he felt strongly enough to say such a thing.

"I am expected back with my regiment soon, but if you will have me, I will make arrangements to sell my commission. We need not be apart for more than a few months."

She smiled, feeling oddly light. "Oh, Captain—"

"Alfred. Do call me Alfred, my dear."

"Alfred." Their closeness felt even more intimate as she used his name. "This... this is so unexpected." Unexpected, but welcome.

He released her hands and stepped back a little, removing his gloves as he did so. Then he reached for her again and removed hers. His hands were warm when they clasped hers, his fingers making circles on her palms. "A week is long enough for me, Joanna. If it is not long enough for you, then I must wait. Only I fear that some

13

other lucky fellow will earn your favour while I am away doing my duty."

"Oh, no. Of course I will wait for you." What was he asking? For her to wait, or to promise more? The latter would set the course of the rest of her life—it was too quick. "My father... I will... I mean, you will..."

"Forgive me, my dear, but I asked permission from your mother to pay my addresses before leaving the house. I hope you do not mind?"

Jo shook her head. How could she mind? This had all happened so fast she could not take it in. But nothing could be settled until the captain... Alfred... returned from Spain again. It would do no harm to promise to wait until he could get leave again.

"Joanna? Do say yes."

"Yes, Alfred, I will wait for you."

That enticing smile lit up his face again. "Thank you, my dear. You have made me the happiest of men." He lifted her hands and kissed the backs of them. She held her face up to his, wondering if he was going to kiss her mouth, but he cupped one hand on her cheek, then stepped back and shook his head. "It tests me to do no more, Joanna, but I would not dishonour you by going further."

She should have felt reassured rather than disappointed, but he was right. This was not the place for her first kiss—not with one of Uncle Henry's grooms watching. "Shall we ride on?"

They went on, along a route they had taken before, not saying much but exchanging happy smiles. When they returned and dismounted, he took her hands again. "I think it best if we do not tell our news, Joanna. Apart from your mother, of course. I would like my family to know before we tell others."

"Very well." She would like Papa to know first, too. "You will write to me, will you not?"

"How could you doubt it? And you—" But the grooms came to take their horses and there was no more chance for private conversation.

Mama was overjoyed at her news, but agreed that they should not tell anyone else just yet. That evening, Jo found it difficult to keep her mind on the talk around the dinner table and in the parlour afterwards. A shared glance from Alfred was enough to fluster her, and she had to make an effort not to keep looking at him, so she wasn't too sorry when he chose to spend his time after dinner in the billiards room instead of the parlour. Things would be so much easier when everyone knew they were courting.

Jo found it harder still the following morning to stand with the Yeldens on the front steps waving goodbye as Alfred rode away, looking more handsome than ever dressed once again in his scarlet regimentals. She had hoped for a few minutes in private to bid him farewell properly, and had lingered in the breakfast parlour after everyone else had left, but all he managed was a quick squeeze of her hand and an intimate smile before they were interrupted by the footmen and maids coming to clear the table.

She watched from the steps until Alfred disappeared around a bend in the drive, then joined Mama in the parlour.

"I think we should return to Town soon, dear," Mama said.

"Are you feeling well enough?" The journey here had been difficult, even travelling for only a few hours each day, but Papa had thought it worth the risk so that Mama could enjoy the clean Hampshire air and the company of her sister.

"I am feeling very well, Jo. I think it is your happy news—I am so pleased. He is such a pleasant young man, and I can't wait to tell your father all about him."

Mama did have a healthy glow to her cheeks, as well as looking happier than Jo had seen her for some time. "Shall I write to Papa to come for us?"

"Wasn't George talking about returning to London now that Alfred has gone? He could escort us."

"Mama, are you *sure* you are well enough?"

"Yes, dear. We need only spend one night on the road, so George will not get *too* impatient. John will send someone ahead to arrange our rooms, I am sure, and won't mind us using his carriage."

"Very well. I will ask Uncle Henry to arrange things."

$\sim$

London, four days later

Uncle Henry had sent a man ahead with a letter for Mr Stretton, so the household was expecting them when the carriage drew up in Russell Square. The journey had gone far more smoothly than Jo had anticipated, and although Mama was tired, she did not retire to her room immediately. Instead, after a quick wash, they had tea in the parlour with Papa while Mama told him all about Alfred.

"I expect he will come to see you as soon as he returns to England," she finished. "I believe his family is in Town, so Lady Bengrove may call on us."

"Indeed, my dear. It will be an interesting meeting." Papa did not seem as happy as Mama about Alfred, but Jo supposed that was only because he had not met him.

"Come into my study, Jo," Papa said, when Mama retired to her room to rest. "I am happy to see you again, but there is—"

"Mama insisted on returning," Jo interrupted, as she sat in her usual chair in front of his desk. "And truly, she does not seem to have suffered from the journey."

Papa sighed. "It is not that. Your mother wrote to me a few days ago, and mentioned that Captain Bengrove was staying at Yelland Court." He picked up a newspaper from his desk and handed it to her. It was folded to show the society page. "Halfway down."

Jo ran her eyes down the column, not noticing the item of interest at first. She didn't usually peruse that part of the paper, and wasn't used to the coy phrasing and use of initials. When she found the item Papa meant, she had to read it twice.

Lord B's troubles may soon be over, if rumours of AB's forthcoming advantageous alliance with a young heiress are to be believed. A small price for the young lady's elevation into an aristocratic family.

"You think this is referring to me?" Jo asked, although she knew it must be. She placed the paper back on the desk, a hollow in her stomach replacing the happiness of the last few days. This was not how she had wanted Papa to find out.

Papa nodded. "It would be too much of a coincidence, don't you think, for another young man with those initials, who is also the son of a lord, to have become betrothed recently to a woman with expectations? I thought you had left your impetuosity behind you."

"I only promised to wait for him, Papa." Although Mama seemed to believe they were betrothed; perhaps because she wanted to believe it. "But how did the paper get this information?" Surely Alfred would not have told them.

"I don't know." He tapped the paper. "This only came out this morning. I sent Farley to enquire, but the editor would not say who sent the information. I will discuss the matter with Lord Bengrove."

"It could not have been Alfred, Papa. He agreed that our families would be the first to know." He would not have broken his word.

"Well, that is irrelevant now, I suppose. I do not want you to become the object of gossip, Jo, and I fear there are enough busy-bodies to work out who is meant." He sighed. "I suspect that trying to deny the implication would only make matters worse."

"I did promise to wait for him, so it is not completely incorrect." Could Alfred have misunderstood her, and taken her agreement as accepting his offer of marriage?

Papa rubbed his forehead. "Jo, I have no intention of dictating who you choose to marry, you know that. But what do you really know about this young man? If nothing else, it would have been polite of him to have discussed the matter with me before suggesting marriage, and certainly before allowing your promise to become public knowledge. I only want to protect you from fortune hunters."

"It wasn't like that, Papa. George swears he said nothing of our circumstances to Alfred, so he cannot be a fortune hunter. And Alfred did speak to Mama first."

"And he had to meet his ship," Papa added, before Jo could. "Your Mama said as much. Tell me about it."

Papa listened to all she had to say, although she was feeling flus-tered and was not particularly coherent. His expression was what Jo called his 'business face', which did not show his feelings. He nodded when she had finished. "Very well, Jo. There is nothing settled, after all, and nothing to be done about any possible gossip."

"Papa—"

He held his hand up. "Now, Jo, I only meant that when he returns, the pair of you may spend more time together before making any final decision. That is all."

"Mama hoped his mother might introduce me into her circle."

"It might be better to wait until Captain Bengrove returns. I have no objection, however, to you getting to know his family."

Lord Bengrove called on Papa several days after their return to London, and Jo was summoned to meet him in Papa's study. She hoped he was more approving of her courtship than Papa had been.

Alfred's father was of a similar build to him, but with a larger girth and a face whose angles were softened by rolls of fat. Jo couldn't help comparing him to Papa's still-trim figure.

As Jo made her curtsey, Lord Bengrove bowed his head briefly and smiled—although with none of the charm his son had. "A pleasure to meet you, Miss Stretton."

"Do sit, Jo. Lord Bengrove came to discuss settlements, but I think we should wait until his son can take part."

"Yes, Papa." That wasn't quite what he'd said to her, but she would not question him in front of Lord Bengrove.

Lord Bengrove cleared his throat and looked at Papa. "I invite you and your family to visit us at Bengrove Hall when Alfred returns to us, Mr Stretton. That will allow the young people to be together while we discuss the settlements."

"Thank you, my lord. We accept with pleasure. Will you stay to take tea? Or brandy, if you prefer? My wife will be pleased to meet you."

"Unfortunately, I have another appointment, Stretton. Pray give my regards to Mrs Stretton."

Papa stood up. "Thank you for calling, Lord Bengrove." He rang the bell and Chivenor came to show Lord Stretton out.

"Was that all he had to say, Papa?" Jo asked, when the door closed behind the man who might become her father-in-law. It did not seem a promising beginning.

"Unfortunately, no. It seems that Lady Bengrove is settled in Staffordshire until the spring. Your acquaintance with the rest of the family will have to wait, I'm afraid."

"Oh, I thought Alfred said he saw both his parents in London. Mama will be disappointed."

"Not you, Jo?" Papa asked, tilting his head to one side.

"I will miss Alfred, but there will be time to meet his family when he returns. I suppose I should break the news to Mama."

Mama was not too displeased. "Alfred did say he would return as soon as he could, dear. I'm sure Lady Bengrove will come to Town then."

Jo hoped that time would be soon—not more than a few months, at most. It was hard to have found someone with whom she might wish to share her life, only to have him leave so quickly.

But Lady Bengrove's absence was not the worst news. That came two months later, a few weeks after Jo had finally heard from Alfred; a disappointingly brief scrawl from him saying little more than that he had arrived in Lisbon safely. Papa came into the library, where Jo was reading, holding a copy of the *London Gazette* in one hand.

"I'm sorry, Jo. Captain Bengrove is reported missing during the army's retreat from Burgos."

CHAPTER 3

Bayonne, southern France, December 1812

In the fading light, Captain Robert Delafield could just make out high stone walls through the windows of the chaise as it came to a stop. They must have arrived at Bayonne at last. Although his broken ribs were healing, they still hurt like the devil at the end of each day of this interminable journey from where they'd been captured in Spain. As did his leg.

"Now what's delaying us?" Captain Bengrove unhooked the strap with his left hand and let the window down. A cold breeze blew through the coach.

"Shut the bloody window, Bengrove," Rob said. "They'll be checking our papers." As they had at every town they'd passed through.

Bengrove swore and pulled the window up. After a few minutes, Sous-lieutenant Fournier opened the door. The young officer was in charge of their convoy with wounded prisoners from Burgos and the Allied retreat towards Salamanca. *"Nous nous arrêtons ici. Je vais vous trouver un logement pour deux nuits."*

"Merci, Lieutenant," Rob said. Fournier nodded and closed the door again.

"What did he say?" Bengrove demanded.

Rob's French wasn't very good, but combined with Fournier's limited English, they managed well enough. There wasn't much to be said, after all. "We're to stay here for two nights. He's gone to find lodgings." Perhaps one of the other wounded officers had taken a turn for the worse. He hoped not, but being jolted along in a carriage day after day was unlikely to speed anyone's recovery.

The chaise eventually took them to an inn. Bengrove headed straight for the taproom; his injured hand was still bandaged, but appeared to be healing well and didn't affect his appetite for ale and brandy. Rob was glad to see him go, cursing once again that Fournier had allocated Bengrove to be his companion for the journey. The man's continual complaints annoyed him, not to mention his boasts of the exploits of his cavalry troop, which only served to make him sound like an impetuous fool. Surely Bengrove couldn't be more than five or six years younger than him? Had Rob himself behaved in such an immature way when younger? He sometimes wondered if he was being too harsh on Bengrove, but then the man would tell another anecdote that only reinforced Rob's original opinion.

The landlady led Rob upstairs to a cramped little room, not bothering to hide her impatience at his slow progress, making full use of his crutch and the handrail. At least the sword slash in his left arm had healed well enough for him to use both hands to help him get up the stairs.

The furniture in the room was worn, the table wobbly on uneven legs, and paint was peeling from the window frame. It would do—it was at least clean, unlike some of the places they had stayed along the way. Unfortunately, the presence of two beds meant he would most likely be sharing this room with Bengrove.

Rob limped over to the nearer bed, dropped his crutch on the floor, and lowered himself carefully onto the lumpy mattress. His ankle was on fire after hobbling in from the coach, and he lay still until the worst of the pain had subsided. Then he stirred himself to wash his face and hands before lying down again. With any luck, Bengrove would spend the evening drinking instead of inflicting his presence on Rob. Bengrove cared as little for Rob as Rob did for him, but for different reasons. Bengrove, as a cavalry officer and the son of a viscount, even if only a second son, considered himself well above the status of a mere infantry captain, particularly one whose family had no connections whatsoever to the aristocracy.

His luck was in, and he didn't see Bengrove until the middle of the following morning. He suspected the man had spent the night with one of the women who frequented establishments like this. Rob was lying on the bed, bored, when Bengrove walked in.

"I need to write to my parents," Bengrove announced.

Rob kept his eyes shut. He should write too, but that meant venturing into the town to find pen and paper, and then finding out how to get the letter sent. That was too much for now. He hoped that someone had already notified his family that he was still alive, but there was not much he could do about it if they hadn't.

"I need to write home," Bengrove said again. "I can't write."

Rob opened an eye to see Bengrove waving his bandaged right hand at him. "No paper. No pen," he said, hoping that Bengrove would just go away again and let him rest.

"I don't know where to get them."

"You can ask Fournier, can't you?" Rob said impatiently.

"The frog doesn't speak English."

Rob suspected that Fournier didn't bother trying with Bengrove. "*Je voudrais du papier.*"

"What?"

"It means 'I need some paper'," Rob said. "Find him and ask him. I'm not walking anywhere."

"You'll have to write it for me." Bengrove held his bandaged hand in front of Rob's face.

The bastard would pester Rob until he agreed. "Very well—if you get enough paper for me to write a letter, too, and pay Fournier whatever it costs to get them sent."

Bengrove scowled. "Pay your own bribes, farm boy."

"Write your own letter," Rob retorted, and closed his eyes. There was a tense silence, then Bengrove stamped out of the room.

Rather to Rob's surprise, Bengrove turned up that afternoon with paper, pen, and ink, and set them on the table. "Letters."

Well, it was something to do, and Rob *did* want to reassure his family. He hobbled over to the table and drew a piece of paper towards him.

"Just write and say I've arrived here safely," Bengrove instructed.

"You want *me* to write to your family? No. You can dictate and I'll explain why it's not your handwriting."

Bengrove glared at him for a moment, then shrugged. "Dear Papa," he started, and then gave a bald account of being wounded and captured. From things Bengrove had let fall on the journey, Rob suspected that the cavalry, as often happened, had got carried away and pursued fleeing soldiers too far. Naturally, Bengrove's account to his parents did not mention that. He finished with a request for them to send some funds to Verdun so he could pay for decent lodgings.

Rob blew on the ink to check it was dry, then folded the paper and wrote the address Bengrove dictated on the outside. Bengrove could get it sealed somewhere else, although he suspected that their letters would be read by the French before being sent on. Thinking he had finished, Rob was about to start his own letter when Bengrove said, "I must write to my betrothed as well."

"You're betrothed? You never mentioned that." In all the blathering about his father the viscount and their estates, hunters, carriages, servants, and status that Rob had been forced to listen to during the journey, he'd not yet heard that Bengrove was to be married.

"Don't want her thinking I've died; she might marry someone else," Bengrove said. "Can't afford to lose her now I've got her." The words didn't sound particularly lover-like, and his tone definitely was not. The letter he dictated included a few phases about missing her and the hope that she would write to him, but was otherwise little different from the letter to his parents. Rob added the same explanation at the top of it; that Bengrove had injured his hand and so Rob was writing for him, and folded it up. He felt a pang of sympathy for the woman who would have to share Bengrove's life and bed, but perhaps they deserved each other.

"You can give them to Fournier when you see him," Bengrove stated, and left without a word of thanks. Rob shrugged—at least with Bengrove gone he could write his own letter in peace. He addressed it to his eldest brother William, knowing that Will would make sure the rest of the family got to hear the news. Then he hobbled downstairs in search of food—tomorrow would be soon enough to give the letters to Fournier.

～

London, January 1813

A weak ray of sunshine shone through the window onto Jo's desk. She looked up from her notes—the clouds of the morning were clearing, and it could turn into a pleasant afternoon. It would not be warm enough to tempt Mama to take a breath of fresh air, though, not even in their tiny back garden. Mama's health, which had improved for a while after their stay at Yelden Court, had declined following the news that Alfred was missing.

In the two months since then, Jo had kept herself busy with her work for Papa, looking into investment proposals and new industrial developments. It was unfortunate that most of the friends she had made amongst the daughters of Papa's business acquaintances had now married and moved away from London, which left her too much time to think and remember. Then, she had to remind herself that Alfred was still listed as missing, not dead—it was possible he was still alive, and she must keep cheerful for Mama's sake. However, in her darker moments, lying awake in bed, she railed against fate for taking Alfred away after she had finally found a man she thought she could marry.

One morning, as she was finishing some notes on a manufactory proposal, she decided that the cold need not keep her indoors. She could exchange her novel at the circulating library, or see if any interesting books had arrived in the shops; she could still lose herself in accounts of travel in distant lands, or volumes of history. The butler knocked on the door as she was wiping her pen.

"A visitor has called, miss." Chivenor held out a silver salver with a card on it. "I informed her that Mrs Stretton is indisposed, but thought that you would wish to see her."

Jo's brows rose as she picked up the card. "Mrs Catherine Bengrove?"

"The wife of Lord Bengrove's heir, I understand. She is awaiting you in the parlour. I took the liberty of ordering refreshments."

"Thank you, Chivenor."

Jo inspected her hands; finding them free of ink stains, she headed for the parlour.

Mrs Bengrove was a petite woman, her soft brown hair arranged in curls across her forehead beneath a lacy cap. She could not have been much above Jo's age, and stood as Jo entered the room. The bulge around her waist indicated that there would be a happy event in several months' time.

"Mrs Bengrove, I am pleased to meet you," Jo said, gesturing for her guest to sit down.

"And I, you." Mrs Bengrove settled back into her chair with a smile.

"It was kind of you to call. We do not have a large circle of acquaintance amongst people who make regular morning calls."

"I came with news, Miss Stretton; good news. Lord Bengrove received a letter from Captain Bengrove. He has been taken prisoner."

Jo couldn't comprehend at first, then hope mingled with fear. "Oh, I am so pleased! That he is still alive, I mean. But is he well? Are you saying he is in prison?" The dire conditions in places like Newgate sprang into her mind.

"I believe he was injured, but not seriously. However, he may not be back with us for some time. He is being taken to Verdun, in the north of France. My husband says that officers give their parole and take lodgings in the town, much as French prisoners do here."

Jo felt limp with relief. Still, someone like Alfred, used to riding about the countryside, would find it terribly restricting.

Mrs Bengrove reached into an embroidered reticule and drew out a letter. "He wrote to you. This came with the letter for his father. Lord Bengrove sent it up to Town."

Jo took it, her hand shaking slightly. "Do you mind if I read it now?"

"Of course not." The door opened, and a maid entered with a tray of tea and queen-cakes. "Shall I pour the tea while you do so?"

"Oh, yes, thank you." She frowned, looking at the direction. It was in a different hand from the brief note she had received from Alfred several months ago. Had he been so badly injured that he could not write?

In some trepidation, she unfolded it. It was short, starting with an explanation from the unknown writer that Captain Bengrove's wounded hand had not yet healed sufficiently for him to write. His hand was injured, nothing more—thank goodness. There followed a brief account of Alfred's capture. Disappointingly, only the last few sentences contained anything personal.

I miss you, my dear. Memories of the conversations we had, our walks together, and your delightful smile, were all that got me through the tedious journey so far, and will ease the rest of the days until we reach Verdun. I hope you will write to me there—I'm afraid we may not see each other until the war is over.

"Is all well with him, Miss Stretton?" Mrs Bengrove asked.

"I believe so, although he says very little." She held the letter up. "He has an injured hand, so this was written by someone else."

"Ah." Mrs Bengrove nodded in understanding. "He could not say all he wished to."

Of course. He would write a more personal missive when he did not have to dictate the words to someone else.

Mrs Bengrove took another letter from her reticule. "Lord Bengrove sent this for your father. He invites you all to Bengrove Hall."

"Oh. Thank you." It would be interesting to see the place where

Alfred had grown up—and perhaps Lady Bengrove would be friendlier than her husband had been.

"Tell me, what is Alfred like, Miss Stretton? If you don't mind me asking, that is. We will be sisters, eventually, will we not?"

"Have you never met him?"

Mrs Bengrove shook her head. "I first met Bengrove just over a year ago, and we were at Bengrove Hall when Alfred came back to England last summer." She paused. "I know what he *looks* like. There is a portrait of him in his regimentals done when he bought his captaincy—he is very handsome. But that is all I know. My husband says very little about the other members of his family."

"He is very charming. And friendly." She could not speak about the way his ardent gaze made her feel; her face warmed at the thought.

"Oh, silly me," Mrs Bengrove laughed. "I'm sorry; it was not my intention to embarrass you. I did not mean to pry into your private feelings."

There was an awkward pause. "Have you been in Town long?" Jo asked, for want of something better to say. The problem with her current lack of female acquaintance was that she didn't get much practice at making polite conversation.

"For a month or so." Mrs Bengrove rested her hand on her midriff. "Bengrove wanted me to be close to the best physicians, as this will be my first child."

"I hope they are not needed," Jo said, trying not to show her feelings; the best physicians had not been much help to Mama. "Will you take more tea?"

"Thank you, but no. I did not intend to stay long—you must have much to think about, with the news I brought. I would like to know you better, though. I cannot go about much at the moment, but if you wish to call, you would be welcome. Mrs Stretton, as well, when she is recovered from her indisposition."

"Thank you." Mama would wish her to go, even if she were too unwell to venture out herself.

Mrs Bengrove pushed herself to her feet, and repeated the invitation to call. When she had gone, Jo went up to Mama's room and found her sitting up in bed watching Halsey set out her clothing.

"Halsey says you had a visitor."

"Yes, Mama. Mrs Bengrove came to call." Jo sat on the end of the bed, in spite of her mother's half-hearted protest. "The family has received letters from Alfred. Mrs Bengrove brought the one that was for me. He has been taken prisoner. He is injured, but not too badly."

"Oh, Jo! Oh, I am pleased for you. And for him, of course. Such a pity he will not be coming back soon, though."

"Mrs Bengrove invited me to call, and you, too, if you are well enough."

"Jo, dear, I'm so happy that you are making friends with the right people!"

Jo frowned. "Mama, Papa's friends are not the *wrong* people!"

"Yes, of course, dear. But I do want you to be able to mix with… well, with people of higher rank, as well."

"Now, Mama, you talk as if you regret marrying Papa!" Jo softened her remark with a smile.

"You know that's not true, dear. I will certainly accompany you if I feel well enough, but you must promise me that you will go without me if necessary."

"I promise." She bent down to kiss Mama's cheek. "You may remind me of the topics allowed for polite conversation when you come downstairs."

CHAPTER 4

erdun, France, February 1813

Rob stood at the window gazing along the narrow street that ended at the town walls. He was grateful to have been given temporary lodgings in the town, rather than in the castle, which loomed menacingly above the rooftops. Although his room left much to be desired.

"Right, laddie, let's have a look at you."

Rob turned at the unexpected voice behind him, almost falling as pain shot up his leg and he lost his grip on the window surround. He reached for his crutch, propped on the wall beside him.

His visitor was middle-aged and greying, but still with a full head of hair. Although dressed in civilian clothes, he had a military bearing. Rob acknowledged his presence with a quick nod. He carefully turned back and pulled the window closed to shut out the cold air. In truth, airing the room had only exchanged the smell of damp bedding for the less attractive aromas from the noisy market outside. Then he reached out and awkwardly dragged the rickety chair close enough to lower himself onto it, his right leg sticking out in front of him.

"Captain Delafield, or Captain Bengrove?" Rob's visitor spoke with a trace of Scottish brogue, consulting a list in one hand. "Arrived yesterday?"

"Delafield." Standing by the window had definitely been a mistake —his ankle was throbbing in complaint again.

"Martin Campbell, assistant surgeon, 24th Foot. I've been here for three years. It's not so bad once you get used to the restrictions. Mind if I sit?" He didn't wait for an answer, but settled himself on one of the two beds crammed into the small room. "What happened to you, then, laddie?"

"Close encounter with a charging horse." Following a rearguard action in which many of his company had been killed, then a difficult retreat through what had felt like a sea of mud.

"A tedious journey from Spain, I imagine."

It was a statement, not a question, and Rob just nodded again.

"And Captain Bengrove has been put here, too, I understand. According to my list, he's suffering nothing more than a broken hand."

"And the indignity of being captive," Rob said wryly, beginning to relax slightly. The prodding and poking of well-meaning but not confidence-inspiring French doctors had been almost as trying as the pain from his wounds. This Scotsman, on the other hand, exuded an air of quiet competence.

"A complainer, eh? Good thing he's taken himself off, then. Now, it's no use looking wary. There's little enough for us to do most of the time, so you canna blame us for taking an interest when we get a new batch to look over."

Rob followed the surgeon's glance around the bare room and grubby bedding, and grimaced. Being more mobile, Bengrove had gone to choose from the few available lodgings for the two of them when they arrived in Verdun. Rob suspected he'd just taken the first one he'd been offered without bothering to look further.

"Might see if we can get you better lodgings, too, eh?" Campbell said. "Nay, lad, don't worry about funds. The Frogs'll give you an allowance. It's enough for the basics, but you'll be more comfortable if you can get money sent from home as well. If needs be, we can tide you over till you can get funds sent."

"I've still got a few silver buttons left," Rob admitted. He indicated the filthy red jacket flung on the end of the bed, torn, and stained with mud and worse.

Campbell nodded. "Now, I can examine you here, or you can come to my lodgings where you can have a bath and borrow some clean clothes. It'll be a bit more private, as well."

Rob glanced down at his leg, sticking out stiffly before him.

"I can try to find a carriage," Campbell added doubtfully. "But it might take a while. I can get hold of a cart, but—"

"Oh, a cart will do," Rob interjected hurriedly. "After all, I've been hauled across half of Spain and most of France like a sack of potatoes. If there is the chance of being properly clean…" He shrugged, hoping he wasn't going to regret it.

Campbell stood. "Verra well, lad. Do you want to leave a note for your friend? You may not want the effort of coming back tonight after I've examined you." He put a piece of paper and a pencil on the table. "Half an hour," he stated, gave a final nod, and left.

Campbell's lodgings were clean and warm. Warmer still was the tub of steaming water that Campbell's manservant helped Rob into, bandages and all. He sighed in bliss as the hot water soaked into him. Most of the inns on the journey had provided only enough hot water for shaving and a wipe with a wet cloth. Even when a bath had been offered, the price asked was extortionate, and Rob hadn't been sure he could get in and out of a tub without making his wounds worse. Consequently, he'd arrived here in Verdun feeling dirtier and smellier than on the muddiest of marches.

When the water had cooled, the servant helped him to wash and then dried him off and gave him a clean nightshirt. Rob inspected himself in the mirror as the man shaved him; his now-clean hair had resumed its usual chestnut colour, instead of the dark lankness of recent days. The cut across his forehead still showed as a red line, but it was fading, and the gaunt look induced by the pain of the long journey would disappear now he would be able to rest properly.

Rob's feeling of contentment vanished when Campbell appeared and soaked off the dressing on his left arm, then poured something astringent on his wound that almost made him leap out of his chair. Campbell tutted over the still-swollen gash, then caused further pain as he prodded sharply all the way down Rob's right leg. Once the examination was over, the manservant settled him in the bed, propped up with pillows, and Campbell pulled up a chair.

"Now then, laddie. Your ribs seem to have healed well. And no sign of swelling where you said you got that crack on the head. No dizzy spells?"

"Only in the first week or so."

"Blurred vision?"

"Only from..." Rob paused, not willing to admit to the cause.

"Drink?" Campbell asked.

"Yes." Rob felt rather ashamed, although there had been no criticism in Campbell's face or voice. He had never been fond of getting drunk, but for most nights on the interminable journey an alcoholic stupor had been the only way to get a little sleep, and cheap wine had also helped him get through the pain caused by the jolting coach.

"No poppy juice?"

"A few of the doctors on the way gave me some, but mostly not."

"Just as well really. It's too easy to get dependent on the stuff, and need more and more of it. Your arm is worrying. Could be a bit of your uniform still in there; may have to dig that out later. *With* a good dose of laudanum," he added.

Rob managed a nonchalant shrug. It wasn't the state of his arm that was his main concern, it was his leg. Although it was becoming easier for him to hobble around, his ankle did not bend, and the pain when he tried was excruciating. He could put up with that if he knew it would eventually heal.

"Walking on that hasn't done it any good," Campbell said, as if he were a mind reader. "Whoever set your leg did a good job; lucky the break was below the knee. But your ankle..." He got up and rummaged around in a cupboard, coming back with bandages and some wooden sticks.

"I'm going to wrap your ankle up so you can't move it. You are not to put any weight on it at all. I'll find you another crutch, so you can get about with those and your left leg. But it would be best if you didn't try to walk at all for a while."

The gentle pressure from the bandages helped to reduce the ache in his ankle, and when Campbell had finished, he lifted it into a more comfortable position on the bed. "I'm not a soothsayer; I don't know how much movement you'll get back, but what I *do* know is that if you continue to walk on it, you will almost certainly cause permanent damage."

Rob nodded. That was one instruction he intended to follow to the letter, for what use was an infantry officer who couldn't walk properly? His ankle *had* to heal.

Campbell left him then and he lay back against the pillows. It was only mid-afternoon; he didn't think he would sleep, but the sheets were clean and the mattress comfortable, and after all the surgeon's prodding and poking, he felt as if he'd been put through a mangle. Again. Then he did fall asleep, so soundly that he didn't awake until the following morning.

The house was silent, and for a moment Rob was confused, vaguely expecting one of the guards to summon him for another day's travel before remembering that he had reached Verdun. His tattered jacket and trousers lay across a chair, considerably cleaner than they had been, and Campbell had left him a clean shirt, too. He managed to dress himself, mindful of his ankle and the pain in his left arm, then hobbled down to the kitchen with his single crutch, hanging on to furniture and banisters to avoid using his right foot. He found a note from Campbell, telling him to help himself to breakfast, that his neighbour would call later to take him back to his lodgings, and that he'd send round another crutch when he located one.

When he reached his room in the lodging house, he found that Bengrove had returned, and was tucking into a breakfast of bread and ale.

"Where've you been?" Bengrove spoke with his mouth full.

"With the surgeon," Rob said shortly, seeing the note he'd left for

Bengrove still resting on the corner of the table—exactly how he'd left it. "Any luck finding better lodgings?" he asked, without much hope. That had been the ostensible reason Bengrove had gone out again almost as soon as they had arrived yesterday.

"No. Hardly any of the frogs understand me; don't speak enough English." Bengrove seemed vaguely surprised by this. "The ones that did wanted payment in advance," he added, disgusted.

Rob didn't bother replying to this and just hopped over to his bed and lay down. The short trip up the stairs had exhausted him. Bengrove finished eating and went out again, leaving the used plates on the table. Rob vaguely wondered how he was to get his own meals —he didn't fancy eating anything prepared by the woman who ran this house. He'd have to send out for food somehow.

He drifted off to sleep again and did not wake until Bengrove returned. He was now sporting a clean bandage on his hand, and a neat sling that kept his right arm close to his chest—Campbell must have caught up with him. A boy followed him in carrying a basket. Bengrove gestured to the table, and the lad removed bottles of ale and several packages wrapped in paper. He didn't leave when he'd emptied the basket—hoping for a tip, Rob guessed, but Bengrove ignored him. With a muttered imprecation, the lad left, slamming the door behind him.

"What did he say?"

"No idea," Rob lied.

Bengrove shrugged and pointed at the table. "There's enough for two there."

The high and mighty Captain Bengrove showing concern for a fellow officer? That was novel.

"When you've eaten, you can write my letters for me." Bengrove put pen and paper on the table. "Campbell said he could get them sent."

Ah—everything as normal, then. The food was a bribe, not a gift. Better than Bengrove attempting to order him to do it, Rob supposed. He hopped over to the table and ate, then picked up the pen.

As before, Bengrove dictated a letter to his father and one to his betrothed, saying that he had arrived in Verdun and was looking for decent lodgings. The letter to his betrothed also said how much he missed her, along with some compliments that Rob felt uncomfortable writing. Rob couldn't help wondering again about the woman who'd agreed to marry Bengrove. He must have been on his best behaviour while courting her.

When Rob finished writing, Bengrove took the letters with a grunt and left, saying only that he'd be back later. Rob sighed. He supposed it was too much to expect Bengrove to wait and take Rob's own letter to Campbell. He wrote to William, asking him to make enquires about sending some funds, then retreated to his bed again. Campbell had said he'd call; Rob could give him the letter then. And Campbell might be able to introduce him to some more congenial companions.

CHAPTER 5

engrove Hall, Staffordshire, February 1813
"Mama would have enjoyed seeing this," Jo said, peering through the chaise window as it turned between the high pillars marking the entrance to the Bengroves' home. The house stood atop a rise to their right, the gravelled drive sweeping round to it in a graceful arc that skirted a lake. The marble columns and entablature that Alfred had described shone pale in the weak late afternoon sun. The proportions of the building were elegant, the rows of tall windows echoing the pillared entrance.

"It is an attractive building," Papa agreed. "But it will still be here in the summer, when it will be safer for your Mama to travel if she feels well enough. She does seem more cheerful since we learned that Captain Bengrove was not killed."

To Jo's dismay, Papa hadn't been enthused about this visit, saying it would give the Bengroves, and society, the idea that her betrothal to Alfred was a definite thing. "I'm not forbidding it, Jo," he said to her protest. "But I *do* want you to get to know the young man better before anything is finalised. However, it will please your mother if we go, and it might be seen as insulting for us to refuse the invitation." And Jo had to be content with that.

The chaise came to a stop, and a liveried and bewigged footman opened the door and handed them out. Jo felt nervous now; she wanted to make a good impression on Alfred's parents.

They ascended the steps to the front door, where a stately, grey-haired butler awaited them. Behind them, the second carriage with Papa's valet and Martha was being directed around the back of the house.

The butler bowed. "Mr Stretton, Miss Stretton, welcome to Bengrove Hall. Lord and Lady Bengrove await you in the parlour."

"Thank you," Papa said as he handed his hat to the butler and removed his coat. Jo pulled her bonnet strings, and the butler passed that and their coats to another waiting footman.

The hall through which the butler led them extended the full height of the house, with ancestral portraits arranged in two rows along its walls. The parlour he showed them into was painted in a deep burgundy, the floor gleamed with polish beneath the richly patterned carpet, and thick brocade curtains framed the windows. Ornate clocks, statues, and ornaments filled the mantelpiece and several marble-topped tables. It was all very opulent, but felt cluttered to Jo. Papa had bought their townhouse four years ago, and she had helped her mother to furnish it; she recognised that the ornaments here were all of the best quality, but there were just too many of them.

Jo regarded Lady Bengrove with interest while their hosts spoke to Papa. She was blonde, like her son, although her hair was beginning to show threads of white. Unlike her husband, she was still slim, and the cut of her gown, together with the delicate lace and jewelled ear drops, lent her an overall air of expensive elegance.

"I am so pleased to meet you, Miss Stretton," she said, as Jo made her curtsey. "Alfred wrote about you in glowing terms." She smiled, but her expression held no warmth.

"Thank you, my lady. I am happy to meet more of Alfred's family." Although any hopes of his mother being more approachable than his father were fast fading.

Lady Bengrove inclined her head regally. "I expect you will wish to refresh yourselves after your journey. The housekeeper will show you to your rooms. Just ask her if there is anything you need. We keep country hours here—we will dine in an hour."

"You described Captain Bengrove as charming, did you not?" Papa asked quietly as they followed the housekeeper up a wide staircase.

"He was."

"He does not seem to have inherited that from either of his parents."

She suppressed a bubble of laughter, but was reassured that Papa's opinion of them matched her own.

"Your room, Miss Stretton." The housekeeper curtseyed and led Papa further along the corridor. The room was more plainly decorated than the parlour, and more to her liking. Possibly because the Bengroves did not choose to spend money on rooms they themselves would not use, Jo thought cynically. Water and towels lay ready on a wash stand, and sounds from an open door indicated that Martha was already unpacking her trunk.

"Tea's on its way, miss," Martha said, emerging with Jo's best evening gown draped over one arm. "I'll just see about getting the creases pressed out of this, unless you need me for anything else."

"No. Thank you. Are they looking after you below stairs, Martha?"

The maid shrugged. "Well enough, I suppose. The maids' rooms are shabby here, not comfortable like at Yelden Court."

Jo crossed to the window when the maid left. After three days' travelling she was feeling the lack of exercise, but the sun was nearing the horizon and it was too late to venture into the gardens. She could scarcely wander around the house, so she drank the tea when it came, and settled into a chair by the fire with a book.

Catherine Bengrove and her husband were still in London, which was a pity—Jo would have felt more comfortable with her new friend here. Jo had called not long after Mrs Bengrove brought the news about Alfred, and several times since then. They had progressed rapidly to first-name terms. However, Jo was not as attracted to Mr Bengrove, who was almost as cold towards her as his parents were.

There were only the four of them at dinner. The dining room was enormous, but the staff must have taken most of the leaves out of the table, for it was only large enough to seat ten. There was little conversation while the food was being brought in and wine served.

"You had a comfortable journey, I trust?" Lord Bengrove finally asked, once the servants had brought in the food and wine. Jo thought he had already made the same enquiry in the parlour, but Papa answered in the affirmative without elaborating.

"Good, good. And Miss Stretton, you must be missing young Alfred, eh?"

"Of course." Particularly when she recalled how special she had felt when in his company. "But I keep myself busy," she added, when Lord Bengrove appeared to be expecting her to say something more.

"You help your mother supervise the household, I expect," Lady Bengrove said. "I am sorry she is unwell."

"Thank you. But our housekeeper needs little supervision. We follow the news from the Peninsula in the hope that the war may end soon. However, it seems that not a great deal is happening there at the moment, although we must be encouraged by Napoleon's disastrous incursion into Russia."

"Read the papers, do you?" Lord Bengrove asked, tapping his glass for the waiting footman to refill it. "Singular! But understandable, I suppose. You will want good news, as an end to the war will bring Alfred home sooner. But you won't need to bother with all that once you're wed."

"Yes, sir," Jo replied meekly. Papa gave her a suspicious look.

"My steward will show you round the park tomorrow, if you wish. See where you'll be living." He didn't wait for a reply, but turned to Papa. "We must talk about the marriage contract while you're here, Stretton. Get it all sorted out, eh?"

"I think we should await Captain Bengrove's return," Papa replied, as he had when Lord Bengrove first came to call.

"No need, no need," Lord Bengrove said. "He's a young man, doesn't know what's what yet."

Papa raised an eyebrow. "Nevertheless, I think the young man should be part of any discussion of his financial future," he said.

"Unless you are telling me he is not competent to be part of such a discussion?"

"Eh? Oh, not at all, not at all; whatever made you think that?"

"Then he should have a say, should he not?"

Lord Bengrove was momentarily speechless, but then changed the subject to ask where Stretton hunted. That topic didn't get far when Papa replied that there were far more efficient methods of removing vermin from farmland, and Lady Bengrove stepped into the gap by asking Jo where she bought her gowns. To Jo's surprise, she seemed to approve of Mama's choice of modiste, but the conversation foundered again when Jo couldn't answer Lady Bengrove's questions about the latest fashions. She was relieved when Lady Bengrove finally rose to withdraw, and even more so when she announced that Jo must be tired after the journey and would wish to retire early.

Jo awoke the next morning to the sound of rain against the window—there would be no tour of the estate today. She could stay in bed, but Papa was an early riser and would be in the breakfast parlour at his usual time.

"How are you this morning, Jo?" Papa asked, when she had filled a plate and sat down beside him. Lord Bengrove had yet to appear, and the footman informed them, when questioned, that Lady Bengrove always took breakfast in her room.

"I slept well, thank you. My room is very comfortable."

"More than can be said for the company." Papa kept his voice quiet so the footman could not hear. "It's going to be a long week. Jo, Bengrove seems to think you will be living here if you marry Alfred. Is that what you want?"

"I... I don't know. It depends what Alfred does when he is released, I suppose."

"Hmm. All the more reason to leave discussion of the settlements, then. I cannot see you being happy living with his parents."

"They seem very... cold. They must still be worried about Alfred, though. In any case, I had hoped to live closer to you and Mama, so we could see each other often." Papa nodded, and they finished their breakfast in companionable silence. Papa asked to be shown to the library, where he soon found a book and settled by the fire to read. Jo wasn't in the mood for that, but did find a guidebook. If they could tour some of the places of interest in the area, the time might pass more quickly. It would be different, so much better, if Alfred could have been here.

Lady Bengrove came into the library an hour later. "Good morning, Mr Stretton, Miss Stretton. I trust you slept well." She ran her eyes over Jo's walking dress and gave a nod and a thin smile of approval. Jo suppressed irritation—she was well past the age of needing advice on appropriate dress.

"Good morning, Lady Bengrove." Papa bowed.

Lady Stretton acknowledged him with a brief nod, then turned to Jo. "I will show you around the house this morning, Miss Stretton. As soon as you are ready."

Over the next two hours, Jo heard all about the Bengrove ancestors in the portraits—and their importance—before moving on to the rooms that she had already seen, and several more, all as richly furnished. Then, although there was a whole wing they had not entered, they returned to Lady Bengrove's private parlour and she rang for tea. "That will be sufficient for today. When Alfred returns, we will have a suite of rooms prepared for you in the east wing. You will have your own parlour and sitting room, of course."

That was a relief—Jo didn't think she could be comfortable always being around Alfred's parents.

"The housekeeper will show you the servants' parts of the house tomorrow," Lady Bengrove went on without a pause. "You won't be in charge of any of that while you are here, of course, but you will learn the running of an establishment such as this for the day when Alfred will have an estate of his own. It is very different from the needs of a town house."

"Thank you, my lady." She already knew how to run a household, thanks to Mama's teaching—the principles were the same no matter how large the establishment. But she should do her best to be on good terms with Alfred's mother, so she made no comment.

A maid arrived with the tea, and Lady Bengrove watched without speaking as Jo made the tea and poured it. "You do seem to be prettily behaved, Miss Stretton; I will say that much for your parents. Once you have settled properly into your life here, I'm sure you will also be included in invitations to dine."

"So kind," Jo muttered, and took a sip of tea. Her wish to impress Alfred's parents was fast dwindling; she doubted anything she did or said would make them welcome her with any degree of affection.

"Do speak up, girl. Mumbling like that is so unbecoming. Alfred will be in great demand, I am sure, as a returning hero."

With Jo as a mere additional extra, no doubt.

"It is possible that some of my acquaintance may call while you are here, so you will need to learn how to behave in such company. What is the correct way of addressing the daughter of an earl?"

Now she was to be subjected to a test of manners?

"I address the one I know as 'Mama'." Jo watched with satisfaction as Lady Bengrove's mouth fell open. "My maternal grandfather is the Earl of Kenton—did Alfred not tell you? Mama had all the usual training in forms of address, precedence, and decorum, and has instructed me likewise." She finished her tea and stood. "Excuse me, if you please. I feel the need to rest again. Thank you for the tour." She gave a curtsey—to exactly the correct depth—and left the parlour before Lady Bengrove could speak.

Once in her room, she took a few deep breaths and went to look out of the window. It had been unwise to answer Lady Bengrove as she had; it would not improve relations between them. Lady Bengrove probably thought she was being helpful, and had been no more condescending than most women of her status would have been. But it was disappointing to find that Alfred's parents apparently set so much more store by rank than he did. Beyond the glass, the skies were still grey, but it was no longer raining. She would walk off her annoyance.

The stroll around the gravelled paths in the garden did her good, and she re-entered the house with cheeks glowing from the sharp air. Papa emerged from the library as she began to mount the stairs.

"Jo, is something wrong? Lady Bengrove said you were feeling unwell."

Jo hesitated. If she upset her ladyship too much, she might try to prevent her marriage to Alfred. She should tell Papa what she had said. "I am well, Papa. Is anyone else in the library?"

"No." He allowed Jo to precede him into the room and closed the door. "I suspect there is a confession to be made."

Jo smiled—Papa knew her well. To her relief, he laughed when she repeated her words.

"Jo, I think the fact that Frances married a man *in trade* would be more acceptable to Lady Bengrove if Frances did not outrank her by birth. Lady Bengrove's father was a mere baron."

"Papa, do we need to stay the full week?" She told him about the promised instruction from the housekeeper. Papa's brows rose as she spoke, and he glanced at the clearing skies outside.

"If this weather holds, we should be able to tour the whole estate tomorrow with the steward, not just the park, so the housekeeper's tour can be put off until the following day. And while you are being instructed, why don't you concentrate on working out all the ways in which Lady Bengrove could run the establishment more efficiently?"

Jo met Papa's eyes and smiled—trust Papa to make her feel better.

"I have a feeling that by the end of that day I will have received a message summoning me back to Town, urgently."

"Oh, thank you, Papa! It would be different if Alfred were with us, of course. If we are invited again, can we at least be sure that Catherine Bengrove will be here?"

"I will do my best. Now, Jo, will you still be unwell when it is time for dinner, do you think?"

Jo looked at Papa's carefully innocent face and sighed. "Unfortunately, I think I will be quite recovered by then. It would not be fair to leave you to face our hosts alone."

"That's my girl." Papa patted her shoulder and returned to his book. Jo went to change her gown—if Papa could manage it, she need sit through only three more dinners with Lady Bengrove. Perhaps, if she and Alfred were to wed, they could buy somewhere to live without having to stay at Bengrove Hall too long.

CHAPTER 6

ondon, February 1813
    Lord Yelden's box at the Covent Garden theatre felt quite crowded by the time Jo and her parents seated themselves. Mama had felt well enough to venture out, partly due to the report of their visit to Bengrove Hall that Jo had given her—emphasising the positive points and omitting her true opinion of her potential parents-in-law. Jo had worried about the freezing February winds that had blown through the tiny gaps around the coach windows, but Mama seemed cheerful enough as she sat with Papa at the back of the box.

Aunt Sarah evicted her son from his seat at the front of the box. "Come and sit here, Jo," she said, indicating the chair George had just vacated. "There's a better view, and it will stop George ogling that trollop." She inclined her head towards one of the boxes opposite, where a young woman with a very low-cut gown was gazing down into the crowd in the pit.

Cousin Lydia, sitting on the far side of her mama, gave an embarrassed giggle. The Yeldens had arrived in Town early for Lydia's first season, and this was one of her first appearances in public.

"I'm so pleased you came, Jo," Aunt Sarah said. "I did wonder if

Frances would be well enough. How is your young man? Have you heard from him again?"

"I had another letter. He is settled in Verdun now." The letter had been written by the same friend and, to her disappointment, had said little more than the first.

"Oh, that's good. George wanted to know how he came to be captured."

"He didn't give me much detail about that."

"Tell me, what is Bengrove Hall like?"

Jo filled the time until the play started by describing the house and its grounds, then the actor playing Duke Orsino began to proclaim about music being the food of love, and Jo gave her attention to the play.

During the first interval Papa and Lord Yelden left—in search of refreshment, they claimed, but Jo suspected it was to have a cigar. Aunt Sarah spent most of the interval looking at the boxes opposite and pointing out various people to Lydia. The poor girl looked bewildered, and Jo sympathised—the people being indicated were too far away for Lydia to see them clearly, and she would never remember all the names and titles.

Jo was once again grateful for her father's lack of aristocratic status. There were hierarchies amongst the bankers and businessmen with whom the Strettons normally associated, but they didn't seem as complex as the various connections that Aunt Sarah was trying to get Lydia to remember. The only people Jo recognised were Catherine Bengrove and her husband, who waved and smiled at them from a box opposite.

"I wonder if they will come here in the next interval," Mama said, looking hopeful. "I can introduce them to Sarah. Or you and Papa could go to their box to pay our respects."

Jo saw the Bengroves leave their box when the next interval came, but they did not call. "I expect they have other people to see," she said, when the play restarted and Catherine and her husband reappeared in their own box.

"They must have a wide acquaintance," Mama commented, trying to hide her disappointment.

"Indeed they must." But Jo wondered if the Bengroves' wave had been nothing more than an acknowledgement, and wasn't sure that they would wish to be seen with the Strettons in public. Catherine had always been alone, or with her husband, when Jo had called, and she was beginning to think that it might not be a coincidence that no other callers had been present. If Catherine didn't want to introduce her friends to Jo, she might not be as much of an ally as Jo had hoped if she became a sister-in-law. Nor did it bode well for Mama's ambition that Jo become an accepted member of an aristocratic family.

Verdun, March 1813

The lodging house that Campbell found for Rob and Bengrove a few weeks after their arrival was cramped, but clean. Rob had managed a quiet word with Campbell, and as a result was shown a tiny room he could have to himself for the same cost as a shared room. There was hardly space to turn around next to the bed, but it was quiet, and with the chimney from the kitchen running up one wall, was reasonably warm in spite of the frigid weather outside. He suspected it would be too hot when summer came, but he'd deal with that when he had to.

After showing them the rooms, Madame Daniau invited them into her front parlour. She was thin, and dressed in well-worn blacks that looked as if they were her permanent attire. Her hair was firmly tucked into a cap, but there was some grey in the few strands that escaped, and lines around her face and mouth showed that she was not young—approaching fifty, he guessed. She was a gentlewoman of some kind—the way the house was furnished and the books in a glass-fronted case demonstrated that. She must have fallen on hard times.

They discussed the rent, Campbell translating for Bengrove, and Rob agreed a price that would include his meals; his leg still needed rest, and he didn't want to have to go out to a local tavern or coffee shop to eat. Campbell paid for a month in advance, explaining in his heavily accented French that funds would take some time to come through for the new arrivals, then stood up to leave.

"Thank you for your help, Campbell," Rob said, leaning on the table to push himself to his feet as courtesy demanded.

Madame tapped him gently on the shoulder. "*Non, restez assis, monsieur.*" She motioned that he should stay seated before escorting Campbell out.

Bengrove looked around the little room with a scowl. To Rob's eye, it was pleasant enough, with a table and chairs, and a couple of comfortable armchairs by the fireplace. Framed prints decorated the walls, and although the carpet and curtains were rather worn, they had obviously been of good quality when new. It was much smaller than the parlour in the large, rambling house where Rob had grown up, so it must have seemed minuscule to Bengrove if his boasts about his family seat were true.

Madame Daniau came back, and this time Rob did stand up. After a pointed glare from Madame, Bengrove did the same.

"*Messieurs, cette pièce est mon salon privé. Capitaine—*"

"What's she saying?" Bengrove interrupted.

"If you shut up, Bengrove, I'll translate when she's finished," Rob said impatiently. "This is her own parlour," he said when Madame had stopped talking. "It is only for guests taking meals, and you have a table and chair in your room if you wish to be in the house."

"Bloody hell, it's like being back at Eton," Bengrove swore. "Can't go here, must go there. If she thinks I *want* to sit in her bloody parlour, she's sadly deluded." He stamped out of the room, rudely pushing past Madame, and Rob heard the front door slam.

Rob started to apologise, but she waved a hand and stopped him.

"*C'est votre ami?*" she asked.

Rob haltingly explained that they were together because they had arrived on the same coach, not because they were friends, and she gave a satisfied nod. She sat down at the table and proceeded to ask him what was wrong with his leg, what he liked to eat, and whether he had any luggage to bring. This took some time, as Rob's French was nowhere near as fluent as Campbell's, having only been used to talk to a few captured Frenchmen over the last couple of years. She finished by saying that *he* was welcome to use the parlour, and it would save him from having to go up and down stairs each day. By this time Rob was feeling ready for a lie-down again, which he briefly explained before awkwardly hauling himself up the narrow staircase once more.

The food that evening was a plain meat stew with potatoes and vegetables, but it was well cooked and tasty. And he was left in peace afterwards to read one of the novels he'd managed to acquire since their arrival in Verdun. Campbell had done them a favour finding this place.

The next few weeks settled into a comfortable routine, apart from the hideous day when Campbell decided that Rob's arm was not healing properly and the wound had to be opened up while he dug around in it for scraps of his uniform that might be festering in there. That had been trying in the extreme, even with the aid of laudanum, and had resulted in him keeping to his bed for several days.

Once Rob was up and about again, the days had a leisurely start when Madame or the girl who came in to cook and clean brought him a cup of coffee in bed. Bengrove was usually still sleeping off his previous night's drinking, and by the time he was awake, Rob had eaten breakfast and was settled in the parlour for the day. Campbell had sent a variety of visitors his way—mostly army men but a few naval officers as well. Some of the visitors had turned out to be more Bengrove's type, and Bengrove went off with them to be introduced to their favourite ale houses. But others stayed for a while, exchanging their stories and sometimes lending Rob books. In between times, he read or watched the passers-by from the parlour window, or stretched himself out in one of the armchairs and dozed. Madame often sat in the parlour, too, mostly with sewing, and the two did not disturb each other.

Madame Daniau had been helpful in other ways, too. Some of his pay had eventually come through, but he had spent most of it almost immediately on what he'd owed for lodgings and food, leaving very little to repair his wardrobe. Madame had unearthed some clothes that belonged to her absent sons, which fitted passably well after she'd taken in a few seams, and she refused to accept anything more than a token payment for them.

Bengrove, to Rob's relief, spent his evenings in the local taverns. But he hadn't finished with Rob's services, and soon after they had moved in, he appeared in the sitting room one afternoon and asked for another letter to be written.

"I thought your hand had healed?" The bandages had gone some weeks ago.

Bengrove held his hand up, flexing it. "Still won't bend far enough to hold a pen properly. I need to write. Mama's concerned that Miss Stretton may not wait for me."

"If she loves you, she'll wait," Rob said, with no idea whether or not that was true.

"Love?" Bengrove shook his head, his expression contemptuous. "She wants to marry up; we need the money. Now I'm likely to be stuck in this place for years, she might decide to break it off and go for a title. Or even someone else without a title. She's more or less on the shelf as it is—most girls are wed by her age. She should be glad I'll have her. But there's probably enough money there for her to aim for something more than a second son."

"She must like you, then?"

"Managed to charm her." Bengrove shrugged.

The woman must have fallen for Bengrove's good looks. As far as Rob could see, the man had no other redeeming features.

"Scrawny stick of a woman, like a beanpole," Bengrove went on. "Bookish too. Frizzy hair. But money talks. The father's a cit, but there's blue blood a couple of generations back on that side, and the mother's well born."

"So kind of you to take pity on the family." As Rob expected, his sarcasm flew over Bengrove's head. He would try to discourage

Bengrove from using him as a secretary again after this, but for now writing the letter seemed to be the quickest way of getting rid of the man.

Bengrove had given this letter some thought, unlike the earlier ones. In addition to the usual words about missing her, he said that he was glad she had gone to visit his family. He described the restrictions placed on prisoners, and being unable to entertain himself because he was short of money. Rob thought it sounded rather self-pitying. There were also passages of endearments that Rob felt embarrassed at writing. The whole thing seemed to be calculated to make Miss Stretton feel guilty if she had any thoughts of not waiting for Bengrove, but the comment about being short of funds came perilously close to begging. Rob wasn't familiar with the ways of aristocratic society, but he was fairly sure that asking your betrothed for money was not the done thing. And the fulsome compliments in the letter were so at odds with what Bengrove had just said that the hypocrisy disgusted him.

"Do you really want to send this?" Rob asked when Bengrove finished dictating. "I'll need to make a fair copy anyway because you kept changing your mind."

"I don't see anything wrong with it. Expert with the ladies, are you Delafield?"

Rob shrugged. "You know best, of course." He hoped that was all Bengrove wanted, but no, there was also another letter to his family, this time asking for funds directly. Thankfully that was short, and Rob was soon left in peace.

CHAPTER 7

*L*ondon, March 1813

"The post, sir." Chivenor's voice carried through the open door to where Jo was doing her weekly task of extracting articles of interest from the *Gazette* and the other newspapers that Papa subscribed to. Farley, Papa's secretary, could do it, of course, but she enjoyed keeping abreast of new ideas and projects, and discussing them with her father. Today's paper had reports about a new steam locomotive and steam passenger services on the River Clyde in Scotland. More worryingly, there was also news of more Luddite machine-breaking in the north-west. That might affect the shares Papa held in a company that made machines for textile mills.

Chivenor came into the library a few minutes later. "Mr Stretton has a letter for you, Miss."

Oh good, Alfred must have written at last! She set the paper aside and went to Papa's study. He pushed a letter across his desk as she entered.

"Is that Bengrove's handwriting, Jo?"

Jo took the letter and glanced at the direction, disappointment replacing anticipation. "No, Papa. You remember he had injured his hand, so his friend wrote for him? This looks like the same hand."

"Ah, yes. I'm surprised he hasn't written more often; he must have plenty of time now."

"I suppose he doesn't have much to write about," Jo said. But they had talked about all sorts of things during their brief time together at Yelden, so should they not be able to do so by letter? "He will probably write more often when he can pen his own letters."

"True, true." But her father had lost interest and was looking at his ledgers again, not at her.

Jo turned the letter over in her hands, but did not open it. It might include some more personal feelings than the last letter she had received, in which case she would prefer to read it while alone. She took it up to her room, where she would not be interrupted.

Dear Miss Stretton,
I am once again acting as an amanuensis for Captain Bengrove. The
text below is entirely dictated by him.
Yours, with respect,
Capt. R. Delafield

The previous letter had started in a similar fashion, but this declaration that the words were entirely dictated by Alfred seemed a bit more... direct?

She read on, thinking that this Captain Delafield's writing was much easier to read than Alfred's scrawl.

My dear Joanna,
I was happy to hear that you visited my parents. If only I could have
been there with you. It seems so long since we were together and I
gazed upon your lovely face.

There followed several more lines in a similar vein. Jo quickly skimmed over them. Somehow the written compliments did not seem as sincere as they had when Alfred said them to her in person last summer.

I am sorry your visit to our future home was cut short. You must have enjoyed seeing where you will be living when I can return to England and claim you as my own. I long for the time we can be together, and the thought of you waiting patiently for me does help the time to pass.

Life is very restricted here. Having given our parole, we are free to wander around the town, and a short distance from it, but we cannot go elsewhere without special permission, and we are required to sign a register in person every five days. There is little to do, and at present I have few funds to allow me to repair my damaged uniform or to relieve the tedium of being incarcerated here.

I am in poor lodgings, not at all what I am used to. Winter quarters in Portugal, although they often resembled the accommodations of the lower orders, were far preferable, and we could ride or hunt and go about as we pleased. If only I had your delightful presence, the days here that stretch before me would not seem so onerous, and I long for the time when I can take you in my arms again...

Jo scanned the rest of the letter quickly, a blush reddening her cheeks. It wasn't just the words about wanting to hold her, but the fact that he had dictated them to someone she didn't know. She hoped that Captain Delafield was a good friend of his, for it seemed very indelicate for Alfred to share such feelings with a stranger.

She put the letter aside to read again later, and returned to her work in the library. That evening, when she retired to bed, she re-read it. Her last letter to him had mentioned Mama's continuing ill health, but he hadn't referred to Mama at all in his reply.

It must be frustrating for a soldier to be kept kicking his heels while there was fighting to be done. On the other hand, her father had said of his short time in the army that being a soldier was mostly tedium interspersed with brief periods of action, so Alfred should be used to long stretches of inactivity. As for restrictions on where he could go—she'd had to live by those rules all her life. By the time she finally blew the candle out she was feeling quite annoyed with him.

Verdun, April 1813

One of the men Campbell sent to call on Rob while he was laid up was Lieutenant Simon Moorven of His Majesty's Navy. He had come late one afternoon, armed with a couple of bottles of decent red wine; Madame had approved of his polite manners and asked him if he wished to stay for dinner. As the two men were well into the second bottle by that time, he had accepted, and sent out for more wine later while they were still exchanging their experiences of the war.

As he related to Rob, Lieutenant Moorven had been captured some eighteen months earlier, after he'd been knocked overboard by a falling spar during an engagement in the Channel. His civilian clothes were of better quality and fit than those Rob saw on most of the British prisoners, which spoke to Rob of plentiful money sent from home. He was the eldest son of the Earl of Claverden, and so more properly addressed as Viscount Moorven, but he chose not to use his title amongst his fellow officers. As he explained to Rob, he had three younger brothers at home, all more interested in managing estates and property than he was, so his father hadn't minded too much when his youthful interest in ships and the sea had turned into a firm determination to join the Navy. Rob found his attitude refreshing after Bengrove's air of superiority.

Bengrove returned just as Moorven was about to leave for his own lodgings. Rob introduced him as Lieutenant Moorven, and was amused to notice Bengrove's supercilious expression until he added "of the Royal Navy". That made them of equivalent rank, and Bengrove's expression turned to a frown. The two men talked for a few minutes before Bengrove took himself upstairs, but in that time he managed to drop into the conversation the fact that his father was a viscount.

"You could have told him your father's rank," Rob commented when Bengrove was out of earshot, giving in to the laughter he had managed to contain until then.

"And spoil the fun?" Moorven grinned. "I'll let him pretend superiority a few more times, I think." He donned his cloak and hat and took his leave, promising to call back in a couple of days.

The following afternoon Bengrove came into the parlour where Rob was reading and dropped a letter on the table. "You thought I shouldn't have sent that last letter."

Rob looked up, wondering what Bengrove was talking about. "Letter?"

"To my betrothed. You asked if I was sure I wanted to send it."

Rob just nodded, bringing to mind the letter in question.

"Read that."

"You want me to read Miss Stretton's reply to you?" Rob asked incredulously.

"Why not? Shows she knows her place properly. That letter worked, d'you see?" He pushed the letter towards Rob.

Rob picked it up reluctantly. Bengrove made an impatient gesture, and Rob looked at it. He skimmed over the first few sentences, which hoped Bengrove was well, then read on.

I have been confined to the house for several days, as my maid is unwell and the footman could not be spared to escort me. And of course I cannot go further afield without permission, and must take the carriage and footman and maid.

It was good to see your family home when we visited Bengrove Hall last month, although it would have been nice if your mama had shown me the apartments set aside for you on your marriage. As she pointed out, I would have nothing to do, as she would continue to run the house and make all decisions about meals and furniture, and most other details. However, she did ensure I was instructed, in detail, about the correct way to run such a house, in case I should live in one at some time in the future. While living at Bengrove Hall, I would be free to spend all my time practising my lady-like accomplishments. And as you would take all important decisions, I would have nothing at all to think about, which, naturally, is the aim of all proper young ladies.

Lady Bengrove also explained all about the neighbouring families, including those of lesser rank who would be prepared to receive me on any future visit to Bengrove Hall, and the ones of higher status who might be reluctant. But she assured me that, once I have demonstrated that I can conduct myself in a suitably lady-like manner, and pay sufficient deference to their superior rank, I may be permitted to mix with them in spite of my somewhat distressing connections with trade. I was very grateful to have my proper place so clearly explained.

I know you failed to ask about my mother's health in your last letter out of concern for me, not wanting to bring distressing facts to my mind unnecessarily. I am happy to reassure you that as I write this, she is feeling a little better.

The final paragraphs said that she hoped the war would be over soon so he could return. Rob's eyebrows rose as he read the letter, but he managed to keep a straight face.

"See, she's looking forward to getting married. Women's minds don't work like ours, you know."

"So she is, Bengrove. And so they don't. I bow to your superior knowledge." Poor woman—betrothed to a self-pitying blockhead who couldn't see sarcasm when it was staring him in the face. Rob handed the letter back and picked up his book. Bengrove smirked and tucked the letter back into his pocket. "I take it you can write your own letters from now on?" Rob asked.

Bengrove shrugged. "The hand isn't quite right yet, but I'll manage. Not much to say, in any case."

Rob kept his eyes on his book, not wanting to be drawn into a further discussion on the subject. Or on any other subject, come to that. Bengrove hung around for a few more minutes, but eventually took himself off out of the house.

Rob was finishing his dinner that evening when Bengrove stuck his head around the door again.

"Is the old bat in?"

"*Madame Daniau* has gone to see a friend," Rob said.

Bengrove grinned, and a few moments later returned with a buxom young woman with quantities of golden hair; so buxom that she was almost falling out of her dress, and hair so golden that it was surely dyed. If that weren't enough, the bright red lips and painted face made her profession obvious.

"Not here, Bengrove. This is Madame's private parlour."

"Oh, be a sport, Delafield. The bedroom's tiny."

"How much space do you need?" Rob asked impatiently, making no move to get up. "I'm not dragging myself upstairs just so you can shag your woman in Madame's sitting room. I don't imagine she'd like it either."

"I'm paying for lodgings."

"Are you?" Madame had complained recently that Bengrove owed her for the coming month.

The woman giggled, making her breasts jiggle, and pulled on Bengrove's hands. With a mutter about the 'bloody infantry', he allowed himself to be dragged upstairs.

Rob sighed. Sure enough there was soon a rhythmic creaking as bed ropes moved under the strain. And, in what turned out to be really bad timing for Bengrove, Madame Daniau arrived home as the noise was reaching a crescendo.

It took her a moment to work out what the sounds were. She glared at Rob, who just shrugged, then she dropped her basket on the table and went through to the kitchen. Rob heard the clank of a bucket and then the pump handle. Now Rob wanted the pair upstairs *not* to finish what they were doing, not until Madame had reached the bedroom. He sat back and listened with glee as Madame crept up the stairs, although he doubted they would hear if she stamped up. Then there was a bang as she flung the door open and a yell from Bengrove and a shriek from the woman, followed by some very loud swearing. He couldn't help laughing.

Madame came back down and headed straight out of the door

again, returning a few minutes later with two men. Rob recognised them as labourers who lodged further down the street. Large labourers, with well-developed muscles. Better and better!

Fifteen minutes later, after Rob had translated Madame's refusal to have such goings on in her house or to allow Bengrove to stay one night longer, Bengrove and his belongings—some of them still dripping—were forcibly deposited on the street outside. The labourers were given dinner in return for their help and, Rob suspected, to keep them around until Madame was sure Bengrove had gone.

By this time Rob was managing to get outside for short periods, hopping along with the aid of his crutches. Campbell's digging around in his arm had set this activity back a bit, but there was hardly a twinge from that sabre slash now, and his leg didn't protest when he moved around. Campbell had removed the splints and bandages on his ankle, but told him that anything that caused discomfort was still to be avoided. Even if he could not get far, or go fast, the opportunities for a change of scenery every day cheered him up enormously. The weather was typical for April, with sunny days interrupted by heavy showers; buds and leaves were unfurling on the trees in gardens and the fields surrounding the town, and daffodils were beginning to flower in window boxes and under hedges. Having spent the last three springs in Spain, Rob appreciated the verdant countryside he could see from the edges of the town.

The day after Bengrove had given him Miss Stretton's letter to read he found a tavern with some outside tables in a sunny sheltered spot, and sat with a pint of ale. He considered the letters again, remembering what he had written for Bengrove a few weeks before, and wondering if he had misunderstood the tone of Miss Stretton's reply. But what she had written was a fair mirror of the complaints Bengrove had put in his letter, and the more he thought about it, the more he was sure that Miss Stretton had written the whole letter in the same vein.

When he finished his drink, he checked how many coins he had left in his pocket and picked up his crutches. He needed more paper, as it was time to write to his family again. And perhaps he'd write another letter as well.

CHAPTER 8

*L*ondon, May 1813

"Have you received another letter from Alfred, dear?"

Jo looked up from the letters she was reading. She'd thought her mother was asleep.

"Yes, Mama. He's doing well." Papa had obviously given orders to Chivenor that letters from France could be given directly to her; one was in Captain Delafield's neat hand, and the other in Alfred's careless scrawl.

Mama nodded with a pleased smile and started removing the shawls that covered her legs. Jo put the letters down on a side table and went over to help. "Would you like some tea?"

"Yes, please. If you would ring for it, dear."

Jo rang the bell, and when Chivenor appeared she requested a tea tray. Then she walked over to the parlour windows, now letting in the afternoon sunshine. Mama had almost taken up residence on the day bed in here, enjoying the light and the sight of greenery appearing on the trees and in the flowerbeds in the small back garden. She had stopped paying calls, as there were so few days on which she had the energy to go out. However, with the stronger tonic her physician had prescribed, she was usually still well enough to receive any visitors that came. That day had been quiet, with only Aunt Sarah and Lydia calling while Jo had been busy with the newspapers in the library.

"Sarah was telling me all about Lydia's admirers." Mama frowned. "You should be attending balls as well, Jo. You know Sarah will take you if you wish to go."

"Now, Mama, you know I don't care for such things." That was true, although it wasn't the main reason she declined Aunt Sarah's invitations. During the few morning calls she had made with Mama or Aunt Sarah she had seen cold looks and whispers behind fans from women who knew that Papa was in business, and had no wish to repeat the experience at larger events.

"You would enjoy a ball if Alfred were here."

"Yes, Mama, but he is not."

"He did seem such a nice young man. Just a pity he had to go back to Spain."

"Yes, Mama," Jo said patiently, for they'd had this conversation several times before. "But at least he is safe now."

"If he hadn't been captured, he could have come home on leave, or sold out, then I would have seen you wed."

"Mama, if he hadn't been captured, he might have been killed in the next engagement. At least this way, he *will* be coming back when this war is over."

"I know, dear, it just seems so hard to have found a suitable young man and then not to see him again for so long." She took a sip of her tea and nibbled on one of the sweet biscuits that Cook had sent up. The staff liked Mama, and Cook was trying very hard to tempt her to eat more. "Why don't you read out some of his letter, Jo. That will cheer me up."

Jo took a mouthful of tea to give her time to think. Then she picked up Alfred's letter from the table.

"He says he is well, and that his hand is better—I can see that because he has written himself this time. He also says that he misses me. Listen: 'I long for the time when we can be together, and the thought of you waiting patiently for me does help the time to pass.'"

"That's lovely, dear," Mama said.

"And he says, 'It seems so long since we were together and I gazed upon your lovely face.'" She hid her irritation that he had used exactly the same words as he had dictated to Captain Delafield in his previous letter. "And he sends his best wishes for an improvement in your health." That sentiment had *not* come from Alfred's letter.

Mama gave her a gentle smile. "All will be well, dear. Have you called on Mrs Bengrove recently?"

"No, Mama. You recall she has removed to Bengrove Hall until she has had the baby." Jo had told Mama that a month ago; she must have forgotten.

"Oh, that's a shame. Now, I'm going to have a nap until dinner. Will you send Halsey to me when it's time to get ready?"

"Yes, Mama." Jo went over and gave her a quick kiss on the cheek. She started when she saw her father standing in the doorway, but he shook his head and put a finger to his lips, so she said nothing. She followed him into the library.

"It does your mother good to hear from Captain Bengrove. He writes nicely, judging by the parts you read."

"Yes, Papa," Jo said reluctantly. She didn't wish to admit to having received a letter from Captain Delafield that had not been written on Alfred's behalf. At least, not until she'd had time to think about what he'd said.

"Mr Felton has invited your mother and me for dinner on Friday, to meet some other people interested in his new venture. May I say that you will accompany me instead?"

"If you wish, Papa. Mr Felton does not care to hear the opinions of women, does he?"

"No, I'm afraid he does not. But it may be instructive if you can converse with his wife. He seemed just a bit *too* keen to have me join him. If he is in financial difficulties for some reason, he may not be making the best of judgements."

Jo sighed. "I'll see what I can find out."

It wasn't the kind of thing she enjoyed doing to assist her father, particularly as the man's daughter was a friend, albeit not a close one. She could see such information would be useful, but she drew the line at explicit questioning. Papa thanked her and returned to his study. Jo went to her room and sat on the window seat with her letters. She read the one from Captain Delafield again.

Dear Miss Stretton,
I hope you do not regard this letter as too much of an impertinence. Captain Bengrove showed me part of your last letter, in which you described your visit to his family home.

Your comments reminded me somewhat of my own childhood. As the youngest of seven children, I was surrounded by over-protective sisters and people who all knew better than I did and told me so frequently. They all had the best of intentions, of course, and were not trying to demonstrate their own superiority. This was little comfort at the time, although in my case I knew I could escape when I grew older, so the situation did not seem too onerous. I had never thought before how frustrating it must be for an intelligent woman to be treated as a perpetual child.

However, and this is the reason I write, I thought you should be aware that Captain Bengrove took the content of your letter completely at face value. If I have mistaken the matter, please forgive me. And please accept my very best wishes for an improvement in the health of Mrs Stretton.

Yours, with respect,
Capt. R. Delafield

She could not understand why Alfred had shown her letter to Captain Delafield. It was not because the captain had needed to see her words to help him to write a reply, for Alfred had written back himself. He had apologised for his untidy writing, saying that his injured hand was not yet working quite as well as it should, but that Delafield—he omitted the 'Captain'—seemed unwilling to write any more letters for him. Jo wondered if Captain Delafield had been as uncomfortable about writing Alfred's lover-like compliments as she had been about the idea of a stranger doing so.

Alfred's letter had also suggested that Delafield might be jealous of Alfred's rank and person, being short, thin, and an old cripple as well. So far Jo had assumed that Captain Delafield was one of Alfred's friends, but that was clearly not the case.

She had wondered, when writing her previous letter, whether Alfred would be annoyed by her sarcasm. And after it had been sent, she thought that she had been too impetuous and should not have written it at all. It seemed she need not have worried—Alfred's answering letter showed no sign of annoyance, and now she knew he hadn't even noticed the sarcasm. Did it not occur to him that a woman could have a mind of her own? That would be worrying, if it were true. Whatever the reason, she was grateful to Captain Delafield for informing her of Alfred's reaction.

The next morning she wrote replies to the letters. Then re-wrote one of them several times. And finally slipped them both into the post after her father had given his own correspondence to Chivenor to send.

Verdun, June 1813

Two letters arrived for Rob; the one from his oldest sister was accompanied by a pair of handkerchiefs embroidered by his nieces. He received letters every week or so from one or other of his brothers and sisters; these contained little about the war, but were full of domestic news and anecdotes that sometimes made him yearn to be back with his family. They were not much different from the letters he'd received on campaign, except that as he was not moving around, they reached him more regularly. Less interesting were Will's letters, which often went into detail about farming matters. Will had inherited most of the family farms, and although he could well afford to employ a bailiff to oversee them all and live the life of a gentleman of leisure, he preferred to manage them himself.

Father had left one of the farms to Rob, but he was perfectly happy to let a tenant run it. However, if his bad leg meant he had to sell his commission when he got back to England, he could end up doing Will's bidding and running the farm himself. He wasn't sure what he wanted to do with his future, but his time in the army had given him a taste for moving around, and being stuck on his farm didn't appeal at all.

The other letter he received was more surprising. He hadn't expected a reply from Miss Stretton, being fairly certain that she *would* consider a letter from an unknown officer to be an impertinence.

Dear Captain Delafield,

My parents would no doubt consider this a most improper correspondence, as we are not related nor have we been introduced; although that would be a trifle difficult in the circumstances, you must agree.

In relation to my last letter to Captain Bengrove, you did not mistake the matter. I thank you for letting me know that he took my words as written. I must also thank you for enabling Captain Bengrove to communicate.

My family and I are grateful for all our gallant soldiers who are opposing the Corsican, and we would be happy to help if there is anything we can do for those of you currently incarcerated in Verdun. I am assuming that the knitted scarves & embroidered items that are made and sent by many gently born women of my acquaintance may not be appreciated quite as much as their donors might hope.

My father has banking interests and may be able to facilitate matters such as the transfer of funds, should you need this kind of assistance.

With my sincere best wishes,
J. Stretton

Rob laughed out loud at the penultimate paragraph, then considered the offer of help. His initial thought was to dismiss it; the main things lacking were his freedom and money, in addition to an ankle that would bear weight and bend without hurting. The first and last she could do nothing about, and money was not something he would ever request from an unknown woman. But then he thought there *was* something she might be able to do for him.

Not long after Bengrove had been forcibly ejected from Madame Daniau's house, Lieutenant Moorven had brought along an engineer. Lieutenant John Chadwick had been too close to the exploding powder in a bridge he was demolishing before the French could cross it, and had badly injured his right leg. The French doctor who tended him after his capture had amputated it below the knee. They made a matching pair, Rob thought, although Chadwick seemed to manage better with his wooden leg and stick than Rob currently did on his crutches. The three men got on well, and it wasn't long before Chadwick asked Madame if he could rent the room recently vacated by Bengrove. Rob had filled the hours with nothing to do by asking Chadwick to teach him some of the knowledge needed for the construction of bridges and defences, and that had developed into the pair of them asking Moorven to explain, in detail, how to locate a ship's position in the middle of an ocean. Suitable books would make that easier.

The next day, after consulting Chadwick and Moorven, he wrote his reply.

Dear Miss Stretton,

Thank you for your letter. Were you a man there would be no harm in it at all, so in view of the sentiments you expressed in your letter to Captain Bengrove, I can quite understand your choice to ignore convention in this instance.

I am hoping to be more mobile soon, but in the meantime I have never had so much time for reading and reflection, although even these activities pall after a while. The main reading material available in

English consists of novels and occasional copies of English newspapers, sadly out of date by the time they reach Verdun. A naval officer is teaching me the elements of navigation, and an engineer has recently taken up lodgings here and is attempting to deliver the mathematical principles of surveying. It is rather too late for me to embark on a new occupation in either field, but studying technical matters such as these will give my mind something to work on and help to pass the time in a moderately constructive manner. If it is not too much of an imposition, my friends ask if you could have some books sent, details of which I enclose. I would ask my family, but they do not travel much and their nearest bookshop would be unlikely to have the required texts, whereas most of these should be readily available in London.

I am also trying to improve my French. If Bonaparte prevails, heaven forfend, it will be useful to speak the language well. Even if the worst does not happen, it is only courteous to the people of this town to attempt to address them in their own language. To this end, a French grammar and dictionary would also be helpful, as my abilities in the language could be described as passable, no more. I will ask my brother to forward the necessary funds to you if you let me know the cost.

With my thanks and best wishes,
Capt. R. Delafield

CHAPTER 9

*L*ondon, July 1813

Jo sat in the window seat of her mother's parlour, enjoying the warm breeze that blew in scents from the garden and reading the letters that had arrived this morning while she had been at the circulating library. Mama, on the sofa, was taking an afternoon nap. There was nothing from Alfred; his last letter had been in response to her making the same offer of assistance she had sent to Captain Delafield, and had thanked her but said that, short of his freedom, his needs in Verdun could be met by having more money. Something his father would deal with, surely.

She unfolded the letter from Captain Delafield first, expecting it to be thanks for the books she had sent several weeks ago. But it was not quite what she expected.

Dear Miss Stretton,
My thanks for sending the French grammar and dictionary, which
arrived safely, although the wrapping on the parcel was torn and any
accompanying letter seems to have been lost.

Things go on here as normal, except that the warmer weather makes my lack of mobility more frustrating. However that is gradually improving and I can get about the town a little now.

I discovered that Madame Daniau, my landlady, is such a kind hostess because she has two sons of military age. One is fighting somewhere in northern Europe, but the other was captured in Spain. He is an officer, although not of high rank, and according to his letters is being treated well in Cheringford, Somerset. In addition, the infantry unit that captured him prevented him falling into the hands of the Spanish, for which he is truly grateful, and so, therefore, is his mother. Thus good deeds and good feeling are passed on. This amity between the prisoners here and the local people who are, in effect, our gaolers, makes this whole sorry business seem even more stupid and futile.

But my apologies for the digression. I wished to ask your advice as to a suitable gift for Madame. She is forty-five or fifty years of age and wears mourning for her husband who died some years ago. She does not wear jewellery, and in any case such a gift might not be proper. Nor, I feel, would a gift of clothing be appropriate. She regards orna-ments merely as objects that collect dust. Any advice you could give me on this matter would be greatly appreciated.

With my best wishes for your health and that of your family,
Yours, with respect,
Capt. R. Delafield

Jo frowned—she had sent more than just the language books. But then she noted again the comment about the parcel having come open and thought that the other items might have been either stolen or confiscated. If her letter were also missing, Captain Delafield wouldn't have known what she had sent—he might just have thought it had proved too difficult for her to obtain the technical volumes.

Could Papa's banking arrangements on the continent be used to send parcels? She would have to ask Papa for permission, although he would expect them to be addressed to Captain Bengrove. She could not explain who they were really for without owning up to writing to someone other than him. Papa might allow her to send the books, as thanks for his help with Alfred's letters, but that would also most likely be an end to their correspondence, and she didn't want that to happen. She was beginning to feel that Captain Delafield was more like a friend than merely a stranger who had helped Alfred.

Could she word her question to Papa so she did not mention the recipient by name?

"Another letter from Alfred, dear?" Mama sat up and rearranged her shawls.

"No, Mama, not today." Jo shuffled the letters together, with Captain Delafield's on the bottom. "One of them is from Aunt Sophie." Papa's youngest sister.

"What does she say? Are the children going on well?"

"They are all thriving. She writes to ask if we want to spend some time with them this summer."

"That would be nice."

"The journey would tire you, Mama. But perhaps we could stay at Yelden for a few days on the way."

"Oh, that is a good idea. I'll ask your father to arrange that. Who else has written to you?"

"Would you like some tea, Mama? Cook made some ginger biscuits this morning—they smelled lovely when I was downstairs earlier." Mama looked doubtful, but Cook's efforts at trying new recipes usually made her at least taste the cakes and biscuits made for her.

Jo got up and rang the bell. She felt a little guilty about distracting Mama from the subject of her letters; corresponding with an unknown man *was* improper, but it was not as if she were writing to someone her own age. Alfred had said he was old, so she was probably communicating with someone nearer to her father's age than her own. That made it perfectly acceptable, she told herself, although she was careful not to examine any of her assumptions too closely.

Later, in the privacy of her bedchamber, she looked through the letter again. The phrase 'according to his letters' gave her pause. The captain, or his landlady, might be thinking that her son was making the best of things in his letters so as not to worry her. Was Captain Delafield asking if she could check? Surely he would have asked directly if that were the case. Or he did not want to impose, and phrasing it like that allowed her to ignore the request if it were too onerous.

There was also the matter of Madame Daniau's gift. Although clothing was not appropriate, a bolt of cloth might be acceptable. However, that would be even more likely to be stolen, and Madame could buy cloth herself in France, so that would not be a particularly good gift, either. And anything distinctly English could raise questions in Verdun that might be awkward for Madame and her lodger.

She would give it some more thought, but she could start by finding out exactly where Cheringford was. One of Papa's business contacts lived in Somerset, and might be able to find out more about Madame's son.

~

Verdun, July 1813

Chadwick deposited two letters on the parlour table and sat down beside Rob. "Lucky man. I wish I received more letters from home."

"It means I have to write more in return." Rob picked up the letters with a nod of thanks.

"And there is so much going on here to tell people about," Chadwick finished for him, as the pair of them had had this conversation before. "Come out for some ale later?"

Rob agreed, and Chadwick left him to his correspondence. The first letter was from his brother Samuel, with the usual news about his family and his parish near Hereford. The other was shorter, and he smiled as he recognised the handwriting.

Dear Captain Delafield,
I was pleased to hear that the books to help you learn French arrived
safely.

*In respect of the loan you requested, my father has made arrange-
ments with the Banque de la Meuse, on the Rue du Marché. If you
present yourself there, the manager will be able to give you the
assistance you need.*

Yours truly,
J. Stretton

Loan? For a moment he wondered if Bengrove had asked his
future father-in-law for a loan, but that would mean that Miss
Stretton had directed the letter to the wrong person, and she was too
intelligent to make that kind of silly mistake. He frowned, trying to
recall exactly what he'd said in his letters to her, and whether he could
have inadvertently hinted that a loan would be useful. But he didn't
think so.

He would have to go to the bank to see what it was about. He
reached for his crutch—he was managing now with just one—and
hobbled towards the kitchen where Madame was supervising the first
preparations for the evening meal. "*Madame, où est la Rue du Marché,
s'il vous plait?*"

She gave him directions, but he lost track of the turnings long
before she finished. Eventually Madame stopped in what sounded like
mid-sentence. "*Demain?*"

"*Nous irons demain?*" We will go tomorrow? Following Madame
wouldn't be a problem, as long as she didn't walk too fast. She
nodded, gave him a smile, and turned her attention back to the maid
chopping vegetables.

It turned out to be further than he'd hoped, and his ankle was
throbbing by the time they entered the bank. Leaning on the crutch
wasn't doing his shoulder much good either. Madame looked into his
face and tutted, and said something to the clerk. As a result a chair
was brought for him to sit on even before he'd stated his business.
Madame looked at him, said something else to the clerk that was too

fast for him to understand, then left him there to go and do her shopping. At least, that was where he assumed she'd gone, and he hoped she'd be coming back for him.

Ten minutes later he was feeling a little more the thing and looked about the room. The clerk caught his eye, and came over from behind the counter to speak to him.

"Capitaine Delafield?"

"*Oui. Monsieur Stretton a—*"

"*Par ici s'il-vous-plait, Capitaine,*" the man interrupted, gesturing and hovering in case Rob needed help to get out of the chair again.

Rob gritted his teeth and managed to stand without help, then hobbled behind the clerk into a spacious office. The clerk bowed and closed the door behind him when he left. An elderly man regarded him closely from his seat behind a desk strewn with papers.

"Capitaine Delafield," he said, his face expressionless. "I am Etienne Allard, the manager. Do sit down."

Rob did, encouraged that the man spoke English, albeit heavily accented. "Mr Stretton, in England, said you could help me."

"You can prove your identity?"

"I have a letter from Miss Stretton."

Allard held out his hand and Rob gave him the short note. Allard glanced at it and handed it back, then pulled open a drawer in his desk and took out a box.

"I have some items for you." He pushed the box towards Rob. Any outer wrappings had gone, and there was no seal on it. Rob lifted the lid—the box contained the technical books he'd requested some time ago. There was also a roll of papers tied with string and a letter, which, at first glance, appeared to have the seal still intact.

"I am a loyal Frenchman, Capitaine," Allard said. "As you can see, I have inspected the items."

He watched to see Rob's reaction to this, but Rob was neither surprised nor offended. He would have done the same had their places been reversed, and it did seem that the man had not opened the letter. He said as much, and Allard managed a smile.

"These books; why do you want them?"

Rob explained about keeping his mind busy, and Allard nodded. "And the newspapers?"

Rob picked up the bundle and pulled the string off. The papers were curled from being tied for so long, and he flattened them on the desk. Miss Stretton had sent him copies of the *London Gazette*, going back to the previous autumn. Flicking through them quickly, it seemed that the issues in the roll all contained dispatches from either the Peninsula or reports of engagements in more northern parts of Europe. Rob looked at Allard uncertainly. "They have reports of battles, monsieur." Allard spoke very good English—he probably already knew that.

"As I thought. In return for me allowing you to have these, you will come back in a few days with a summary of what your paper says has been happening."

Rob was without words for a moment.

"You are surprised?"

"Yes."

"I am loyal to France, Capitaine. This does not mean that I always trust what our government tells us about the war."

"You would believe the English?"

Allard shrugged. "Not necessarily. But between the English and the French we may find something near the truth. Your payment to me for allowing this..." he waved a hand at the books and papers, "...is to keep me informed of what the English are saying about their war."

"I am sure you could get this information yourself," Rob said carefully.

Allard smiled, without humour. "I could, yes. But I do not have the time to read every copy of your *Gazette*, and you will know the significance of what is happening better than I. It will be easier for me if someone brings me the important points. In return for this small effort, I am willing to continue to allow parcels to be passed on."

Rob thought for a few moments, but he couldn't see anything wrong with the idea. "That sounds a fair trade."

"*Bien.* There will be a carriage to take you home shortly. I apologise, but I must see someone else. But do return soon, Capitaine, with my summary."

Rob pushed himself to his feet and shook the hand offered to him. He opened the letter while he was waiting for the carriage, but it was almost as short as the one delivered directly. Miss Stretton had written only that she had sent the parcel via the bank because the first copies of the technical books she'd sent had been either stolen or confiscated, she was happy to obtain any other books he might need, and she hoped he found the newspapers useful.

She had sent the books he wanted, and more, so why did he feel disappointed?

The back copies of the *Gazette* kept Rob busy for some time. Moorven and Chadwick were interested too; copies of British newspapers were sometimes to be had in Verdun, and they had managed to piece together some of what was happening in Spain, and with the fight against Bonaparte's armies in the rest of Europe, but it was much easier when they had all the published dispatches to refer to. Madame's tiny front parlour was too full when all three of them were together, especially on the evenings when Madame wanted to use it as well, so they started going to a tavern a few streets away. The place served reasonable food and ale, and they commandeered a corner table and read through the papers while Rob made his summary.

Other captives asked what they were doing, and word spread; soon the hardest part of the exercise was preventing others from borrowing copies. Not that Rob minded people reading them, but he wanted to make sure he'd been through them all himself before someone possibly forgot to give one back. Reading them in the tavern seemed to be the answer.

The tavern keeper appreciated the extra customers who bought ale while they came to read the papers, and by the end of a fortnight the three friends had become a fixture in the tavern. When they were not poring over the dispatches or joining others in trying to work out what exactly had happened, they studied their engineering or navigation or French.

A week or two after the parcel of books arrived, a messenger came asking Rob to call at the bank to discuss his loan. Rob went on foot the next day, and was given a small packet in return for handing over his summary of recent battles. The last few weeks had almost completed his healing, and although he was still using the crutch, he could just about put his full weight on his bad foot—but not for too long. So he took the packet to a nearby tavern to rest before attempting the walk back.

The packet contained a letter and another, slightly heavier, item wrapped in paper.

Dear Captain Delafield,

I hope the replacements for the missing books arrived safely, and you are making good use of them. I took a look inside and could make neither head nor tail of their content. This disappointed me somewhat, as I consider myself reasonably proficient with numbers. It would appear that dealing with business accounts is a rather different, and easier, skill from mastering the mathematical ideas behind navigation.

But I write about your request for advice. Not knowing your hostess, I could not think of anything you could buy for her. However, I found that my father has a business contact in a town not fifteen miles from Cheringford, and I asked if it were possible for him to meet your landlady's son. My father's associate met and talked to Lieutenant Daniau, who assured him that his letters saying he is being treated well are the truth. The associate also took his daughter with him, who produced the enclosed. I hope you will find this adequate as a gift for Mme Daniau.

I hope you are getting about more now, and that the weather is being kind to you in France.

With my best wishes,
Joanna Stretton

His letter thanking her for the technical books and newspapers must not have reached her yet. He picked up the heavier packet and unfolded the wrapping, finding that the extra weight was due to a piece of pasteboard preventing a sketch becoming creased or bent. The drawing was a head and shoulders portrait of a smiling young man, bare headed but dressed in a proper coat and cravat. Madame's son—the likeness was clear, even if he hadn't had Miss Stretton's letter to explain.

How thoughtful of her. Miss Stretton had gone to a lot of trouble for an unknown woman, merely at his request. She would be wasted on an oaf like Bengrove.

Madame would love it, but it would be better in a frame so she could hang it on the wall. He carefully wrapped it up and tucked it into a pocket. He'd see what he could do tomorrow—their local tavern keeper was bound to know of someone who could frame it for him.

CHAPTER 10

London, August 1813

L "Jo?" Papa's voice came from his study as Jo removed her bonnet and handed it to Chivenor.

She found her father sitting at his desk with the usual piles of papers in neat rows in front of him. "Is something wrong, Papa? Has something happened to Mama?" she added, with sudden anxiety. The doctor had been due to call this morning.

"No, no. She's much as usual. No worse, but no better, either. Doctor Walsh prescribed a stronger tonic, which he said would help. No, this is about you." He waved a hand, and she sat down. "Can you explain this?"

Papa picked up an opened letter from his desk and held it out. He usually had a smile for her, but now, although he wasn't looking angry, he clearly wasn't pleased with her.

Dear Mr Stretton,
I write to thank you for sending materials to my brother in France.
He did not know exactly how much you had expended on his behalf,
but hopes that the enclosed will cover it.

My thanks again.
Wm. Delafield, Esq.

Oh. Her anxiety returned—no, that feeling was disappointment that Papa would now forbid her correspondence with Captain Delafield. But that was silly; it wasn't as if she even knew the captain, not really.

"Explain, Jo."

"It is repayment for the two books I sent. You recall, Papa, I asked if they could be sent by the bank to stop them being stolen or confiscated?" She realised she was twisting the fabric of her skirt in her fingers and made an effort to still her hands.

"I remember very well. What I do not recall is you intending to send them to anyone other than Captain Bengrove."

"I don't think Alfred is interested in those kinds of books," Jo said.

"Don't change the subject, Jo. I can well believe he is not, but that is not the point. No, no," he went on as she was about to speak. "I'm sure you did not lie to me. You're too clever for that. You just managed not to mention that you are corresponding with a man other than Bengrove!"

"There's no harm done, Papa, is there? He is the one who helped Alfred to write when he was injured. Alfred says he is old."

Papa leaned back in his chair and looked at her thoughtfully for a few moments, until Jo wanted to squirm. "Whether harm has been done remains to be seen. If word of it gets out, the Bengroves will not approve, and nor will your mother."

"Who is going to tell them?"

"Bengrove, perhaps? If Delafield is his friend—"

"I don't think they *are* friends, Papa." Alfred certainly didn't like Captain Delafield—there had been further disparaging comments in Alfred's letters. And surely, if the captain liked Alfred, he would have said something to Alfred about the sarcasm in her letter, rather than writing to her to say that Alfred had not understood it?

"Oh?" Papa waited a moment with raised brows, but Jo did not elaborate. "It is most improper, whether or not they are friends. In fact, it might be better if they *were* friends! We don't know anything about this Delafield. How did he come to ask you for those books? Did Bengrove ask for them?"

Jo shook her head.

"Does Bengrove even *know* that you are writing to another man?"

"I don't know. I don't think so."

Papa put his fingers to his forehead for a moment before looking back at her. "How did it come about? Did you write to him first?"

"No, Papa. It just... well... happened."

"You have kept the letters?"

Jo nodded.

"Go and get them."

She had to obey. But there was nothing improper in the letters themselves; if her father saw that he would not be too angry. Would he?

She took Captain Delafield's letters out of the drawer in her dressing table and, after a moment of hesitation, added Alfred's letters as well. Back in the library, she sat down opposite Papa again and handed over Captain Delafield's letters.

Papa read the first one, looking puzzled. "What sarcasm had you written to Bengrove?" he asked.

She handed him the letter from Alfred that had annoyed her. "I replied to that letter, Papa. I was... not pleased that he had dictated such things to a stranger, and his complaints seemed self-pitying. I wrote him a very sarcastic letter about how gracious his mama had been when we visited, and how good it would be if I lived there and I didn't have to think for myself at all. And how I always have to have permission to go out and be accompanied."

"Sarcastic, Jo? You?" To her relief, Papa was beginning to look amused. "So Bengrove detected no sarcasm, but this Captain Delafield did?"

"Yes, Papa. Alfred has not asked after Mama's health at all, either." To her disappointment; he had not seemed so uncaring when they were together at Yelden. "You can read his letters, too, if you wish."

"They are full of these lover-like phrases?"

"Yes, Papa," she said demurely. "But generally the same ones each time."

He raised an eyebrow at that. Jo sat while he read the other letters from Captain Delafield, trying to discern from his expression what he was thinking, but failing completely. When he finished, he stacked them neatly and set them to one side. "What, beside the books, did you send via the bank?"

"Only some back copies of the *Gazette*. Mostly ones with Lord Wellington's dispatches, or reports about the battles in northern Europe. And, er…"

"Go on."

"I, er, took the liberty of writing to Mr Pakenham in Frome on your behalf. He visited Lieutenant Daniau. I sent his letter and a picture his daughter drew to the captain."

He frowned. "That *was* rather a liberty, Jo."

She looked down at her hands clasped in her lap. "I'm sorry, Papa."

Papa sighed. "So sending the picture was a final gift?"

"Papa, he was very glad to have the *Gazettes*. He says, as you saw, that there is no *regular* supply of newspapers, and many of the other officers also enjoy reading them. I'd thought to continue to send such things."

"What do you know of him, Jo?" Papa still had Alfred's letters spread out before him, and turned to the first one written in his own hand. "Your betrothed does not seem to care for him much."

"He was injured serving our country. I thought to ease the boredom of captivity for him and his friends."

Papa looked at her, his expression thoughtful, then just nodded. "I need to think about this, Jo. You will promise not to write again unless I give you permission. And should any further letters arrive, you will give them to me without opening them."

"Yes, Papa. I give you my word."

"Very well. Send Farley back in, will you?"

Relieved to have escaped without a reprimand, Jo went to her room.

.   .   .

It was five days before Papa spoke to her again about the letters. She'd wanted to ask him when he would decide, but she held her tongue—appearing too eager might sway him against allowing her to write at all. Finally, not long after Chivenor had brought in a letter, he summoned her to his study again.

"You may continue to send *Gazettes*, and any other books or similar items that are requested. You will, however, keep any letters you receive, and I may ask to see them at any time. You will also keep copies of any letters that you send. Is that understood?"

"Yes, Papa. Thank you." She was surprised by the sudden relief she felt. Surprised, too, that her father had not forbidden her from writing —after all, it was not essential that the *Gazettes* were sent with accompanying letters. What had he been doing these last days? Had he found out more about Captain Delafield?

He reached into a drawer and handed her all the letters. "The top one arrived two days ago. Jo, if there is anything untoward in *any* of these letters, you will bring it to me immediately."

"Yes, Papa."

"And by 'untoward', I mean anything that could not or would not be written to a *sister*, is that clear?"

"Yes, Papa."

In her room, Jo sat at her dressing table with the unopened letter propped against the mirror. Why had she felt so relieved that she was not forbidden to write back? She had only had a few letters from the captain, and they had mostly been responses to her offers of assistance.

No matter—she had permission now, and she would continue. She reached for the letter and broke the seal.

Dear Miss Stretton,
My thanks for the news of Lieutenant Daniau, and the portrait.
Madame was so touched by it, and so pleased to have it, that she wept
on my shoulder for a full ten minutes. It was very much appreciated
and now has pride of place above the mantelpiece in the parlour. I

cannot think of a more suitable gift for her, nor how to thank you properly for your efforts in obtaining it.

You mentioned in your last letter that you deal with business accounts. I have to admit to being curious, for this is surely unusual for a woman? Please be assured that I intend no criticism, and do not feel obliged to answer my query if you do not wish to.

You also mentioned not being able to make head nor tail of the content of the two books you sent. You are not alone in this; it took me some time to understand the first chapters, and that was achieved only with the help of my friends, who are more used to such things. For anyone to understand without the aid of a tutor would be beyond most people I know.

I am now able to get around with just one crutch, and hope to be promoted to the use of a stick before too much longer. This will be a great boost to my dignity, as one can attempt to convince oneself as well as onlookers that the stick is used merely for effect.

Yours, with respect,
Capt. Robert Delafield

Still smiling at that last paragraph, she wished, not for the first time, that she knew a bit more about the captain. At least she knew his name now.

Her assumption that he was old was based on a comment in one of Alfred's letters. But how old *was* he? It might be better not to find out too much. She did like his letters; they made her feel like a person and not merely a dutiful potential wife, as Alfred's did. Would it be even more improper if Captain Delafield turned out to be younger than she thought?

∾

Verdun, September 1813

Rob received another packet of *Gazettes* about a month after the first, accompanied by a letter from Miss Stretton. He was pleased to see it, for it had occurred to him that Mr Stretton might not know of his daughter's correspondence. If so, a letter from Rob's brother with money for the books could have let the cat out of the bag. As he hadn't told Will to send it to her, he would naturally address it to her father.

The afternoon was sunny, so he walked to a tavern near the river and sat outside to drink ale and read the letter. It started by thanking him for the money, but went on to say that there was no need do so again; he could repay anything he owed once he arrived back in England.

> *You asked me about dealing with business accounts. Papa invests in many different enterprises, including shipping, canals, and various manufacturing ventures. He allows me to take part in many of his investment decisions, some of which involve looking through account books, and I make some small investments of my own. I am an only child, so Papa thinks it important that I understand something of his financial affairs. It is most satisfying to look into a business to see if it is worth investing in, and helping him to consider whether doing so could bring about changes to make it more profitable.*
>
> *I hope you have progressed to using a stick. Be sure to buy a stylish one, to carry off the deception that it is merely a fashion choice.*

He read through the letter again, carefully. What it did *not* contain was any indication that he should not write back. He was unaccountably pleased by this. More pleased than he should be.

Folding the letter, he replaced it in the packet, wondering what Miss Stretton was like. Bengrove had given a disparaging description of her—he recalled something about a scrawny beanpole and being bookish. But Bengrove wasn't the type to marry someone ugly or old just for the money, so he must have been exaggerating. And the bookish remark might simply have been due to her intelligence. Rob had heard some of his brother officers belittling women who read too much, or took an interest in business or politics. Others had talked about their wives in quite the opposite way, being glad that they were capable of making sensible decisions and could deal with things at home while they were away.

And what did looks count for, really? He absently rubbed the scar across his forehead. It had faded to a thin white line, now more visible as his face was going brown in the summer sun. He thought of his niece Eliza, his eldest brother's daughter. She was pretty, but although she could seemingly prattle on for hours about fashion or gossip, she had little else to say. And she giggled. If he ever married, it was *not* going to be to a girl who giggled.

But what was he doing thinking about marriage? He had to sort his life out first. And at the moment his life included Miss Stretton's letters, which he enjoyed reading. It felt like corresponding with... well, with what?

Not a sister; his sisters were all older, and he still felt mothered by them. If he told them his worries about the future, they'd just tell him to cheer up, find a nice pretty girl, and settle down on his farm. Getting away from that benevolent but overbearing management was why he'd joined the army in the first place.

A friend? He supposed so, although it felt different from his friendship with Moorven and Chadwick. When he'd mentioned his trouble deciding what he would do with the rest of his life, they had not sympathised much. It wasn't that they didn't care, more that they didn't understand. Moorven was destined to be an earl one day, and to Rob's mind, having to manage several large estates and take his seat in the Lords was a bit different from Rob's prospects of being stuck in a small farm in rural Gloucestershire. Not that he disliked the countryside, far from it, but it was the 'small' and the 'stuck' parts of that description that were dispiriting. And Chadwick, whom Bengrove would have considered well beneath him due to his father's background in commerce, had decided he was going try to get work as a consulting engineer and build bridges or canals.

He'd had enough introspection for one day, so he finished his ale and limped back to his lodgings. Unfortunately, the war meant that he'd have a lot more time to contemplate things before he had to make a decision about his future.

CHAPTER 11

erdun, September 1813

By the end of September, Rob's ankle had progressed to the point where he could walk for short distances without his stick. But even though walking did not cause too much discomfort, the joint would not bend as it should, and as a result he had a distinct limp. Campbell, when consulted, had recommended massaging it daily, but had had to admit in the end that he didn't know if it would ever mend completely.

"Damned lucky they didn't take your leg off," he pointed out when Rob showed his disappointment. "And you're lucky, too, that it's healed without leaving permanent pain. There's many who need to use laudanum for some time after injuries such as yours, and that rarely ends well."

"I won't get approval to rejoin my regiment like this, will I?" Rob asked, knowing full well what the answer would be.

Campbell shook his head. "Think on it, laddie. After Wellington gave the frogs a pasting at Vitoria, it's looking as if we might prevail. Once Boney's gone there'll not be the need for such a large army as we have now. So even if your ankle is working properly, there'll be a lot of fully fit officers put onto half pay. Best to think what you might do instead."

But no matter how much Rob thought about it, the fact was that fighting was the only profession he was qualified for. If he had to leave the army, he wanted to earn a living in a way he found interesting.

Rob still had his mind on his future that evening as he joined Moorven and Chadwick in their usual tavern, but he distracted himself with a discussion about the war. Wellington's Allied army had taken the coastal fortress of San Sebastian, and his next move must surely be towards the Pyrenees. Near the end of the evening, Bengrove came into the tavern with a couple of his friends, accompanied by three women. The one with Bengrove was just as well endowed as the girl he'd been with when Madame Daniau doused his ardour with a bucket of water. This one was a very young blonde, too, although her hair looked more naturally light-coloured.

Rob turned back to the discussion of possible tactics and routes across the Pyrenees. They were about to make their way home when an argument started across the room. Bengrove's girl had jumped up off his knee and was haranguing him loudly about her payment.

"Pay up first, Bengrove, like she wants," someone called.

"Tell her I'll pay her after, will you?" Bengrove asked. Had the man *still* not learned any French?

"Tell her yourself," the man said shortly. Bengrove felt in his pockets, but came up empty-handed. The woman stepped away from him with a pout and cast her eyes around the room. Her gaze paused on Rob's table, and she headed for Moorven. Rob nudged his friend.

"You're in luck, by the looks of it." Moorven was the best dressed of them, and the woman had likely picked him because of that. Her hips did sway nicely as she walked over.

"*Chéri,*" she started, but Bengrove had come up behind her and swung her round.

"We have an arrangement," he said, lips thinning in annoyance.

"*Eh bien, paie-moi donc!,*" she said, knocking his hand off her shoulder and holding her own out, obviously understanding what he meant even if she didn't comprehend the words.

"I'll pay you after," he said. "I've money back at my lodgings." She was shaking her head before he'd even finished speaking, and turned back to make eyes at Moorven.

"Delafield, lend me something, will you?"

"No. I need all the money I've got." Which wasn't true—he could afford what the woman would charge, but Bengrove was the last person he'd consider lending money to.

"I'll pay you back tomorrow."

Rob just raised his eyebrows and shook his head, not bothering to speak.

"I give you my word," Bengrove said through gritted teeth, his face beginning to turn red. Rob shook his head again. "Moorven?"

"No, Bengrove. Find a moneylender."

"The word of a gentleman," Bengrove said, facing Moorven now. "Don't you understand the idea?"

By this time everyone in the room was watching him, most sitting back waiting for the fun to start. "What makes *you* a gentleman, then?" Moorven asked, carefully keeping his voice polite.

"Lord Bengrove. Viscount Bengrove, my father." There were a few grins now, from the men who knew Moorven well.

"Is there a hierarchy in these things?" Rob asked, feigning an air of innocent interest. "I mean, are you more of a gentleman, as the *second* son of a viscount, than someone who is the heir to an earl?"

"What the hell's that got to do with it?"

"You seem to be claiming that I am not a gentleman," Moorven said mildly. Someone behind Bengrove sniggered.

"You going to challenge him, Moorven?" a voice called. "My lord Moorven, I should say." The man bowed with an exaggerated flourish, amid laughter.

"Oh, I don't think I'll dirty my—"

"Lord?" Bengrove interrupted, glowering at Moorven.

Moorven nodded. "Correct. Viscount Moorven; my father's the

Earl of Claverden. And it's *Lord* Moorven to you. Now toddle off, won't you, and let us get on with our discussion."

Bengrove gaped for a moment, then turned to Rob furiously.

"You introduced him as Lieutenant Moorven."

"So I did. Unlike some, he doesn't see the need to flaunt his *gentlemanly* background." Rob couldn't help laughing, which made Bengrove even more furious. He looked around at the grinning faces, snarled something crude, and slammed out of the room.

The tart eyed up Moorven again, but someone else called out behind her. "I'm no *gentleman*, love, but I've got money!" This raised another laugh and the woman, once again readily understanding the meaning, took herself over to her next customer.

"Amusing," Moorven said seriously, "but I think you've made an enemy there, Rob."

"More than you?"

"Ah, but you're an inferior sort poking fun at your betters, so yours is a worse crime." Moorven looked down his nose at Rob, managing quite a good impression of Bengrove's sneer, but couldn't quite keep a straight face.

"Poor, delicate little flower, that Bengrove," Chadwick added, raising another laugh, and stood up. "I'm for my bed. Rob?" They gathered up their papers and finished their ale, then, sticks in hands, set off for Madame Daniau's.

Not long after the encounter with Bengrove, Rob found himself near the Rue du Marché on one of his daily walks. As it was some time since he had received a packet of *Gazettes*—or a letter—from Miss Stretton, he decided to call at the bank in case a message to Madame Daniau's had gone astray.

"I was about to send for you, Capitaine," Allard said, when Rob was shown into his office. "There are more books, and more newspapers."

The *Gazettes* looked as if they had been leafed through already. But no matter—their contents held no secrets.

"Now Austria is fighting on your side," Allard went on. "This is welcome news for you, *n'est-ce pas?*"

It was, but alliances had been formed and broken again before now. "Only if our armies win the next battles," Rob said honestly. "You do not seem too worried about this?"

"France is not Napoleon, and Napoleon is not France. I would prefer that we win, obviously, but I think peace will be better for France even if it means we have the old order back in charge."

Rob was surprised; he could not imagine the people at home being so sanguine about a possible French victory.

"But you will come back with your opinion when you have read these?" Allard put his hand on the pile. "As a *capitaine*, you will be able to… to read things that are not said?"

"Read between the lines," Rob said, nodding. This was new—he had continued to make summaries of what the *Gazettes* reported, but Allard had not shown any interest in discussing things before.

"And we can compare what the French papers say with your English papers?"

Rob had to agree. Then he thought that a friendly contact in France could be useful in the future, no matter what the outcome of the war was. "I will come back soon. Is that acceptable?" It would be helpful to discuss the matter with Moorven and Chadwick.

Allard nodded and pushed the box towards Rob. Rob took his leave, heading for a nearby tavern to find out what Miss Stretton had sent this time.

Dear Captain Delafield,
I enclose a copy of the Philosophical Transactions of the Royal Society *published this year. Papa subscribes to this, as the occasional paper may prove of relevance to his commercial activities. If you or your friends find this of any interest, I can obtain other volumes.*

Papa and I wondered if you might find the book about steam engines interesting. As ever, I could not make sense of it. This is only to be

*expected, as the man in the shop from whom I ordered it explained
very carefully, almost in words of one syllable, that attempting to read
it would only lead to a brain fever. It was only following my explanation that I was enquiring for such a book on behalf of a male friend of
the family that he deigned to help me decide on the best one.*

Rob smiled at that and picked the books out of the box. Turning to
the contents page of the *Philosophical Transactions*, he found that it
included a couple of articles on new detonating compounds, and
something about an air pump. Chadwick should be interested in
those, if nothing else. The other book was *The Steam Engine*, but that
simple title was a mere cover for a great deal of mathematics that Rob
would need help to understand. Still, it would keep him well occupied
for some time.

However, the next paragraphs in the letter removed any trace of
amusement, and he put the books aside.

*Next month we will be removing to Bath for a time, in the hope that
taking the waters will do Mama some good. Mama's physician is
cautiously optimistic when I ask him how she goes on, but has been
more honest with Papa. Mama spends much of her time in bed or
reclining on a sofa in the parlour, and has little energy or interest in
anything. Even when the doctor provides a stronger tonic, its beneficial effects do not persist for more than a few weeks. I am trying to
remain hopeful, but it is difficult, as Mama is getting steadily weaker.
My only comfort is that she does not appear to be in pain, as she was
at the beginning of this illness over two years ago. Taking the waters
is all our physician can recommend, although he does not hold out
much hope. Papa will not be able to spend all his time in Bath, due to
his business affairs, but Mama's sister will come with her family, so
Papa's absences will not be too difficult.*

*My apologies, Captain, for burdening you with my troubles, but it is
refreshing to be able to be honest about this without some well-*

*meaning person immediately attempting to contradict me and say
that all will be well in the end.*

*Pray do not think you will be aiding me by saying I need not continue
to send news; I am grateful for useful tasks, as they help to distract me
from our family's present sadness.*

Yours,
Jo Stretton

Rob almost smiled at this last—he had just been thinking that he
would write to say exactly that. He finished his ale and returned the
books and the letter to the box to take them back to his lodgings. He
cried off the tavern that night, not feeling in the mood, and instead
read through Miss Stretton's letter again. He wished there were something he could do to help, but he knew full well there was not.

His mother had fallen ill when he had been ten years old, when
he'd had a house full of older brothers and sisters to talk to, and to
comfort him. And Father had been well into his seventies when he
died; Rob had been in Spain, busy with campaigning. All of those
things had helped him through his grief. He hoped she was close to
her aunt and cousins, so they could provide comfort.

Miss Stretton had said she needed distractions, and he could
understand that very well. He could at least write to take her up on
her offer to obtain the previous year's *Transactions*. He'd see if Chadwick or Moorven wanted anything else sent, too.

But when he finished writing his letter he did not seal it. Instead,
he sat and looked at it—it was short and sympathetic, but not very
personal. Her letter to him had been the opposite, talking frankly
about her feelings and fears. It also appeared that her father knew she
was still writing to him. Did that mean this correspondence was no
longer quite so improper?

There was something else about her letter that nudged his
memory, and he read through it a third time. Then he tore up what

he'd written and reached for a new sheet of paper. He needed to see Campbell before he finished the letter—he could do that tomorrow. That would also give him time to sleep on it before sending something that would be much more personal than anything he'd written to her before.

CHAPTER 12

Bath, November 1813

Jo followed Aunt Sarah into the Pump Room, with Cousin George beside her. This was only the second time she had come with Aunt Sarah. She had accompanied Mama here every day for the fortnight Papa had spent with them in Bath, and had hardly left her side. As a result, the only people she recognised were the few women of Mama's age who had spoken to her then.

George was looking about the room as if he, too, knew no-one present. That was entirely possible—he and a friend, James Newman, had taken rooms rather than staying in the house Lord Yelden had rented for his family, and had accompanied his mother to only a few entertainments.

"Shall we take a turn about the room, Jo?" George said, offering his arm.

Jo fell into step beside him, her hand resting lightly on his sleeve. "Thank you for accompanying me, George. It was kind of you to volunteer."

He grinned, and she couldn't help smiling back. She knew Aunt Sarah had all but ordered him to come.

"Are you to take some water back for Aunt Frances?"

"No. Chivenor sent one of the footmen this morning, when Mama said she could not come." Jo had tried to persuade her, but to no avail; she had insisted that even being carried in a chair was too fatiguing, and Jo had given up when Mama showed signs of becoming tearful.

George patted her hand in unspoken sympathy, and they walked slowly on. A few older women nodded at Jo, but not in a way that encouraged her to approach and speak to them. She was glad of it; beyond relating Mama's continued poor health, she didn't know what else to say.

"Miss Stretton, how pleasant to find you here."

Jo turned, surprised to find Mr Bengrove behind her. She nodded. "Mr Bengrove. I didn't know you were coming to Bath. Is Catherine with you?"

"Indeed." Mr Bengrove indicated his wife in a group of other women at the far side of the room. "She will come over directly."

"I will be pleased to see her. May I introduce my cousin, George Yelden? George, this is Mr Bengrove, Alfred's brother."

The two men made their bows. "Do you stay in Bath long, Yelden?" Mr Bengrove asked. "We are to return home shortly—hunting season, you know."

"I have no plans to leave," George said. Catherine approached, and George was introduced. He turned to Jo. "Shall I leave you to women's talk, coz?" He couldn't completely hide his hopeful expression.

"By all means," she said, and was unable to resist adding, "I hope you will accompany me again tomorrow." She smiled at the dismay that briefly crossed his face.

Catherine took Jo's arm, and they walked to a quieter part of the room. "I was sorry to receive your note telling me that your mama had taken a turn for the worse." Her gaze followed Mr Bengrove and George, as they talked a few yards away. Jo could see from the way George was standing that he wanted to be gone.

"Have you been in Bath long?" Jo asked. Catherine seemed to be ill at ease—perhaps she was as uncomfortable with strangers as Jo was. She had only ever met Catherine in private until now.

"We only arrived yesterday."

"How is your baby?"

Catherine's expression softened. "She is doing well. I was sorry to have to leave her with Nurse while we were here."

"Is she not a good traveller?" It must be trying to be in a carriage with a crying baby for several days.

Catherine grimaced. "When we took her from London to Bengrove Hall, the journey was rather difficult." She was interrupted by a loud burst of laughter from a nearby group. "We cannot talk properly here," Catherine said. "Will you call? Or should I come to you one morning?"

"I will call, if you give me your direction. Thank you."

"I am at home most afternoons." Catherine took a card from her reticule and gave it to Jo. "I hope to see you soon."

As Catherine walked away, Jo wondered why Catherine seemed so keen to see her now, when the only communication she'd received since Catherine had gone to Bengrove Hall was a brief note to say she'd been safely brought to bed with a little girl. Then she shrugged and looked around for Aunt Sarah. She had satisfied Mama's wish to come here, and Mama would be happy to know she had met Catherine Bengrove again. There was no need for her to stay any longer.

Jo's life in Bath soon settled into a routine. Each day she went for a walk in Sydney Gardens or attended the Pump Room in the company of Aunt Sarah or, sometimes, a reluctant George. She had also called on Catherine Bengrove several times, which helped to pass another half hour or so.

"Is Mama still in her room, Chivenor?" Jo asked as she removed her bonnet and gloves after a trip to the circulating library. She had been looking for an undemanding story that she might read to Mama.

"I believe she is dozing in the front parlour, miss. Some letters have arrived for you—I have left them in the back parlour."

"Thank you." She went to change into her working gown before going to the small back room she used during the day—it hardly justified the name of 'parlour'.

There was a letter from Papa, mentioning a couple of the investments that Jo had helped to research, and hoping that Mama was still taking the waters. A sealed packet from Papa's secretary contained copies of the London newspapers, and also a letter that had arrived for her in Russell Square. It was from Captain Delafield.

She hesitated before unfolding the paper. This could be a reply to the letter in which she'd expressed her worries about Mama. After she'd sent it, she had wondered if she had been too personal, and if that might have made Captain Delafield uncomfortable with their correspondence. She hoped it was not just a single sentence of sympathy, which was all she'd had from the briefer news she'd sent to Alfred.

It wasn't. The captain hadn't written a great deal, but what he had written was heartfelt and sincere. Jo blinked away a prickling in her eyes and read the rest of the letter.

I hope it is not too impertinent of me to mention this, but what you say about your mother's illness bears a resemblance to the trials of some of the officers here in Verdun. It is sadly too common that those who need opium in some form to ease the pain of severe wounds become dependent on it if it is needed for some time, and still require its use in ever-increasing quantities when their injuries have healed. This is to the detriment of their body and sometimes their faculties as well.

I do not pretend to any medical knowledge, and hope I have not distressed you in any way. This may, of course, be completely unrelated to your mother's case, but I thought it better to write this rather than fail to say something that might be of some use.

Mama's medicine was making her ill? No, it couldn't possibly be.

Jo put the letter to one side, surprised that Captain Delafield could have written such a thing. Turning to the newspapers, she began her usual search for items of interest. But when she had had to re-read the same article for the third time, she gave up.

The captain's idea sounded preposterous. Could Mama's medicine really be harming her? Mama's physician would not poison her deliberately, she was sure. With a sense of unease, she recalled that Doctor Walsh had provided what he called 'stronger' tonic several times.

She must tell Papa. He could talk to Mama's physician in London and find out what the situation was. If the captain were wrong, she could put it from her mind. If he were right, could anything be done? She didn't know. But she would not say anything to Mama—she would leave it to Papa to decide what to do.

Papa arrived three days later, long after darkness had fallen. Jo had been on tenterhooks since she'd sent her letter with a messenger, wondering if she was making a fuss out of nothing, and even if Papa might be angry that she had mentioned Mama's illness in a letter to Captain Delafield. She heard Papa's voice from her back parlour and went to greet him.

"Jo." He gave her a quick hug, and the trace of a smile. "You were right to pass on what your captain said. I will speak to you in the morning—I'm afraid all I want at the moment is my bed. But do not worry—I have everything in hand."

Jo comforted herself that there must be some hope of improving Mama's prospects to make him travel so late in the day.

She had to wait longer still, for Papa came late to breakfast. He ignored the food set out on the sideboard and poured himself a cup of coffee before coming to sit opposite Jo.

"I went to see Doctor Walsh as soon as I received your letter, Jo. It was not a pleasant interview." He rubbed one temple. "I did not accuse him of anything; I merely asked if there was any possibility that some of Frances' symptoms were due to the tonic. He said I was impugning his professional competence, and I was free to find another physician."

"Oh dear." Jo frowned. "That sounds very... defensive?"

"It was. I spent some time trying to find a physician who both had the time to see me and was willing to do so. I managed to find two. Understandably, they talked only in vague terms about the likelihood that the symptoms of the original problem may have been worse than the potential harm from the laudanum."

"So giving it to Mama in the beginning may have been the right choice?"

"Indeed. They did also confirm that Frances' current symptoms could be the effects of laudanum, and described the difficulties of stopping its use. It seems that not only does the person wish for more of it, but the effects of stopping its consumption can be painful and distressing."

"So is it *possible* that she could stop taking it?" Was there some hope?

"It can be done, but is not easy. Not at all, from what they told me. However, one of the physicians did give me the names of a couple of practitioners here in Bath who take an interest in the subject. I have written to them this morning, but it may be several days before they can examine your mother."

Jo nodded.

"And Jo, even if it is the case that Walsh's tonic is poisoning her, it does not follow that stopping or reducing what she takes will help. It sounds as if the cure for her current problems may be worse than the problem itself, in some respects. Your Mama will have to *want* to stop using it."

"I understand, Papa. It is hard to wait, though, knowing that she might be well again."

"Keep yourself busy, Jo. Farley will forward only the most urgent matters for now, so I will have plenty of time to sit with her. She will be reassured to know that you are going into society."

"Mama was happy to know that the Bengroves—Mr and Mrs Bengrove, that is—are here. I called on Catherine again yesterday."

"Then pray continue to do so. But Jo, it would be best not to say any of this to your Aunt Sarah, not until we know more."

Jo did as he asked, going to the Pump Room with Aunt Sarah later that morning, with George's rather unwilling company, and accompanying her aunt on calls later in the day. And the following day she called again on Catherine Bengrove. Jo still had too much on her mind to make conversation easily, but Catherine was happy to chatter about the weather and the local gossip.

"Do you go to the concert in the Assembly Rooms this evening?" Catherine asked, when those subjects had been exhausted and Jo was about to take her leave. "You could accompany us if you wish, unless your mother is well enough to go? I understand your father is in Town at the moment."

"Thank you, but I will be accompanying my aunt and cousins," Jo said. She didn't tell her friend that Papa had returned to Bath, in case Catherine asked her why. She had no wish to invent a reason.

"I will see you there," Catherine said, before taking her leave.

But Jo did not go. She would not be able to concentrate on the music, and politeness would keep her trapped there for the length of the concert. She sent a footman to Aunt Sarah with a note of apology and spent the evening trying once more to go through the latest batch of newspapers.

Chivenor knocked on her parlour door the next morning. "Mr Yelden has called, Miss. He is awaiting you in the parlour."

"Mama sent me," George explained when Jo joined him. "She is worried that you are staying at home too much, so I'm under orders to take you for a walk on such a fine morning." He tilted his head to one side. "Are you well, Jo?"

Jo sighed. "I am worried about Mama, but that is nothing new. I will gladly walk with you." She managed a smile. "Am I your escape from escorting Aunt Sarah?"

He grinned in return. "You are indeed. Shall we go to Sydney Gardens? Wrap up well. It is very cold, even in the sunshine."

George was good, and undemanding, company as they walked briskly among the bare trees and shrubs. He talked about a horse he was considering buying, the places he intended to ride to around Bath, and his amusement at the way his friend James Newman was trying to court his sister Lydia—all without requiring much of a response from Jo. It suited her mood, and she felt better for the exercise. The following morning, Mr Newman came along, too, and they climbed Lansdown Hill to the racecourse. That was far more strenuous than the walk in the gardens, but Jo enjoyed it, and was pleasantly tired when she returned.

"Mr Stretton wants to talk to you, miss," Martha said as she teased the tangles out of Jo's windblown hair. "He said to join him in the parlour when you're ready." She pushed in the last pin, stood back to admire her efforts, then started to remove Jo's chemises and petticoats from the drawers of the clothespress.

"What are you doing?"

"Mr Stretton said we'd be staying with Lady Yelden in Sydney Place for a week or two."

"What...?" Jo stopped; Papa would not have explained why to Martha.

"Is Mama worse?" Jo asked her father, as she hurried into the parlour. "She was much the same as usual yesterday—what has happened?"

"No, no, don't worry. It is good news. Well, it could be good news. Come, sit down and I will explain."

Not completely reassured, Jo sat. "You have spoken to the doctors?"

"Yes, and two of them have examined your mother."

While she had been safely out of the house with George. Jo tried not to feel put out about it; Papa was only trying not to worry her.

"They both concluded that at least some of her ills are due to the amount of opium in Walsh's tonic. They suggest we start by trying to reduce the amount she takes—but even this could be very unpleasant."

"Does Mama know?"

"Yes. I have explained it all to her, and she has agreed to try." He gave a slight smile. "No, more than 'agreed'. She *wants* to try. Jo, I know she has been somewhat confused at times, but be assured I talked to her about this on two separate occasions, and I am sure she understands what is involved. *She* wishes you to stay with your aunt, so you do not need to witness any distress she may suffer. Will suffer."

"Oh, Papa!" Jo's voice wobbled.

"Now, Jo, no tears! Your mother is a *very* determined woman. She will have me to look after her, and Halsey, and the physicians will call daily."

Jo nodded. She could not be any more worried about Mama than Papa was.

"I want to hear that you have been out with your aunt, or for a walk, at least once a day, so I may tell Frances."

"Very well, Papa."

Three days after Jo moved to the Yeldens' rented house, George and Mr Newman accompanied her up onto Lansdown Hill again. She preferred walking with her cousin and his friend to going about with Aunt Sarah; she found it difficult to make polite conversation at the best of times, and felt even more awkward in company when worry about Mama was in her thoughts.

Today, the sun was almost warm enough to take the chill from the breeze. The two young men waited for her at the top of the hill, leaning on a fence admiring the view. Jo stood next to them, regaining her breath.

Eventually, George broke the companionable silence. "Funny chap, that Bengrove."

"I didn't know you'd met him," Jo said.

"Mama introduced us in the Pump room. But I was playing cards at Lord Elverton's last night, and he came up to me. Started talking about his brother, saying how he was looking forward to coming back to see you."

"What's odd about that?" Jo asked, feeling some guilt that her concerns about Mama's health had meant that she had not given Alfred much thought recently. "You aren't saying he shouldn't be keen to see me again, are you?"

"Ha, no! Of course not. But then he said, looking right at me, how ungentlemanly it was for a chap to go around with another man's betrothed when the man couldn't be here himself."

Jo frowned. What business was it of Mr Bengrove's? "How did you reply?"

He grinned. "I said I didn't see why you should have to be a hermit. Then I said how much I enjoy your company, and that the Bath air suits you, as you're looking very well. He went rather red in the face. Then James said you were a jolly good sort and it wasn't any effort to escort you around. Thought the man was going to hit one of us."

"Really?"

"It's true," Mr Newman corroborated.

"Why didn't you just say we are cousins, George?"

"Oh, I did! But cousins can marry, you know."

"Don't be silly, George. We are friends, that is all, and neither of us wishes it to be different."

"True enough. And James wants to marry Lydia…"

Jo looked at Mr Newman, raising an eyebrow. He went very red. "Well, it must be perfectly plain!" he protested. "Lydia doesn't like long walks, but she doesn't mind me escorting you!"

"And I am happy to have your company."

"But George is right, Miss Stretton. Bengrove was very strange. He more or less came right out and asked George if he was… was interested in you."

"So you said no?" Jo asked, looking back at George.

"No, I said it was none of his damned business!" George looked genuinely angry now. "I wouldn't blame you if you were having second thoughts, Jo. I mean, you didn't know Bengrove—Captain Bengrove—for very long, and your father never met him. If he's anything like his family…" Words failed him, and he shook his head. His friendly feelings for Captain Bengrove, so evident last year, seemed to have worn off.

"We'll have to see what happens when he comes home," Jo said, not willing to discuss this any further. "But George, do try not to tease Mr Bengrove about it if he speaks to you again. He must be worried about his brother."

George was about to say something else, but obviously thought better of it and instead started bickering with his friend about exactly how far they could see—leaving Jo to wonder, yet again, how she was going to manage to live in the same house as the rest of the Bengrove family if she married Alfred.

CHAPTER 13

erdun, December 1813
In the weeks after his last letter to Miss Stretton, Rob wondered many times whether he had been right to say what he had about opium addiction. His doubts were not eased when he received a reply, for it was very brief, only thanking him for his kind wishes and for the information, which she had passed to her father.

Was that a final letter? He hoped not, for that would mean he had offended her, or her father. Or both. The note had come with another batch of *Gazettes*, although those had been sent by Mr Stretton's secretary. But the alternative explanation for the lack of Miss Stretton's usual entertaining communication was not something to be hoped for —that her mother had declined further, or even died.

That the latter might be true was indicated later in the week he came across Bengrove once again in their usual tavern, while he and Chadwick were waiting for Moorven to arrive. Bengrove was at the far side of the room, complaining about his future prospects to anyone who would listen, and clearly already in his cups. Unfortunately, he was talking so loudly that everyone in the room had no choice but to hear him.

"...wait until I get married. I'll sort everything out then."

"Thought you were complaining about that being delayed, Bengrove?" one of the players said.

"Not if I can help it. But the house is closed up, and the mother hasn't been seen out for weeks. Hope the old trout doesn't turn up her toes, or the family'll be in mourning."

"Being in mourning don't have to stop you getting married," someone pointed out.

"Oh, stow it, Bengrove. Just don't play if you can't pay!"

"I'll pay, I told you! As long as the woman doesn't play the jilt."

Rob started to listen more carefully. He wandered closer to Bengrove's table and leaned against the wall.

"Should have married her before I left, then I wouldn't be having these problems. Dragged her off to Gretna, maybe, or had my way with her and then her father would have had to get a special licence before I went back to Spain." Bengrove emptied the brandy glass he was holding.

"I say, Bengrove, that's a bit much," one of the other men around the table protested weakly. Rob bit his lip, muscles tense as he fought the inclination to dive over the table and shove Bengrove's teeth down his throat. But he knew he could not rush to Miss Stretton's defence without betraying their correspondence. That would *not* go down well with Bengrove—with good reason. Rob felt a pang of guilt, swiftly suppressed when he remembered that Bengrove had never mentioned her with respect, but always with some disparaging remark. If Miss Stretton's betrothed had been someone honourable, like Moorven, then Rob would not have continued with the correspondence. Indeed, he would never even have thought of writing to her.

There was a movement beside Rob, but he ignored it, still focused on Bengrove and the men around him.

"Why do you think she might jilt you?" someone else asked. "Not that I'd blame her."

"My brother says she's being squired about by a couple of youngsters," Bengrove said, seemingly oblivious to the insult. "My father tried to get her old man to sign the settlements a couple of times after I was captured, but he wouldn't. Damned cits, no sense of honour. If it weren't for the money, I'd not go near the woman."

Rob felt a hand on his shoulder, and looked around to see Moorven standing beside him.

"Let me deal with him," Moorven said.

Moorven didn't know about Rob's correspondence with Miss Stretton, but he must have seen his anger at Bengrove's words. With his rank and a cooler head, Moorven was in a better position to make Bengrove stop, so Rob nodded.

"Such touching devotion to your betrothed, Bengrove," Moorven said. "Such gentlemanly conduct, talking about a respectable woman like that behind her back! How *did* you manage to persuade the poor woman to become engaged to you?"

"Mind your own damned business, *my lord*," Bengrove snarled. "This is nothing to do with you."

"It *is* to do with *us*, though." One of the card players spoke up as Bengrove refilled his glass and drank from it. "You're promising money you haven't got yet. What if she gets to hear about the way you talk about her? If the woman had any sense, she'd run a mile before tying herself to you. And then you'd have no chance of paying your debts."

"I told you—she wants to marry into a good family."

"A debt-ridden one," someone muttered. "Poor girl must be desperate."

"Who's to tell her, anyway?" Bengrove protested.

"Oh, perhaps I will," Moorven put in. "If she's as rich as you say, and desperate for improving herself, I dare say my title might swing the odds in my favour. Not to mention my future prospects."

"If Moorven doesn't, my old man's a baronet," someone called. "Not a viscount like yours, Bengrove, but I'm the *eldest* son!"

"You'll have to get rid of your own wife first, Johnny boy," another voice shouted, amidst laughter.

"Ah, well. It was a nice thought while it lasted!"

That brought another laugh from most of the listeners, who were now treating the whole conversation as a jest. Bengrove would have done well to leave it there, but he didn't. He stood up, staggering slightly, and walked over to where Moorven and Rob stood against the wall, breathing brandy fumes in their faces. "She's betrothed to *me*." He poked Moorven in the chest. "*You* don't know who she is."

"I'm sure I could find out," Moorven replied quietly. "Even if Delafield here doesn't recall the address from the letters he wrote for you. I would be doing her a favour, I should think, to warn her off."

Bengrove turned a bleary eye on Rob. "You, you countrified oaf, should know your place and not interfere with your betters." Then back to Moorven. "And you can mind your own bloody business!" Bengrove drew his fist back and took a swing at him. Moorven, being sober, dodged it easily and Bengrove hit the wall behind him instead. He gave a howl of frustration and pain and bent over, moaning and clutching his damaged hand. Moorven gazed down at him for a moment, shrugged, and turned away.

"Fancy a different location, Delafield? Company's a bit below par in here."

Rob followed him out, pausing only to let Chadwick know they were leaving.

"Do you know his betrothed?" Moorven asked.

"In a way," Rob replied. He said nothing for a few minutes. He should not betray Miss Stretton's confidence, but his anger at Bengrove needed some explanation, and he trusted Moorven not to tell anyone else. He gave Moorven a brief outline of events. There was a long silence when he had finished.

"It seems Bengrove has some cause for annoyance, even if he doesn't know it," Moorven remarked at last.

"I'm not trying to... I mean, I've never met the young lady, how could I...?" Why had Moorven's question flustered him so much? "There has never been anything said—written—that was other than between friends."

"I doubt Bengrove would see it that way."

"I hope he'll never know," Rob said shortly, still uneasily aware that it really was not proper to correspond with a young woman who was in no way related to him.

"You are really just friends?"

Rob had asked himself that from time to time. How could they be anything more? Liking someone to any degree beyond ordinary friendship based purely on what they wrote in letters was foolish—wasn't it?

"In all fairness," Moorven went on, "I think someone should at least tell her father what Bengrove is like. If you don't feel that you can tell me, I'll find her name and direction somehow."

"I'll see her father when we get out of here," Rob said firmly. And he would. Never mind the idea that it wasn't the done thing to interfere in another man's marriage—*future* marriage—no-one deserved to be tied to Bengrove without at least being warned of what he was like. Bengrove had crossed a line tonight. The way he had disparaged her when he was talking to Rob was bad enough, but to do so in public went well beyond the pale.

And if Miss Stretton took Bengrove anyway? Could she really want to have titled relatives so much that she would happily live with him? Surely not. Her letters... her letters showed she had a keen intellect and a dry sense of humour. How long would it take for Bengrove to wear all that out of her?

"More ale, Moorven?" Rob said abruptly. "I feel a sudden need to get drunk."

Bath, December 1813

Jo stayed with Aunt Sarah for three weeks. During that time she received daily notes from Papa that said she wasn't to worry. George continued to take her for walks on fine days, in spite of the frigid air, and she visited Catherine Bengrove several times. Then Papa came in person one morning and Jo was summoned to the parlour.

Jo felt a momentary dread, but yesterday's note had said nothing ominous, and she dismissed the feeling. Aunt Sarah was already in the parlour with a smile on her face. "Good news, my dear."

Her knees feeling suddenly weak, Jo sat down.

"It *is* good news, Jo," Papa said, coming to stand in front of her. "The last weeks have been very... unpleasant... for Frances, but she has been free of the worst effects of opium for three days now."

"Is she still..." Aunt Sarah hesitated. "I mean, Frances needed laudanum after losing the baby because of the pain she was feeling."

"She says there is no pain now. Doctor Saunders thinks it is possible the original damage has healed."

"Oh, Papa." Jo stood up, and her father enveloped her in a hug. "Oh, I am so glad!"

"It is not a cure, Jo." Papa held her away from him a little. "You must understand that. You, too, Sarah. She is likely to need to take a weak form of the tonic from time to time—she will never be entirely free of it, and the craving for more may come upon her again. Halsey and the other servants will have to be warned not to buy extra laudanum for her, even if she pleads for it. You, too, Jo."

"Yes, Papa."

"Sarah?"

Aunt Sarah sighed. "Of course. And I will be vigilant whenever she comes to Yelden Court. It will not be easy, I think, if she says she is in pain."

"You should talk to her yourself about this. She is more lucid and aware now than she has been for some time, although still weak from her lack of appetite these last months."

Jo thanked her aunt for letting her stay, and returned to Queen Square with her father. She found Mama lying on the chaise longue in the parlour, swathed in shawls, as usual. There were shadows beneath her eyes, and her face looked drawn. But she held a hand out when Jo entered, her smile happier than Jo had seen in many months. Jo ran over and knelt beside her, tears coming to her eyes.

"Now, don't cry, dear. All will be well, you'll see."

Jo sniffed, swallowed hard, and nodded.

"It will be some time before I am up and about properly again. You must promise me, Jo, to go about with your aunt as long as the Yeldens stay in Bath."

"I will, Mama." She might enjoy the assemblies and concerts more now she did not have the worry about Mama always in her mind.

Life settled into a new routine in the following weeks. Mama began to go to the Pump Room every few days, first with Papa, then with Jo and Aunt Sarah when Papa had to return to London. Snow curtailed many of their activities, but they went out when the streets had been cleared enough to be safe.

Jo made a point of attending as many concerts and recitals as she could, and went to the weekly assemblies. She even put up with Mama summoning a dressmaker to measure Jo for new evening gowns and walking dresses—an exercise that she normally disliked. The Bengroves returned to Staffordshire before Christmas, so she no longer had a particular friend to call on, but she found she did not miss Catherine as much as she'd expected to. Jo liked her well enough, but they had few mutual interests to talk about.

One afternoon, several weeks after Jo had returned from Aunt Sarah's, Jo sat at the table in the front parlour while Mama took her usual afternoon nap. She had finished with the latest batch of newspapers, and left one folded to show the invitation to invest in a new canal project that she wanted to discuss with Papa when he arrived from London later this evening—if the state of the roads permitted. Feeling somewhat at a loose end, she watched the street for a while, but the cold was keeping many people indoors and dusk was gathering. The novel she was reading from the circulating library didn't appeal to her at the moment. Instead, she opened her portable writing desk and took out the bundles of letters she kept there.

There were two, the smaller one containing Alfred's brief notes. She rarely looked at those more than once, for they were all remarkably similar, being limited variations on the theme of missing her and frustration at his continued incarceration. The ones from Captain Delafield made a much larger bundle. Since she had confided her fears for her mother in October, and then sent the good news of Mama being on the mend, their letters had become longer. Reading them and writing back felt like holding a conversation with a friend in whom she could confide her hopes and fears, albeit one with long gaps between exchanges. She flicked through them, reading the odd paragraph here and there: sympathy for her troubles, anecdotes of happenings on his walks about the city, comments on the progress of his studies, including admitting to struggling with some of the mathematics involved. And the all-important one with his thoughts about laudanum, for which she would be ever grateful.

She picked up his most recent letter.

The news of the continuing French retreat, and Wellington's victories
in the south of France, is giving us hope that the Allies may soon
succeed in ousting Bonaparte and we may all return home.

She wanted the war to end, of course she did, but then Alfred would return, and she would have to decide what to do. The Alfred in his letters was not the Alfred that she remembered meeting at Yelden. Perhaps it was just that he was not very good at putting his feelings into writing? She flicked through a few of his letters. If her memory of him *were* faulty and she had just been flattered by his attentions, could she really marry him? It wasn't just his letters that gave her doubts, but also the prospect of being part of the same family as his unlovely parents. She sighed—she had no choice but to wait and see what transpired when he came home.

Almost as if she had read her daughter's mind, Mama's voice made Jo look up. "Is that a new letter from Alfred, dear?"

"No, Mama. I am re-reading old ones."

"Read some to me, Jo. At least writing still keeps you two in touch."

Jo reached for Alfred's letters and then paused. She had read out the trite compliments too many times in the worrying days when Mama had not seemed to recall that she had heard the same things before. Mama had so set her heart on Jo's marriage to Alfred that Jo didn't want to voice her doubts yet. So she sorted through Captain

Delafield's letters, finding one that included something that she could discuss with Mama. "Here's an interesting one, Mama," she said, unfolding one from last summer. "He writes that he has heard from his family that some wounded men from his company have gone there to ask for help. Then he says, 'but when this war is over—whoever wins—there will be many more with little or no provision that I know of to help them earn a living once the army no longer needs them.'"

"That's very thoughtful of him, dear."

"Then he goes on, 'When I return, I would like to help any former soldiers who need it. Any form of assistance will require money, but no doubt funds could be raised with enough effort. But money is not the only requirement; there is also the problem of how to spend it wisely, and that is possibly the more difficult to solve.'"

"Soup kitchens," Mama suggested. "Several well-born ladies organise such things for the poor."

"That does not help people permanently, Mama."

"No, I suppose not. Does he have any ideas? Do read the rest."

"All right." It was good to see Mama taking a real interest again, after her forgetfulness and changeable moods while she had still been suffering the effects of the tonic. "He says, 'Wellington has referred to his soldiers in disparaging terms on several occasions, and I know of some men in my own regiment who will easily return to a criminal life, but others who started out that way have learned discipline and self-respect, and deserve a chance to earn their own living and not depend on charity—particularly the kind dealt out by the workhouses.'"

"That's a good point," Mama said. She lay back and Jo wondered if she'd fallen asleep again, until she spoke. "I suppose some could find work in the new factories. But most will not be skilled in anything other than fighting. The funds you spoke of could be used to train them for other occupations." Her gaze slid away from Jo towards the door. "Nathaniel!"

Jo spun around. "Papa! You are earlier than we expected. We did not hear you arrive."

"I managed to get on an earlier coach, and you were engrossed in your letters." He looked at Mama, and his face softened. "How are you, Frances? You are looking well."

"I am feeling well." Mama sat up, swinging her legs to the floor, and Papa went to sit beside her. The look they shared made Jo feel very much *de trop*, so she crept out of the room. Would she have that degree of affection with Alfred when he returned?

CHAPTER 14

Bath, February 1814

"Lord Bengrove is here to see Mr Stretton, miss," Chivenor said, looking uneasy as he stepped into the back parlour. "Mr Stretton asks if you can wait outside the parlour, in case he wants to see you."

"Surely he can just ask you to come…" Jo stopped in mid-sentence. It was most unlike the staid butler to look so… *furtive* was the only word for it. Papa must have a reason. "Very well."

She followed Chivenor as he crept down the stairs and gestured her to a chair just outside the parlour. The door was ajar, and Jo could hear Lord Bengrove's voice. Chivenor did not meet her eyes as he gestured to the chair once more, then retreated towards the baize door to the servants' quarters.

Jo sat.

"…waste more time, Stretton."

Lord Bengrove's words were clear now she was sitting so close. Papa must want her to hear what was being said.

"My lord, I don't understand why you are so keen to discuss this now. When we were at Bengrove a year ago, we agreed that the matter should await your son's return from France, so he can have his part in it. It is *his* marriage after all."

It was *her* marriage as well, Jo thought.

"The boy will be keen to get married. It's been a long time." Lord Bengrove's words were sympathetic, but his tone was more one of impatience. "He'll want to get on with his life, eh?" he went on, his voice a little softer. "After being locked up for so long. Will have been very hard on him."

"As it will have been for all the prisoners. However, as you say, it has been a long time. I think the two of them should have a chance to get to know each other again before we think about contracts and settlements. They were only together for a just over a week. And we should allow some time for Jo to think about what her life will be like as a married woman."

"Eh? What do you mean, Stretton? Just like any other married woman!"

"My daughter is used to helping me with my business matters. She will—"

"Good of you to humour her, but it's time she gave that up, surely? Women have no head for business. It's not natural."

Did Alfred think the same? She hoped not. But she recalled, with sinking spirits, that she had avoided mentioning her involvement in Papa's business interests when they had been together at Yelden. He might well share his father's view.

Papa was still talking. "You think that women are incapable of making important decisions, do you?"

"Everyone knows it, eh? That's why we do it for them."

"So you consider that women should not be allowed to make contractual arrangements?"

Why was Papa continuing this? A simple refusal to discuss the settlements would have been enough to get rid of Lord Bengrove.

"Of course not," Lord Bengrove replied. "Some have to, of course. Widows, and so on. But not when they have a man to rely on. I don't understand your wish to delay, Stretton. The betrothal was announced—you are not going to break your word, are you? That would not help your business interests if it became known."

That sounded like a threat.

"I have given you several reasons, Bengrove. There was no betrothal, or any announcement of one. And it is not a matter of me going back on my word, as my agreement would have been required before any betrothal took place. In fact, I understand that my daughter agreed only to wait until your son could return from Spain. That is irrelevant, however. Jo was with my wife at Yelden Court when your son met her. She was only twenty years of age at the time, and the only permission asked was of my wife. A *woman*, and therefore, as you have stated, not capable of giving such permission. You had sent the exaggerated details to that gossip column before I could be consulted on the matter."

There was a silence, and Jo smiled slightly. She imagined Lord Bengrove gaping like a landed fish. He had, in fact, been skilfully played.

"What… what are you saying, Stretton?"

"I'm saying," Papa repeated calmly, "that they need to spend some more time together before any further announcements or arrangements are made. And that I need to *meet* your son before giving him permission to marry my daughter."

"Your daughter is of age now. She doesn't need your consent."

"Have you asked *her* what she wants?" There was a pause. "No, I thought not. Don't forget, Bengrove, that although Jo can marry without my consent, she only has the dowry or other income that I choose to give her. And if she *does* marry without my consent, that amount could be very limited indeed."

"Hmph!" Lord Bengrove cleared his throat a couple of times.

"If that is all, Bengrove?"

A scrape of wood on wood indicated that Lord Bengrove might be about to leave, and she quickly stood up. She didn't want to be caught eavesdropping. She crept into the dining room across the entrance hall, and was just out of sight when she heard her father summon Chivenor to fetch their visitor's hat and coat. She waited until she heard the front door close behind him, then went to join her father in the parlour.

"Well, Jo?" he said seriously, waving her to a chair. "I assume you heard most of that?"

"Yes, Papa." Her father seemed to be waiting for some further comment. "He seems very anxious to get a contract signed. Did George tell you what Mr Bengrove said to him last December?" Papa shook his head, so Jo told him about Bengrove's assumption that George was courting her.

"And George did not deny it?"

"No. He said it was none of Bengrove's business."

"Good lad. But it could explain why Lord Bengrove continues to try to get contracts signed." He hesitated. "Jo—I will do something about the contracts if you wish it."

"No. You were right in what you said to Lord Bengrove." The Alfred she knew from his letters was not the man she remembered from that week at Yelden Court. Could the feelings she recalled be rekindled?

"Jo, he may not be like his father. Those parts of his letters I over-heard you reading to your mother last week impressed me. I hadn't thought he was so considerate."

Jo felt her cheeks heat. "Er, those weren't Alfred's letters I was reading from."

Papa nodded, unsurprised. "I did wonder about that. Why, Jo?"

"Mama is still pinning her hopes for me on marrying Alfred, and I have read his letters out to her so many times..." She sighed. "I was adding a bit of variety for Mama's sake, and found something to discuss. I should own up to having deceived her, I suppose."

"No, Jo. At the moment she is still rather fragile, in mind as well as body. Let her continue to think well of the young man. When he returns, I will ask your aunt if she is willing to host a small house party at Yelden Court. Both of us wish you to be happy in your marriage, and that will give Frances time to know Alfred better, as well as you. If you then decide against him, Frances will be able to see that the marriage will not make you happy." He paused a moment.

"And Jo, had you met another young man worthy of you, I would not have allowed those considerations to stand in your way had you wished to go back on your promise to wait for Alfred to return."

"Thank you, Papa." Although the reassurance was moot. "Why did you allow me to continue writing to Captain Delafield?"

"He seemed a sensible man, from his letters, and you were helping him and his friends to pass their time in captivity. I did make some enquiries as to his character before I gave you permission to continue."

Jo wondered what he had found out, but stopped herself from asking. Papa could still rescind his permission if she seemed *too* interested.

"And as it was Captain Delafield's observation that led to your mama's better health, I am very happy that I did allow it. But Jo, it would be best if you did not read any more of his letters to her."

"I won't, Papa."

If the Alfred who came back from France was the man she had agreed to wait for, Mama probably wouldn't even recall the letters. She would not worry about that until Alfred returned.

Verdun, March 1814

"Capitaine, thank you for coming." Allard stood to greet Rob, and shook his hand. "Do sit down."

Rob did so, assuming this would be the usual hand-over of a letter or batch of newspapers from Miss Stretton. Her letters had resumed their previous frequency in late January, with the welcome news that Mrs Stretton was much better, thanks to his suggestion.

There was a stack of *Gazettes* on Allard's desk, but also some back copies of French news sheets. As he sat, Allard brought out a map of France. "I do not wish to wait for you to summarise the news this time," he said. "In here," he tapped the pile of *Gazettes*, "there is news that your Marquess Wellington has defeated Maréchal Soult's army in France." He peered at the map, and pointed to a place just north of the

Pyrenees. "Here." His finger moved on to various places further north. "And there have been battles here, and here, and..." he hesitated a moment, "and here, not far from Verdun."

The last was no surprise to Rob, as Verdun had been rife with rumours for the last month or more, mostly about the movements of Napoleon's troops or the various armies of the Coalition forces in north-western France. Some of the soldiers must have passed nearby, but the prisoners were no longer allowed out of the town for exercise. Reports of who had fought where and who was winning were garbled, but, to Rob's surprise, there seemed to be a general feeling among the townspeople that the Coalition forces were prevailing, and that this was not necessarily a bad thing.

"This is... well, this is good news for me, monsieur," Rob said carefully, not sure what Allard's opinion was.

"I think it is good news for France, Capitaine. The emperor..." He shrugged. "There have been a lot of good French lives lost, and for what? He gave Spain to his brother, who has lost it now to your Marquess Wellington. And the attack on Russia? Pah! We are all war weary."

"Thank you for telling me," Rob said. "Your information is... correct?"

"As far as I know. I have news from various commercial contacts. I think there will soon be a battle for Paris. Then we shall see."

There was an uneasy pause. Rob thought that Allard wanted something else, but he seemed reluctant to say anything. "May I take these to read them?" he asked eventually, pointing at the *Gazettes*.

"*Oui!* There is a letter, too." Allard picked it up, but did not immediately hand it over. "You are acquainted with Mr Stretton?"

Rob hesitated. He was not about to explain the details of his connection with Miss Stretton, but it was clear that her father allowed the correspondence, so he just agreed that he was.

"You will let him know I have been helpful?" Allard asked. "I think it will be important to keep good business dealings when this mess is over."

"Certainly, if you wish it. There is a way you could assist me, if you are willing, monsieur." With the news of Napoleon falling back towards Paris, he had been thinking about what would happen when he could leave Verdun, and when prisoners from the ranks were released. "I was not the only one in my company captured, I think. If my men were not too badly wounded, they may be still held in France. I did hear the officer escorting us talking about it when we were a few days' journey south of here. If they are nearby, I would like to make sure they have the means to get home safely."

"You wish me to find where they were taken?"

Rob nodded.

"*Bien*. You will write down the details, and I will ask for you. And when the time comes, you may apply for a loan if you need it. You will repay me via Mr Stretton, yes?" Allard was rolling up the *Gazettes* as he spoke, and handed them to Rob. Rob thanked him, then headed for his lodgings.

He shared the news with Moorven and Chadwick that evening, and they drank rather too much wine toasting the successes of the Allies and the prospect of a final defeat of Bonaparte. Now all they had to do was wait for that to happen so they could all go home.

And he would have to warn Mr Stretton about Bengrove.

CHAPTER 15

*L*ondon, April 1814

"Lady Yelden has called, Miss Stretton," Chivenor said, entering the library. "She requests that you join her in the parlour."

Jo put a marker in her book and stood. Aunt Sarah called on Mama every few days, but it was unusual for her to ask Jo to join them. When she entered Mama's parlour, Aunt Sarah was still standing, her smile wide, and Mama's face was more animated than Jo had seen it for a long time.

"Jo, Sarah has brought good news! The Allies have entered Paris!"

Jo sat down, her legs suddenly wobbly. "Truly, Aunt? There was nothing in today's newspaper." From recent reports of the war, she had hoped that matters were reaching a conclusion but had not expected it so soon. "Surely the war must be over, then?" England had been at war almost all her life; it would feel quite odd to no longer have that in the background. Odd in a good way. A very good way.

"We must hope so. Yelden heard about it in the Lords," Aunt Sarah said. "The news will be all over town within a few hours, I should think. I had to tell you both."

"Just think, Jo," Mama added with a happy smile, "Alfred will be back soon!"

"Yes, Mama," Jo said faintly. Now that meeting Alfred again was imminent, instead of being in some undefined future, she found herself feeling nervous. They had known each other for such a short time, and been apart for so long, that it would almost be like meeting a stranger again. She felt she knew Captain Delafield far better than she knew Alfred.

Then she realised that Mama and Aunt Sarah were already planning her wedding. "Mama...," she tried to interrupt. "Aunt Sarah!" she said more loudly.

"...bride clothes from Lydia's modiste and..." They finally realised that Jo was trying to gain their attention.

"Jo? What is the matter?" Mama asked. "Are you not pleased?"

"It does not seem real." She rubbed her forehead, trying to work out why she felt rushed. "Papa... Papa said that Alfred and I need to spend more time together before..." Before anything was settled, but she did not say that. The idea of Jo marrying into a titled family had been a comfort to Mama this last year. "Before we finalise arrangements," she finished. "There are the marriage settlements to be worked out as well. That might take some time. And don't forget, the war is not won yet."

"But you have been writing to each other," Mama said. She turned to Aunt Sarah. "They were good letters; he seems a most considerate and thoughtful young man."

Oh dear—Jo had been hoping Mama had forgotten the details she had read aloud. "Aunt, Papa said he was going to ask you to invite the Bengroves to Yelden Court. But none of that can happen until we know when Alfred will return."

Mama sighed. "I suppose not. But now we know he *will* be returning soon, we must see to your wardrobe, Jo. I will accompany you to the modiste."

Jo was about to protest, but hesitated. She had not seen Mama so enthusiastic about anything since before she lost the baby, over two years ago. "I will ask Madame for some fashion plates, so we may look at the latest styles before we visit the salon."

"That's a good idea, Jo." Aunt Sarah nodded in approval. "And of course you may all come to Yelden in the summer. Now, I will take my leave."

To spread the good news, Jo suspected.

It was nearly a week after Aunt Sarah's call that news reached London of Napoleon's abdication, and everyone knew the war was over at last. And a week after that, one of Papa's contacts at Horse Guards let him know the French authorities had ordered the release of all prisoners of war. But even they did not know how long it would take for the men to return home—they thought it would most likely be done in order of capture. That would make Alfred amongst the later prisoners to be released. That was disappointing, but at least she knew Alfred would be returning before the summer. No matter her trepidation about how they would like each other after so long apart, at least her future would be settled soon.

Captain Delafield would be returning, too. Would he call? He might wish to thank her for sending the books and papers.

Yes, she thought with relief. He would do that.

A few weeks later, the faint echo of a knock on the front door distracted Jo from her perusal of the papers in the library. There followed a murmur of voices. Male voices. It was unusual for Papa's business acquaintances to call in Russell Square, and Jo thought, with a thrill of anticipation, that enough time had passed for some of the prisoners at Verdun to have reached England. Had Alfred arrived?

She crept to the door and opened it a crack to look into the entrance hall. The visitor was being shown straight into Papa's study, and all she caught sight of was his back view—a tall, slim man with blond hair, in a well-fitting dark blue coat. For a moment, the blond hair made her think it was Alfred—but he was broader in the shoulders. Then the door shut behind him and she retreated into the library. Her disappointment vanished when it occurred to her that it might be Captain Delafield. She could ask Papa when his visitor had left, of course—but if it *were* the captain, she should thank him in person. Wouldn't that be the polite thing to do? She gave it some thought, then rang the bell.

"Could you send tea up, please," she said, when Chivenor arrived. The butler bowed and was about to leave when she asked, as casually as she could, "Papa has a visitor?"

"Yes, miss. A Lieutenant Moorven."

Oh. Her stomach returned to normal.

Lieutenant Moorven was one of Captain Delafield's friends—but why had he called? If he knew of her at all, it would only be as the supplier of *Gazettes* and books to the captain. Could he have brought bad news of some kind?

She wanted to go and find out, but Chivenor would have said if the lieutenant had asked for her, and it would be impolite to intrude. After pacing back and forth for a few minutes, she forced herself to sit down and take several deep breaths. It would not do to seem agitated when a maid brought the tea. She could find out why Moorven had called from Papa when he left.

She drank the tea when it came, leaving the library door ajar so she could hear when the lieutenant departed. The clock on the mantelpiece ticked away the time until, nearly an hour later, she heard voices in the entrance hall again. The lieutenant had stayed far longer than usual for a mere courtesy call.

Smoothing her skirts, she stepped into the hall and turned towards the stairs as if she were going to her room.

"Ah, Jo!"

At Papa's call she turned to face the two men. Lieutenant Moorven had an open, friendly face, his grey eyes crinkling at the corners as he smiled at her. His coat, buckskin breeches, and Hessians were all finely made and fitted him well.

"My daughter, Joanna," Papa said. "Jo, this is Lieutenant Moorven."

"Miss Stretton," he said, making a quick bow. "It is a pleasure to meet you. I called to thank you and your father for your efforts in keeping us all informed this past year. The reading materials you sent were most gratefully received, I assure you."

"My pleasure, sir," Jo said, with a curtsey. "Has Papa offered you some refreshment?"

"Some very fine brandy," he replied. "I have an appointment now, but I hope to see you again." He bowed, shook her father's hand, and allowed Chivenor to show him out.

"Was that really all he came for, Papa?" Jo asked when he was safely out of hearing. He had taken an awfully long time to say thank you.

"Er, no." Papa hesitated a moment. "He also said that Captain Bengrove has been delayed in his return from Verdun. As has Captain Delafield."

"Is something wrong?"

"No, no. They are both in good health, as far as I can gather. Delafield wanted to make sure that the men in his company who were captured with him have the means to reach their homes safely."

"That is good of them."

"I... Yes, yes it is. Now, how are you getting on with those summaries of Luddite troubles in Lancashire?"

"I finished this morning, Papa. Shall I bring them in?"

"If you would."

As she fetched the papers from the library, Jo thought that it would have taken no more than a few minutes for Lieutenant Moorven to pass on the two captains' reasons for not having returned yet. What *had* they been talking about?

London, May 1814

As the footman brushed the shoulders of his jacket, Rob marvelled again at the painted wallpaper on the bedroom walls and the rich bed hangings and curtains. Moorven had invited him and Chadwick to stay at his parents' town house on Grosvenor Street whenever they needed to be in London, whether or not he was there. Moorven's lack of regard for class was the more remarkable now Rob saw that the family was not only titled, but wealthy with it.

"Thank you," he said, when the footman stood back.

Rob inspected himself in the full-length mirror as the footman bowed and left. The man had done a good job pressing out the creases in the uniform that had been stored in a trunk for over a year. The trunk that his fellow officers had returned to his brother in Gloucestershire when Rob was captured, and Moorven had sent for on his behalf. Without that kind thought, Rob would be presenting himself in Russell Square in one of the made-over sets of clothing that Madame Daniau had altered for him. He was pleased that the uniform still fitted him properly; he had been concerned that Madame Daniau's cooking, and the relative lack of exercise over the last year, might have made him too fat for it.

He had arrived in London two evenings before, and had presented himself at the front door after paying off the hackney. He smiled at the memory of the butler's transformation on his arrival, the man's initial disdain giving way to dignified politeness when Rob handed him Moorven's letter. His lordship, the butler had informed Rob, was absent at present, but expected back within a few days. The other staff here were friendlier, for which he was grateful. He'd spent most of yesterday resting, buying some new shirts and cravats, and getting a decent haircut.

Downstairs, he checked his appearance one last time while a footman summoned a hackney for him. Not that it should matter what he wore, he told himself. He would thank Miss Stretton for her kind actions in sending materials to Verdun, hand over the small gift he had bought for her, and find an excuse to talk to her father alone. Mr Stretton, at least, should know what Bengrove had been saying about Miss Stretton. Her father would also know how much of that to pass on to her; she must have felt some affection for the man to become betrothed to him, however unlikely that seemed to Rob.

His intention felt uncomfortably like telling tales at school, but it should not. Bengrove had made no secret of his dislike for Miss

Stretton and her family, and Rob owed him nothing. It wasn't as if he were trying to get Bengrove out of the way to his own advantage.

Not at all.

Rob straightened his jacket when the hackney deposited him on the pavement in Russell Square. The address he'd been writing to for the last year was a tall house in a terrace of similar properties, with a large front door atop a short flight of steps, and a railed-off area with steps leading down to the servants' entrance. He plied the knocker, and asked the footman who answered it if he might see Mr Stretton.

"Whom shall I say?" the footman asked, holding out a silver salver for Rob to leave his card.

"I'm afraid I have no card, but please let Mr Stretton know that Captain Delafield wishes to pay his respects."

To Rob's surprise, the footman immediately stood back and gestured for Rob to enter. "Please come in, sir. Mr Stretton was expecting you to call at some point. If you will wait in the library, I will inform him that you are here." He took Rob's shako and gloves and set them on a side table before showing him the way.

Although the room was not large, it contained a great many books. He moved closer—the floor to ceiling bookshelves held volumes on a wide variety of topics, including atlases and a fair selection of scientific and technical works. The wood of the shelves and the large desk in one corner shone with a gentle glow that indicated much polishing. The four leather wing-back chairs near the empty fireplace looked well used, but, to Rob's untutored eye, to be of excellent quality.

It wasn't long before footsteps in the entrance hall alerted him to his host's approach. Although he had only asked to see Mr Stretton, he was hoping to meet Miss Stretton as well, and turned in suddenly breathless anticipation.

CHAPTER 16

The man who entered the library was about Rob's own height, with clear blue eyes and hair that was going grey but not yet thinning. He was alone.

"Mr Stretton. Thank you for seeing me." Rob made a bow, ignoring his disappointment at Miss Stretton's absence.

Mr Stretton inclined his head with a welcoming smile. "Captain Delafield. Won't you sit down?" He waved towards the chairs. "What can I do for you?"

Rob set his parcel down on a table beside his chair and rested his stick against it. "I… er…" He swallowed, and cravenly decided to start with the least contentious part. "Monsieur Allard, of the *Banque de la Meuse* in Verdun, asked to be recommended to you, as desirous of maintaining good relations now that peace is with us."

"Thank you for passing that on. Monsieur Allard has been most helpful, it seems."

"He has, yes. I also wished to thank you for sending books and news."

"You should rather thank my daughter." There was a dry note to his voice.

"I would be glad to, if you permit."

Mr Stretton did not reply immediately, and Rob had to stop himself squirming under his host's scrutiny. Corresponding with another man's betrothed might not have been an honourable thing to do, but her father had known about it. Or, rather, he had found out and allowed it to continue. He could not have disapproved completely.

"Before I answer that, Captain, tell me something about yourself."

"Captain Robert Delafield, 2nd battalion, 30th Foot," he started. Mr Stretton smiled and raised one brow. "Er, I expect you knew that already, sir."

"Why do you say that?"

Rob took a deep breath. "You allowed your daughter to conduct what many—most—people would regard as an improper correspondence. I assume you would have carried out some kind of check on who or what I was."

"You are correct. Were you also aware that I have read some of your letters?"

Rob felt his face get warm as he hastily tried to think of anything improper he might have written—particularly in the last few months, since their correspondence had begun to be more frank and open.

"When your brother wrote with a bank draft to repay me for the first few books that Jo sent," Mr Stretton continued, "I asked her to show me the letters you had exchanged to that point."

He'd never written anything that he could not have said to his sisters, he was sure, but he still felt some relief that no-one else had read the most recent ones.

"Why did you continue the correspondence, Captain? I am aware of the reason for your first letter, but after that?"

He'd expected to be asked something like this. "Miss Stretton replied and asked if there was anything she could do or send. As there *was*, I asked for books and news. It grew from that. Miss Stretton seemed happy to confide some of her thoughts to me."

Mr Stretton nodded, his face more serious. "And you to her. Captain, I can never thank you enough for conveying your speculation about the overuse of opium. Without that, we might never have realised that the physician my wife trusted was slowly poisoning her." His lips thinned and his brows drew together momentarily. "It still makes me angry to think of the harm..." He ran a hand through his hair.

"I am glad to have been of use, sir."

"Tell me more about yourself, Captain. You must have had other correspondents while you were in Verdun. I believe you have a large family?"

"Two brothers and four sisters."

"With you the youngest of the family."

It was a statement, not a question; Rob gave a wry smile. "You *have* been checking up on me." Mr Stretton chuckled, and Rob began to relax. This conversation still felt rather like an interrogation, but a friendly one. "Yes, I am the youngest. I had plenty of letters from them, but almost all about their families. Miss Stretton's letters were different—more wide-ranging, and recently more on how things go on in England. And... well, my sisters are all quite happy doing the usual female things. I mean, the things that society decrees are suitable for women. It was a novel idea for me that not all women thought like that."

"You approve?"

"It is not up to me, sir, to approve of your daughter, or to not approve."

"Hmm." There was a short pause before Mr Stretton went on. "Are you remaining in Town, Captain?"

Rob was relieved at the change of subject. "I'm not sure yet, sir. I need to go to Horse Guards, where I expect I'll be given leave." And after that? Campbell hadn't held out much hope of his ankle ever working properly again. It was possible that Horse Guards might still find a use for him, but it wasn't really likely. Although he should at least wait to find that out for certain before getting too worried about it. "I also need to go into Somerset."

"You have family there?"

"No, most of them live in Gloucestershire. My landlady's son has been held in Somerset since being taken prisoner, and I promised to ensure he had sufficient funds to return home safely. I will go on from there to see my family."

"Did you manage to see your men before you left France?"

Rob frowned. He didn't recall writing to Miss Stretton about that. "Sir?"

"Lieutenant Moorven called on me and explained why you had been delayed."

That was odd; Rob hadn't asked Moorven to do that. "Yes, I did. They seem to have been treated reasonably well." That reminded him of another part of his errand here. "I loaned them—gave them, rather —some money to ease their journeys. Sir, if I send you a draft on my bank, could you arrange to forward the money to Monsieur Allard? He was kind enough to advance me some extra funds."

"With no collateral?"

"He took my word," Rob said stiffly. "We had several discussions about the progress of the war. He did know me a little."

"I meant no offence, Captain, I assure you. Do send the draft when you have it, and call again when you are back in London." Rob's expression must have looked doubtful. "I mean that, Captain. Apart from anything else, my daughter is not at home at the moment. I assume you wish to thank her in person?"

"Er, yes. Thank you, sir." He *would* be allowed to talk to her, then. That was good, albeit somewhat unwise. Although Mr Stretton's words had been a clear signal that the interview was at an end, Rob did not stand up. There was still the matter of Bengrove.

"Is that all, Captain?"

Rob took a deep breath. "No. Sir, you may consider this not to be my concern, but I must say something about Captain Bengrove. He—" Rob stopped as Mr Stretton held up a hand.

"Please say no more, Captain. No, don't look so worried. I should tell you that Lieutenant Moorven had quite a bit to tell me about Captain Bengrove, so there is no need for you to repeat it. Unless you know anything he does not?"

"Er, possibly different details, but I imagine our opinions of him are very similar."

"Very well. Thank you for your concern for my daughter, Captain, and be assured that I have her best interests at heart."

Rob wasn't quite sure what that meant, but he had quite clearly been dismissed. He stood, picked up his parcel, and took his leave. Horse Guards next, although he doubted he'd get any answers right away. He'd be lucky to achieve anything more than getting an appointment. Then to a coaching office to find out how best to get to Cheringford to see Madame's son.

A carriage turned into the square as he was leaving it. It began to slow as it passed him, and when the noise of hooves and wheels ceased, he looked back. The carriage stood outside the house he had just left, with a footman letting down the step. Was this Miss Stretton returning?

The first person out was a young man, who handed down the other occupants; an older woman, possibly in her forties, dressed in emerald green, then two younger women, one in a lilac pelisse, the other in dark red. He couldn't make out their features from this distance, but neither matched his mental image of Miss Stretton, so he turned and walked on.

Then it occurred to him that his idea of Miss Stretton's appearance was based solely on what Bengrove had said of her, and was not to be trusted. He spun around again, but the party had already gone into the house. Damn!

He contemplated going back. But if Miss Stretton were not one of the young women, what possible excuse did he have for returning so soon? No, he would have to wait until he after his visit to his family.

"Oh, look, Jo—is that Alfred back at last?" Cousin Lydia said excitedly, pointing out of the window of the carriage. "You've just missed him!"

Jo had been looking the other way, and did not see who Lydia was pointing at, but George stuck his head out of the window and glanced backwards.

"No, that's not a cavalry uniform."

"How can you tell from this distance?" Lydia asked.

"Headgear," said her brother with an air of superiority. "That chap was wearing an infantry shako."

"Oh," Lydia said, her interest waning as Jo's intensified.

If it weren't Alfred, could it have been Captain Delafield? However, there were any number of reasons why an infantryman could be in Russell Square; he might not even be an officer.

"Oh, that's a shame," said Aunt Sarah. "I wonder what's keeping him away. You haven't heard from him recently, have you Jo?"

"No, Aunt." At that moment the coach came to a halt, and they gathered their purchases while the door was opened. George handed them down, and Jo paused to glance up the street, but all she saw was a man in a red coat as the soldier walked away.

"Come on, Jo, why are you dawdling there?" Aunt Sarah sounded impatient.

"Coming, Aunt."

George took his leave to walk home, but Aunt Sarah and Lydia followed Jo into Mama's parlour. They were describing the new walking dresses and evening gowns they had ordered when Papa joined them, a note in his hand.

"It seems your preparations are just in time," he said, smiling at them all. He waved the note. "This is from Lord Bengrove. They have received word from Captain Bengrove that he expects to be home within a se'ennight, or perhaps a few days longer."

"Oh, good!" Mama exclaimed. "I am so happy to hear that. Aren't you, Jo?"

"Of course, Mama." Jo managed a smile, but felt as much trepidation as happiness. How *would* they deal together after so long apart? It would almost be like starting again.

"Bengrove invites us—the three of us—to dinner two weeks hence, so we can all meet the captain."

"I'm sure he will call as soon as he can, dear," Mama said. "You will see him before then, Jo."

"Yes, Mama." She hoped Mama was right—the idea of their first meeting happening under the eyes of Lord and Lady Bengrove was daunting.

"However, I have a better idea," Papa went on. "I thought it might be less awkward for Jo and Alfred to meet again if… well, without his parents being almost the only other people there. So I intend to invite them all here, instead." He turned to Aunt Sarah. "Would you act as hostess, Sarah? That way Frances won't feel obliged to remain if she becomes too fatigued."

Aunt Sarah nodded. "Yes, of course. I will bring George and Lydia as well as Yelden—that will be ten in all."

"Catherine Bengrove will be in Town by then," Jo said. "Should we invite them?"

"Yes, indeed. And there's an acquaintance of mine, a Lieutenant Moorven, who has also recently returned from Verdun," Papa said. "It might be nice for Captain Bengrove to have someone with similar experiences to talk to."

"If you wish," Aunt Sarah said doubtfully. "But this lieutenant will put the numbers out."

"It's an informal dinner. If the Bengroves are such sticklers for 'correct' behaviour that they object to one extra man at dinner… Well, I'm not sure that Jo would thrive in such a family."

Aunt Sarah nodded thoughtfully. "Or Yelden may be busy, or George; we shall see." She stood up. "We must be off—I'll call in a few days to check the arrangements, Frances."

Mama thanked her, and went to her room to rest before dinner. Jo followed Papa into his library.

"Yes, Jo? I presume the arrangements for the dinner meet with your approval?"

Jo narrowed her eyes slightly. "Would it make any difference if I said no?"

Papa waved at a chair, and Jo sat down. "*Do* you object?"

"No. But you are plotting something, Papa. You remind me of when you are about to make an investment that you think will do well. But this isn't about investments, and Lieutenant Moorven is not an acquaintance."

"He is now."

"You *are* plotting something!"

"Not really a plot, Jo. Nothing as complicated as that—and I mean it all for the best, trust me. Now, was that all you wanted to talk to me about?"

"Er...." It seemed wrong to ask about Captain Delafield when they had only just been discussing Jo seeing her betrothed again.

"Well, never mind," Papa said. His lips twitched. "I had a visitor while you were out."

"Oh?" Jo tried to feign indifference.

"Yes. Captain Delafield came to thank us... well, you... for sending the books and so on."

"I'm sorry to have missed him." She should not feel so despondent that she had. Would he call again? He was unlikely to write, now there was no more reason to, and she should not regret that.

"I have to say he is not quite what you might be expecting," Papa went on. "How was it that Bengrove described him?"

"In various uncomplimentary ways," Jo said, unwilling to demonstrate that she recalled perfectly well what Alfred had said about him, or to ask Papa *how* the captain was different.

"Hmm. I think young Alfred is not terribly accurate in his descriptions. Captain Delafield has gone to Somerset on an errand, but he will likely call again when he returns to London."

"Oh, that's good. It will be interesting to see him." She would have to contain her curiosity until then—if he *did* call again.

"No doubt," he said. "Now, I must write to Lord Bengrove about the change in dinner arrangements."

"Will he mind, do you think?"

"Whatever he thinks, I doubt he will actually protest. He is keen on this marriage, after all."

But would Alfred still be? Would she?

CHAPTER 17

The day after his call in Russell Square, Rob was contemplating how many clean shirts and neckcloths would fit in his portmanteau when there was a tap on his bedroom door and Moorven walked in.

"Delafield! Back at last! Glad you took me up on my invitation." He gave Rob a welcoming slap on the back, then looked at the clothing spread out on the bed. "You're not staying?"

"I'm off in an hour to catch the Mail to Somerset, to check on Madame's son—make sure he's got enough blunt to get home. Then I should see my family before I do anything else, so I'll go on to Gloucestershire."

"Then back here?"

Rob nodded.

"Good. Come downstairs for a drink."

Moorven led the way to a small back parlour, furnished in dark colours and with worn but comfortable chairs, and poured brandy for them both. "I've been to Devon to see my parents. Chadwick went north to see his—not sure when he'll be here. Has Bengrove returned, too?"

"Ha, no. The gendarmes wouldn't let him leave the city until he'd settled all the tradesmen's bills. The last I saw him he was cursing them and drowning his sorrows in cheap brandy while he waited for his father to send more funds."

"Couldn't happen to a more deserving man," Moorven said, shaking his head. "You've been to Horse Guards, I suppose. Any news?"

"No. Just an appointment in a few weeks."

"And how was Miss Stretton?" Moorven had an air of studied innocence.

"I... What makes you think I've called?"

"Haven't you?"

"Yes. But I only met her father. And found that you had been there before me!" he added indignantly.

Moorven shrugged. "I thought he needed warning about Bengrove. You were delayed..." His lips curved slightly. "And this way, no-one can say that you carried tales about Bengrove with an ulterior motive."

"I don't know what you mean." But he did.

"Nice-looking young lady," Moorven added.

"*You* saw Miss Stretton?"

"Calm down, Rob. I'm not poaching on your preserve."

"She's not... I'm not..." Rob took a breath. "She's promised to Bengrove. And she's too rich."

"Wasted on Bengrove," Moorven stated, ignoring the last part of Rob's comment. "Still, if you're not interested in what she looked like..."

Rob choked on a mouthful of brandy. "Moorven!"

"Black hair, curly," Moorven said, with a knowing grin. "Tallish for a woman. Slim, blue eyes. Not beautiful, but pretty." He took a sip of his brandy. "Not what you were expecting?"

"I only had Bengrove's description to go on." Rob grimaced. "Stupid to believe a word he said, I know."

"What did he say? The main complaints I heard were that she wasn't sufficiently well born."

Rob thought for a moment. "'Scrawny' and 'beanpole' came into it."

"Ah. I think Bengrove's definitions of those words would differ from many people's. If you remember his taste in whores…?" Moorven cupped two imaginary melons in front of his chest. "Scrawny probably just means a woman with normal proportions. Beanpole?" He shrugged. "As I said, she is tallish for a woman, but not overly so."

"Frizzy hair?" Rob said, remembering another term.

"Curly, certainly; perhaps unfashionably so. But I seem to remember Bengrove prefers blondes." He laughed. "Whether naturally blonde or not!"

"Bluestocking?"

"More intelligent than he is," Moorven translated. "Although that doesn't appear to be a high bar."

"You like her?" There was a strange weight in his stomach that felt very like jealousy—but that was ridiculous.

"I saw her for two minutes, Rob. She came into the hall just as I was taking my leave from her father."

"Sorry," Rob said contritely, then remembered the end of his own interview with Mr Stretton. "I tried telling Stretton about Bengrove, but he stopped me. Said you'd told him, and I was to be assured he had his daughter's best interests at heart."

"That's what he said to me, too."

"But what if *his* idea of her best interests is marrying up, even if it means marrying her to an arse like Bengrove?"

Moorven shook his head. "I don't think it is."

"What makes you so sure?"

"How did Stretton refer to me?"

"Lieutenant Moorven—what else would he call you?"

"I told him my title, and what I stand to inherit. He was quite happy to continue to refer to me without the title, and with no difference in manner, either. I've met enough of the ingratiating sort to know how such a one would have reacted."

"That's reassuring."

"What you ought to be wondering," Moorven said with a wicked grin, "is what she's expecting *you* to look like. Unless you've described yourself to her?"

"Of course I haven't!"

"Then she'll be going on however Bengrove may have described you."

"Good grief!" Rob closed his eyes.

"But then, as she's not your... your anything, it doesn't really matter, does it?"

"Oh, sod off!" Moorven was right, though, it *shouldn't* matter. But he liked her, even though they had never met.

"Pax!" Moorven said, holding his hands up. "Have a safe journey."

Gloucestershire, May 1814

Rob had written to Will to let him know when he expected to arrive, and as a result, he had ridden only halfway along the drive when a boy ran down the gravel towards him. "Uncle Rob!"

"Hello, young Sam. You've grown since I saw you last!" He reached down, and Will's youngest child swung himself up to sit in front of Rob for the final few yards up to the house. Rob dismounted and slung his saddle bags over his shoulder, and Sam took the horse round to the stables. Beatrice, his brother's wife, was waiting in the doorway, and he gave her the obligatory peck on the cheek.

"Come in, Robbie, do!" Beatrice led the way into a parlour. "Here are Eliza and Jane to welcome you back. I'll go and make sure cook is preparing tea." She bustled off, leaving Rob with two young women who were almost unrecognisable as his nieces—both looking so much more grown up now compared to his memory of his last leave, over three years ago now.

Will arrived back from the fields as tea was being poured. "Good journey, Rob?" he asked once they had shared a quick hug.

"Not bad. Hired a horse in Chippenham for the last few miles." He'd wondered if his stiff ankle would be up to riding, but although it was now aching, he'd had no trouble with the docile gelding they'd given him.

"Bea wanted to invite our sisters to welcome you home, but I thought you might not want everyone exclaiming over you at once." Will gave his wife an affectionate smile.

"I'll ride over and see them while I'm here," Rob said. They all lived within a couple of hours' ride of the farm.

"So, what was it really like in Verdun?" Bea asked, and they spent the next hour exchanging news. Much of it had already been told by letter, but he didn't mind. It was easier to talk about things than to write; he managed to convince them that Verdun had mostly been tedious rather than unpleasant, and they were happy to hear about the friends he'd made. They continued during the large dinner Beatrice had prepared for his return, sitting over the meal for most of the evening.

The next morning, Will took Rob to see the farms. They rode through the fields as Will described many of the same things that he had written in his letters about the land and its management. They visited the tenanted farms, and Rob was taken into a few of the houses to greet the tenants and their families, and be plied with ale. He remembered some of them from many years ago, and had to repeat the story of his injury and captivity several times. By the time they left the third one, Rob was becoming decidedly bored. Will was a farmer through and through, to the extent that he apparently could not comprehend that others might not share his enthusiasms. And, worryingly, Will was talking as if it were a given that Rob would soon be assisting him with all this management, including the farm left to Rob by their father.

The final part of their tour was around the edge of the land that would become his. Will pulled his horse up on a slight rise and gazed across the neighbouring fields. Rob dredged the depths of his memory for a name.

"Tennson's land?"

"Yes. Josiah's not well, unfortunately. Hasn't been in full health for some time, but he's just about managing. It's a shame—he's a young man yet, a year or so younger than I."

Rob gave a grunt that he hoped showed sufficient interest, and Will glanced at him sharply.

"Sorry, Will. My ankle…" Rob tapped his right boot with his whip, and Will's face cleared.

"Well, we've been touring the fields long enough for one day." He turned his horse and led the way back.

After their evening meal, when the younger children had gone to bed, Beatrice asked after the families they had seen that day. "I'm pleased you called on them," she said, when Will had passed on any news. "I will arrange a dinner soon—you will want to meet the neighbouring landowners as well, now you are home for good. For you will be resigning your commission, won't you?"

"I may have little choice."

"You should have got soldiering out of your system by now, Rob." Will's tone carried a distinct hint that it was time Rob grew up. "I thought sitting around in Verdun for so long would have turned you off it."

"It was better than the alternative," Rob muttered.

"What do you mean, Robbie?" Beatrice asked.

"Better than being dead," he said bluntly, and Beatrice gave a gasp.

"Rob, not in front of the ladies," Will said sternly, making Rob feel as if he were a mere youth again.

Beatrice returned to discussing the dinner party. "We must have the Jeffersons, and the Browns. And the Tennsons. If Josiah isn't well enough to come, Dinah can surely come without him and bring Linda." She nodded to herself in satisfaction.

"Such a shame there's no son to manage the land," Will said. "A woman cannot manage such things alone."

Rob suspected that Miss Stretton could, if she set her mind to it. Then he wondered what that smile of Bea's had been about. She was still listing other people who might come, a string of names he didn't recognise.

"Where will they all sit?" he asked Will quietly.

Will shrugged. "Many won't be able to come at short notice."

"There's no rush, is there?" Rob didn't want to be catapulted into the middle of a busy social life, especially if Will and Beatrice were going to put it about that he was to be back here permanently. That might be forced upon him in the end, but he wasn't going to submit to it without exploring other options first.

A letter from Moorven arrived the next day while he was out again with Will, being shown parts of the home farm in more detail. Much more detail. Beatrice waited expectantly when she handed him the letter on their return, but Rob just thanked her and put it into his pocket. She gave a little pout, and told them that tea would be ready in a few minutes.

"I expect Uncle Rob needs to stretch his legs after riding for most of the day," Eliza said, coming to stand behind her mother. "Shall I show you the vegetable garden?" She nodded her head vigorously.

Although mystified, Rob was nothing loath. "By all means." He waited until they were on a path between rows of peas and beans. "What's going on, Eliza. You're no more interested in vegetables than I am."

Eliza sighed. "It's Mama. And Papa," she added, being fair. "They have decided it's time you settled down and showed Nick a good example by resigning from the army." Nick was Will's eldest son, a lieutenant in the Rifles.

"What makes them think that my resigning would have any effect on Nick?"

"It was your fault he went into the army," Eliza said, with enough of a grin to show that she realised how silly this sounded.

"Your mother thinks that?"

Eliza shrugged. "It sounds that way when she talks about it, but I don't think she really means it. She wants you to marry Linda Tennson and settle down, and Linda's mama thinks it is a good idea, too, and—"

"*What?*"

"That's why I'm warning you, Uncle Rob. Linda doesn't want to marry you, either. She wants to marry Nick."

Rob grimaced. Beside him he could hear Eliza giggling.

"It's not funny."

"Yes, it is!" Eliza said. "It makes me feel better too. Mama and Papa are always telling me what to do. And I can't run off and join the army like you and Nick did." She looked at him with interest. "Is there someone else you *do* want to marry?"

There might be, if she weren't already promised. But even if there were not, Will and Bea were not going to push him into a marriage of their choosing. "When would I have had the chance to meet someone like that?"

"That's what Mama says. She says you need to settle down, and there's Linda's papa needing someone to look after the farm, and their land is next to yours and—"

"Thank you, Eliza. But your mama no longer has the power to tell me what to do."

"She'll go on and on—"

"Yes, I know. Why do you think I joined the army?"

Eliza giggled again. "Your letter might summon you somewhere on urgent business."

"I haven't even read it myself yet!" Rob protested.

"Oh, it doesn't matter what it *actually* says. But you can tell Mama and Papa—"

"Good grief—Will should lock you up, young Eliza! Plotting to lie to your parents?"

Eliza looked shocked, thinking he meant it, then shrugged. "If they would just *listen!*" she said, and Rob had to sympathise. "Mama is looking out of the window," Eliza said a moment later. "We had better go back in for tea."

As it happened, there was only a little prevarication required. Moorven's letter said that Chadwick would be in Town at the end of the week, and that Mr Stretton had invited all three of them to dine with him and his family. Rob had planned to be back in London by then in any case, but he was *not* going to meet Miss Stretton for the first time with Moorven and Chadwick looking on. If he returned to London a couple of days before the dinner, he would have time before he left here to call on the two wounded men from his company for whom Will had found employment.

"But you can't leave so soon!" Beatrice protested when he broke the news that he was leaving within a few days. "What about my dinner party? I've even found the chest in the attic with your civilian clothes so you can look your best."

"I'm sorry, Bea, but that was your idea, not mine. You haven't sent the invitations out yet, have you?"

"No," she admitted. "But you need to meet people in the area again, Robbie. You'll be living here—"

"Will I? Bea, I haven't settled what I'm going to do yet."

"Nonsense, Rob, you'll farm here. You know it's always been planned."

"Not by me," Rob said firmly.

"Linda will be disappointed," Beatrice said.

"I'm sure she'll get over it," Rob said, ignoring Eliza's giggle.

"And you haven't seen your sisters yet!"

"I will come again soon." When Bea might have realised that he no longer needed—or wanted—to be mothered.

"But Robbie—"

"Bea, dear, that's enough," Will said sternly, to Rob's relief.

He wouldn't waste Bea's efforts in finding his clothes, though. Wearing his uniform when he was soon to be out of the army felt wrong, and even if the garments Bea had unearthed were a trifle old fashioned by now, they would be smarter than the ones that had come back from Verdun with him.

And he did want to make a good impression.

CHAPTER 18

L ondon, May 1814

On the evening that the Bengroves had been invited to dine, Jo donned a new evening gown, its primrose yellow subtly trimmed but well cut to show off her figure. Martha had managed to tame her curls into a bandeau, and she wore a simple string of pearls with matching eardrops.

A knot of excitement and nervousness stirred in her stomach as she inspected her appearance in the mirror. Alfred had taken longer to return to England than anticipated, arriving only the previous day. A brief note from Lady Bengrove had conveyed his regrets for not being able to call before the dinner engagement. Was she looking pretty enough for their first meeting? Had his memory of her changed with time, thinking her more attractive than she was?

Jo was descending the stairs when the Bengroves arrived, and she paused to watch the party entering. Lady Bengrove and Catherine came first, followed by their husbands. Then Alfred appeared, in a dark jacket and pale breeches like the other two men.

Even seen from above, it was the face she remembered—square-jawed, with his blond hair styled in the windswept manner. His face was not as tanned as she recalled it, but when they first met he had just returned from a Spanish summer. The sight of him didn't induce that warm, shivery feeling she recalled—and surely it should have?

Papa was already greeting their guests, bowing as he was introduced to Alfred. Jo took a deep breath and continued down the stairs. Lady Bengrove was the first to notice her approach, running assessing eyes down her figure before poking her younger son with her fan. Alfred seemed to square his shoulders before turning to face her, then a dazzling smile curved his lips and crinkled the corners of his eyes.

That was the smile that had charmed her two years ago. She began to relax.

"Joanna!" He stepped forward eagerly and mounted several steps to meet her before she reached the bottom. She held a hand out; he kissed the back of it, then tucked it under his arm and led her back to the others. "Joanna, it is so good to see you again!"

"And you, Captain." She felt her smile must match his own, and his spoken words held a sincerity that his written ones had not. Perhaps he really was just a poor letter-writer.

Papa ushered the Bengroves into the parlour. The Yelden party had already arrived, and George was interrogating Lieutenant Moorven about his experiences at sea in one corner.

"Have you met my wife?" Papa asked, leading them to where Mama sat.

"I believe we met, many years ago." Lady Bengrove inclined her head the tiniest amount. "Lady Frances."

Mama's face flushed, but she did not deny her rank. "Lady Bengrove. Lord Bengrove. I'm so pleased you could accept our invitation. And you, Captain Bengrove. I am happy to see you returned to us safely."

Alfred bent over Mama's hand. "It is good to be back. To see Joanna again."

"You know Lord and Lady Yelden, of course," Papa said, moving them on. "And their son George and daughter Lydia."

Alfred stiffened beside Jo as George made his bow, and he

muttered something under his breath. Puzzled at the reaction to her cousin, Jo glanced at his face to find that he wasn't looking at George at all, but at Lieutenant Moorven, standing behind the Yeldens.

"And may I introduce Lieutenant Moorven, of the Royal Navy," Papa went on. "He has recently returned from Verdun, and I thought Captain Bengrove would enjoy having someone to talk to with common experiences. But perhaps you already know each other?" he added, disingenuously.

"We have met," Lieutenant Moorven said. "Good evening, Bengrove," he added pleasantly. "I trust you were not too long delayed in Verdun?"

Alfred's expression was decidedly less friendly than the lieutenant's. "Not too long, no. A minor misunderstanding, that was all."

"Good, good." The lieutenant turned to Jo and greeted her warmly —far more warmly than was warranted by the few minutes of their previous acquaintance. Jo hesitated, but there was a friendly twinkle in his eye, so she said it was a pleasure to see him again.

"Would you like a drink, Joanna?" Alfred said hastily, and took a glass from the tray a footman had been about to offer. He handed it to her, then guided her towards the sofa. He sat down, half-turned to face her. "I have missed you, Joanna. It seems... it *has been* a long time!"

"Indeed it has," Jo said. "Are you well? It took you some time to get home, did it not?"

"There were... complications," Alfred said, his gaze flicking briefly sideways, to where Lieutenant Moorven stood talking to George. Then he leaned forward and looked directly into her eyes. "We cannot speak freely in company. Would you care for a drive in the park tomorrow?"

"Thank you, Captain. I would love to." His intent gaze was doing odd things to her breathing.

He reached for her hand and gave it a brief squeeze. "You must call me Alfred, please. We are on less formal terms, are we not?"

"Alfred," Jo repeated, with a happy smile. "My family call me Jo."

"Jo," he said, warmly. "Papa tells me you wish us to know each other better before we wed. Do not keep me waiting too long, will you? After so long apart, a further delay..." He sighed.

"Lady Yelden has invited—" Jo broke off as Chivenor opened the parlour door and announced that dinner was ready.

"Later," Alfred said in a low, intimate voice, then stood. He gave her that smile once more, and offered his arm.

As the senior lady present, Lady Bengrove had to accept her host's escort to the dining room, although she looked as if she were smelling something bad. Jo found herself seated between Alfred and Lieutenant Moorven. The bustle of filling plates seemed to have dried up Alfred's conversation. He paid a few compliments to her and to the food, but then confined himself to enquiring whether he could serve her some of this chicken, or those vegetables, or summoning a footman to fill her glass, while glancing at the lieutenant several times. The rather awkward silence around her was broken when George, sitting opposite, asked Lieutenant Moorven how he'd been captured.

"Not across the table, George," his mother said quietly, but Papa spoke up from the head of the table.

"Nonsense, Sarah, this is a family dinner; no need for such formality!"

Lady Bengrove gave an audible sniff at this, but support came from an unexpected quarter.

"No, indeed," Lieutenant Moorven said. "In my own family, dinners such as this are very informal. I am happy to be included here." He raised his glass to Mr Stretton.

"And who *are* your family?" Lady Bengrove enquired, looking down her nose.

Alfred cleared his throat. "Er, the lieutenant is actually Lord Moorven, Mama. Heir to the Earl of Claverden. He chooses not to use his title while he is in the Navy."

Jo was surprised, as were the Yeldens, but stunned was the only word to describe the expression on Lady Bengrove's face. Papa was trying to hide his amusement—he must have guessed something like this would happen.

"Oh, well, in that case…" Lady Bengrove said, when she recovered the power of speech.

"In that case, let us by all means be informal," Lord Bengrove finished for her heartily, from the opposite end of the table.

"Nevertheless," Moorven put in, "I think descriptions of naval engagements are not for the dinner table." He gave a friendly smile to George, who flushed slightly and subsided.

"While we are gathered here," Papa spoke up, "I have a proposal for you all. As you know, Captain Bengrove and my daughter met two summers ago, only a few weeks before the captain was captured. A long absence after such a short acquaintance is not, I think, a suitable basis for an immediate marriage. Lord and Lady Yelden are holding a house party in July, to which they have kindly invited you all. That will provide an excellent opportunity for them to spend more time together. I hope you will all be able to attend, including you, Lieutenant." He looked at Lieutenant Moorven.

There were various murmurs of agreement, and Mr Bengrove thanked him.

"Now, Sarah," Papa went on. "You must invite that other friend of Captain Bengrove's, as well. The one who wrote the letters for him when he first arrived in Verdun. What was the name?" He stared into space for a moment, and Jo suddenly paid a lot more attention. Papa had *not* forgotten the name.

"Delafield," said Lieutenant Moorven. Jo turned her gaze on him. His lips were slightly compressed, as if he was hiding amusement.

"Ah, yes. Captain Delafield."

"He's not—" Alfred started to say, but Papa carried on talking.

"He must be a very good friend of yours, Bengrove. Jo said how lovely those first letters were; you wouldn't have dictated that kind of thing to anyone who wasn't a good friend, I'm sure."

Alfred stared at him, speechless.

"Is he another who doesn't use his title?" Lady Bengrove asked.

"No, Mama." Alfred spoke through tight lips. "I believe Delafield's family are farmers."

Aunt Sarah frowned, but when Lady Bengrove sniffed, her expression changed to amusement. "Any friends of Captain Bengrove will be welcome at Yelden Court," she confirmed.

Alfred's knuckles tightened on the stem of his wine glass; Jo dropped her gaze to hide her puzzlement. Why would the invitation anger him? She knew he didn't like Captain Delafield, but that reaction seemed excessive.

"What are your plans for the future, Captain?" Papa asked, breaking the awkward silence. "Do you intend to stay in the cavalry?"

"I won't need... I mean, I have not yet decided. I thought to..."

"Not good for a wife if a fellow is away for long periods," Mr Bengrove said.

"Ah, buy an estate and settle down, eh?" Papa said. "Excellent."

Alfred opened his mouth, and closed it again. Jo frowned at her father; what was he doing? He seemed to be going out of his way to make his guests feel uncomfortable—although why that supposition should do so, she had no idea. When she and Papa visited Bengrove Hall, Lady Bengrove had mentioned that Jo would have her own establishment. Mama appeared to be just as bewildered at the undercurrents.

"That's a prettily detailed gown you wear, Lady Yelden," Lady Bengrove said into the silence. "Who is your modiste?"

Jo took little part in the conversation after that, as it limped along from fashion to theatre visits, then the plans for celebrating the peace. That was a safer topic, and everyone stuck to it. Finally Aunt Sarah, after a close look at Mama's pale face, rose and led the ladies to the parlour for tea.

"Shall I accompany you upstairs, Mama?" Jo asked.

"Very well, dear, but you must rejoin the guests afterwards." In her room, Mama sank into a chair and shook her head. "I don't know what your father was doing, Jo. It felt as though he were deliberately antagonising your captain. I do hope he's not going to change his mind."

Jo wasn't sure whether she meant Alfred or Papa. "I'm sure he won't, Mama. You'll feel better about it when you are not so tired."

"Go to the parlour, Jo. Halsey will be here in a moment to help me."

Jo bent to kiss Mama's check, and went back downstairs. In the parlour, Lydia and Catherine Bengrove sat talking in one corner, and Lady Bengrove was next to Aunt Sarah. Jo joined the older ladies; she would have to encounter Lady Bengrove often in the future, so she should try to get on better terms with her.

"Well, Sarah," Lady Bengrove was saying. "It appears that you allow your brother-in-law to dictate who you invite to your parties."

Aunt Sarah's eyes narrowed slightly. "I accept suggestions for my guest list, yes, Gabriella. Is there something wrong with inviting your son's friends from Verdun?"

"He was forced to associate with such persons in the army; he has no need to do so now."

"Such persons?" Aunt Sarah looked annoyed now, which was unusual for her. "If your son does not wish to associate with my guests, he is free to decline the invitation."

Alfred not come? "Aunt—"

Lady Bengrove spoke before Jo could finish her protest. "Really, Sarah, do not take on so. I meant nothing of the sort. It's just that you do not know this captain that Stretton was talking about."

"I didn't know your son when George invited him to Yelden two years ago, but I welcomed him. It might have been better had I not done so. You would not then be put into the position of having to associate with... with farmers and families like my sister's."

"Aunt!" Jo protested, loudly enough to attract the attention of Lydia and Catherine. What might have happened next, she didn't know, for the gentlemen walked in.

Lady Bengrove stood. "Ah, Bengrove. I trust you recall we are promised to the Cholmondeleys this evening. Stretton, thank you for your hospitality. It has been most enjoyable."

Her tone belied her words, but Papa seemed more amused than offended. "A pleasure, my lady." Behind him, the other men stood silently, uneasy in the tense atmosphere.

Mr Bengrove and Catherine approached; their excuse was the

same, but Catherine's thanks sounded more sincere. Alfred, too, but he turned to Jo afterwards and took her hand. "I will call for you at two. The time will pass slowly until then." He gave her fingers a gentle squeeze, and turned for a last smile as he left the room behind his parents. She began to feel more confident that all would be well between them.

"That was a sudden end," Papa remarked, bringing Jo back to the present.

"I'm afraid it was my fault," Aunt Sarah admitted. "Jo, I do hope you don't need to have much to do with that woman once you're wed. I think we had better depart, too, Nathaniel. After that encounter I'm in no mood for conversation. Yelden?"

Lord Yelden nodded. "As you wish, my dear."

Jo thought, not for the first time, that all her uncle wanted was to live his life in peace.

"Sarah, I *do* appreciate your help with all of this, you know," Papa said. "As does Frances."

"Yes, well. Family is family."

Lieutenant Moorven took his leave at the same time. When the front door closed behind them all, Papa turned to Jo. "What happened?"

"Lady Bengrove took exception to a 'farmer' attending the same house party as her exalted self," Jo said. "Aunt Sarah spoke her mind." Which might not have been polite, but Jo couldn't blame her for it. She was nearly as cross with Papa as with Lady Bengrove, however; he had needled Alfred during dinner, even though she didn't know why Alfred should have taken exception to his words. And it seemed very odd that he had asked Aunt Sarah to invite two men to her house party whom he hardly knew.

"How did you get along with Alfred, Jo?"

"We started well, but there wasn't much time for conversation." Thanks to Papa; she tried to keep her annoyance from showing. "He is calling tomorrow afternoon to take me for a drive."

"That's good."

With all the guests gone, Jo retired to her bedroom, feeling sadly flat. Although meeting Alfred had rekindled the feelings she remembered, she hadn't had much time to talk to him, and their conversation had felt a little awkward. He had talked more freely at Yelden Court—with her and Mama, and with others when Aunt Sarah had invited the squire and his family to dinner. But then his parents could put a damper on any conversation.

Could they use the Dower House at Bengrove Hall until they bought somewhere of their own? She must talk to Alfred about that.

CHAPTER 19

*A*lfred came the following day as the hall clock was striking the hour. Jo, sitting in the library, heard the knock. She arrived in the hall, bonnet in hand, as Chivenor opened the door and Alfred stepped in bearing a bunch of roses.

"Joanna," he said, with his charming smile. "I hope I find you well today?"

"Yes, thank you, Alfred. And you?"

"All the better for seeing you, my dear." He held out the roses with another smile.

"Thank you, they are lovely." They must be hothouse blooms, to be available before June.

"Not nearly as lovely as your beautiful face, my dear."

Jo felt a blush rise, glancing at Chivenor, who was standing close enough to hear. He maintained his impassive expression, but Jo found it uncomfortable to be complimented in such a way in his hearing. In anyone else's hearing, really. "Thank you," she said again, handing the flowers to the butler. "Have them put in water, please."

She turned to the mirror to don her bonnet, its deep amber ribbons matching her new pelisse. Alfred held out his arm, and she took it for the few steps out to the waiting curricle. It was a smart vehicle, its body a glossy black and the wheels picked out in red and gold. Once she was settled in the seat, Alfred took the reins. The tiger jumped up behind as the curricle moved off.

It wasn't far to the park, and Alfred drove at a rather faster pace than Jo was used to with her father's coachman. She winced as they came close to knocking over a delivery boy.

"Don't worry, my dear," Alfred said. "You are perfectly safe. We're nearly at the park, too." They turned through the gates into one of the main drives, which was almost as crowded as Park Lane. Jo was relieved when Alfred slowed to the more sedate pace of the other people taking the air. Acquaintances hailed him—mostly military men by the look of them—but he waved or nodded without stopping.

"The horses are a handsome pair," Jo said, when Alfred didn't speak. There was less traffic further into the park, and he wouldn't need to concentrate on his driving here. "Are they yours?"

"My brother's. His curricle, too. A captain's income—" He frowned. "That is, he was happy enough to lend them to me until I can buy my own."

Did that mean he was planning to leave the army? But if so, why had he not just said so last evening when Papa asked him? She didn't feel she could question him about that, though—not yet. Nor the question of living apart from his mother. "Are you settling in properly now you are back in England?"

"Well enough," he said. "I can go where I wish to now, and there is more to do."

"How did you pass your time in Verdun? You didn't describe much in your letters."

"I'm not a great hand at letter-writing." He glanced at her, a brief frown changing to his charming smile. "Don't normally have the time."

"What did you find to do in Verdun?" Jo asked again. He must have had plenty of opportunity to write; he had even complained about not having enough to do.

"Oh, the usual." He kept his attention on the horses. "Same things that most gentlemen do."

"They didn't keep you locked up, then?" Jo asked, knowing full well from Captain Delafield's letters that they had not. "So it wasn't really like being in prison?"

"Bad enough," he said abruptly. "Not allowed out of the town at night, having to sign a damned book every few days to show we hadn't escaped. As if the word of a gentleman were not good enough." He glanced at her again, giving her the full benefit of his most charming smile. "But that is over, now, and I am back with you. How did you spend your days while I was gone? Did you miss me?"

"I kept Mama company a lot of the time," Jo said. "She has not been well."

"I'm sorry to hear it. She seems recovered now, though."

"Yes, she is." She had mentioned Mama's illness several times in her letters, and this was the first time he had expressed any sympathy. "I read a lot," she added, when he didn't speak.

"Novels, eh?" he said genially.

"Mostly the *Gazette* and other newspapers." She had told Alfred about Papa's business interests when she first met him, but had not told him that she was involved. It was an occupation she would be reluctant to give up.

"Unusual! Oh, well, you won't need to bother your head with that in future. Women don't need to get involved in politics and the like."

That was not promising. "What *will* I do with my time?" Jo was beginning to feel irritated. "If we are to live with your parents, I won't even have the house to manage."

If they were to live at Bengrove Hall.

"Oh, women's things, I suppose. Embroidery and what not," Alfred said airily. "You'll enjoy the leisure, you'll see. And we will be in Town for the season, of course."

"We will go to the theatre together?" Jo asked. "And other events?"

"Mama will take you, I'm sure."

Jo grimaced—she'd rather scrub chamber pots.

Alfred must have noticed. "I'm sorry if Mama was... unpleasant last night." He spared a hand from the reins to pat her arm. "I'm sure she'll like you once you get to know her ways."

Once *she* had adapted to Lady Bengrove's ways, no doubt.

"I cannot dance with your Mama at balls," Jo pointed out.

"Oh, no-one expects husbands and wives to dance with each other," Alfred laughed. "Don't you worry about that, my dear. We'll go on swimmingly, I'm sure."

What more could she say? It would not do to abuse his mother to his face, no matter what she thought of Lady Bengrove. She made an effort to smile, and looked about her for another topic of conversation. "I do enjoy being in the park; it makes a nice change from the noise of the city streets. Do you prefer Town or the country, Alfred?"

"They both have their attractions. Can't have a good gallop in Town, but there's not much fun to be had in the country apart from hunting and shooting."

"You enjoyed walking at Yelden."

He frowned momentarily, then turned his breathtaking smile on her. "I was with *you*, Joanna. Your presence makes any activity a delight." He drew the horses to a halt, and half-turned to face her. "I am sorry, my dear, if I seemed less than enthusiastic about escorting you about Town. I'm not very good at making polite conversation..."

Jo could sympathise with that—neither was she.

"...and having been confined for so long, I am unaccustomed to polite company. I'm sure escorting you will make such events enjoyable."

"We will enjoy more walks at Yelden," Jo said, comforted by his words and manner. "You will be joining us there in a few weeks' time."

"I look forward to it." He turned the horses towards the gate. "Do you mind if we return now? I have an appointment with my tailor shortly."

"No, of course not." She didn't say much as they drove back through the streets, and Alfred helped her down from the curricle.

"When can I see you again?" he asked, when Chivenor let them in.

"I would like to go to the exhibition at the Royal Academy." Jo handed her bonnet and pelisse to Chivenor. "Would you escort me?"

"Paintings." Alfred said, not looking terribly enthusiastic. "Interested in that kind of thing, are you? I'll call in a couple of days, and we'll see, eh?"

"Thank you, Alfred, that's very good of you," Jo said, as he bowed over her hand. "I'll see you *tomorrow*, then. Shall we say eleven o'clock? The crowd is likely to be thinner in the morning."

He frowned.

"The exhibition closes in a few days," Jo went on. "If I don't see it tomorrow, I probably won't be able to. I *would* like to go." He still hesitated. "Never mind, Alfred. It *is* short notice. I will see if my cousin George will escort me instead."

"Oh, in that case…" he said quickly, and a good deal more pleasantly. "I'll call for you, shall I?"

"Thank you, Alfred."

Today's drive had been considerably more enjoyable than last night's dinner, Jo reflected as Chivenor closed the door behind Alfred, although there had still been some uncomfortable moments. Perhaps that was to be expected; they *had* been apart for a long time. And she had not managed to ask him where they would live.

"A note arrived for you, Miss Stretton." Chivenor proffered the silver salver.

She broke the wafer and read the few lines. Catherine Bengrove had written, asking if she would be at home this afternoon. "Chivenor, please send to Mrs Bengrove that I will be at home if she wishes to call."

"I am sorry for such short notice," Catherine said, as they sat in the parlour an hour later. "I wanted to apologise for… for last night."

"What need have you to apologise?" Jo couldn't recall that Catherine had said anything to offend; she had not said much at all.

"For my mother-in-law. She was… less than polite at times. I understand she was feeling unwell."

"I see." That was no excuse; when Mama was unwell, it did not make her rude. And although Catherine had apologised, it would have been better had Lady Bengrove done so herself. "Well, it cannot be helped now."

"Did you enjoy your drive with Captain Bengrove?"

"Yes, thank you." Although it had also given her much to think about.

"Perhaps we can go together one day, and I can introduce you to some of my friends."

"Do you think they will wish to associate with me?" Jo recalled some of Lady Bengrove's words after dinner yesterday, and when Jo had visited Bengrove Hall with Papa. "Many families do not like the fact that Papa takes a hand in the enterprises in which he invests."

"I'm sure that won't cause a problem," Catherine said, a little too quickly. "Not everyone is as particular as Lady Bengrove." She leaned forward. "Does it surprise you to know that Bengrove and I live in the Dower House when we are in Staffordshire?"

Jo shook her head. "Oh. No, it doesn't surprise me." But it *was* disappointing news. "I had been wondering if Alfred and I might do so."

"I'm sorry." Catherine looked sincere, and Jo smiled. At least there would be one member of the family that she liked. One *other* member, she corrected herself hurriedly. "Don't be silly! Alfred and I will soon buy somewhere for ourselves, I'm sure."

"I... Yes, of course. Um, Bengrove—my husband, that is—was wondering how your Papa comes to know Lord Moorven."

"Through a mutual acquaintance, I think." That was the truth, even if only a part of it. "Why? Is it so odd that my father should know someone like him?"

"No, not at all. At least, *I* don't think so, of course." Catherine managed a bland face for this, but then they both laughed. "Shall we drive together the day after tomorrow? If the weather permits, of course."

"I'd like that, thank you."

. . .

Jo was reading in the library the next morning when Chivenor knocked on the door and entered, holding a salver with a sealed note resting on it. "This was just delivered, Miss Stretton, together with flowers. I have sent them to be put in water."

Flowers? They must be from Alfred, but why did he not bring them himself, later? She picked up the note, recognising Alfred's scrawl, and broke the seal with a sinking feeling in her stomach. The note was short, apologising that he had been suddenly called out of town on urgent business and expected to be away for some days.

"Is everything all right, miss?" Chivenor asked.

"I... Yes, thank you, Chivenor. Please tell Martha we will not be going out this morning."

"Very good, miss."

Jo sighed as Chivenor left. Before Mama lost the last baby, she had enjoyed going to the annual exhibition with Jo, and often bought one or two paintings. Last year, Jo had been too worried about Mama's health to attend, but she *did* want to this year. Her disappointment mingled with irritation as she recalled Alfred's words before they parted yesterday. He hadn't been enthusiastic about accompanying her—had he intended to cry off even then?

No, surely not. She had no reason to doubt the explanation he had sent.

Could she go with only Martha for propriety? Possibly, but part of the enjoyment of viewing the exhibition was discussing the art with someone else. She dismissed yesterday's idea of asking George to take her if Alfred could not; even if George were free at such short notice, he didn't care for 'gawping at daubs', as he put it, and she would not enjoy herself knowing that he was bored.

The exhibition still had a couple of days to run. Perhaps Catherine would accompany her tomorrow instead of driving in the park? She would write and ask—Catherine might also know what had taken Alfred off so suddenly.

Papa entered her parlour as she was finishing the note. "Chivenor tells me you are not going to the exhibition—has something happened?"

"Alfred was called away on urgent business."

"That's a shame." He glanced at the clock on the mantelpiece. "Shall I accompany you? I have a little time... No. Give me half an hour to finish some business, then we can spend several hours there. Does that suit you?"

"Oh, yes, Papa. Thank you!" Papa would be a better companion than Alfred, given his initial lack of enthusiasm for the outing.

"I think your mama is not yet well enough for such an event," Papa went on, "but perhaps we could choose a painting for her."

They walked there together, enjoying the warm weather and hazy sunshine. Papa paid for a catalogue, and they toured the exhibition rooms discussing the merits, or otherwise, of the paintings on display. Papa put his name against one of the remaining unsold landscapes—a restful scene of bucolic life. But the image that fascinated Jo depicted the storming of a citadel in Spain. Consulting the catalogue, Jo found it was San Sebastian; Wellington's forces had captured it the previous year. Seeing the masses of troops amongst the smoke, and the walls and steep ground they had to scale, was vastly different from reading dispatches in the *Gazette*. She returned to it before they left the exhibition.

"It is already sold, Jo," Papa said as they peered up at it.

Jo shook her head. "I don't think I'd want it hanging on the wall even if it were available. I cannot imagine what it must have been like to be there. Alfred would not have been involved in something like that, would he?"

"The cavalry would not, no. But Captain Delafield might have taken part in similar actions before he was captured." He laid a hand on her shoulder. "The war is over now, though."

Jo nodded, and took Papa's arm as they left Somerset House. "How do you like Captain Bengrove now he is here with us?" he asked as they walked home.

Jo thought for a moment before answering. "Sometimes I like him very well—very well indeed." That smile! "But I still hardly know him, and I wonder how we will live together. He thinks I will not want to read the papers, and will do 'women's things.'"

Papa chuckled. "Things your mama enjoys, like embroidery?"

Jo shrugged. "He mentioned that, yes. It passes the time, I suppose."

"Many men—and women—think the same, Jo. You may find it difficult to find a husband who does not need to be persuaded that you're genuinely interested in such things, not merely helping me."

Perhaps she could persuade Alfred, but she wished she did not need to.

"He's had a frustrating, and probably tedious, time being shut up in Verdun," Papa went on. "It will be a big change for him now he's back, and he probably had some urgent business to see to that kept him away from you today."

"Do you approve of him, Papa?"

"Not necessarily, I want you to have time to make up your own mind about him. You liked him well enough to promise to wait for him two years ago, and I need to know him better before giving my permission. We can do that at Yelden." He patted her hand where it rested on his arm. "I will do my best to persuade you against it if I think you will not suit. And if you do decide against it, your mama will accept it more readily if you have spent more time together. However, you are of age, and I will not cause a rift between us by forbidding you if we disagree. After all, he may not be as obnoxious as his parents."

"Being worse than Lady Bengrove could be quite difficult, I think."

Papa chuckled. "Indeed."

CHAPTER 20

A few days after the visit to the exhibition, Chivenor opened the door to Jo as she returned from a walk. "Mr Stretton wishes to see you in the library," he said, as Jo removed her gloves, bonnet, and pelisse and handed them to Martha.

"You wanted to see me, Papa?" Jo came to a halt a few steps into the library as her father and another man stood. "Oh! I'm sorry, I didn't realise you had a guest."

The stranger was of a height with her father, his chestnut hair cut short, and what could be laughter lines beside his brown eyes. He was too young to be one of her father's contemporaries—he looked close to Lieutenant Moorven's age. A walking stick rested against the arm of his chair.

"Miss Stretton." He bowed, an uncertain smile on his face. "I am pleased to meet you at last."

At last? Then as Papa started to speak, she suddenly knew what he was about to say.

"Jo, this is Captain Delafield come to thank you for your correspondence and help."

She stared, completely taken aback. Even after making allowance for Alfred's unaccountable dislike of him, her mental image had been wildly inaccurate. For one thing, he looked so much *younger* than she had been expecting.

His expression changed from uncertain to quizzical as she gazed at him, and his smile faded as she still said nothing. Then she realised that the two men remained standing, so she hurriedly sat down.

"Jo, do speak." Papa was clearly amused.

"I'm sorry, Captain," she managed to say. "I… was I frowning?" She still felt off balance. What a silly question to ask a stranger! But not really a stranger.

"Positively scowling!"

"Papa!" she protested indignantly, but that helped to remove some of her constraint. "I'm sorry, Captain, I am not normally so bird-witted."

"I take it that I am not what you were expecting, Miss Stretton?"

The captain's wry smile reminded her of the self-deprecating humour often evident in his letters, and her feeling of awkwardness began to fade. She felt her lips curve in response.

Rob had a few moments to take in Miss Stretton's appearance while her attention had been focused on her father. Moorven had been right —she *was* pretty and, to his mind, just the right height. Wisps of her black hair had escaped from their pins and curled attractively around her face.

He was glad now that Moorven had seen her first and given him some idea what to expect—otherwise he might be feeling as dazed as she appeared to be. He watched in some trepidation as she took in his appearance, hoping that, although she was obviously surprised, he might be an improvement in some way on what she had been antici-pating. Then she gave a smile that animated her face and changed her from pretty to beautiful.

"No, Captain, you are not what I was expecting. But it is not easy to form an accurate impression from a few words written over a year ago."

It was probably best not to wonder how Bengrove had described him. Nor should it matter, he told himself firmly. He had come here for a purpose. "As your father said, I called to convey my thanks for all the books and papers you sent. They did a great deal to help the time pass productively."

"Can you now design steam engines?" A twitch to her lips betrayed her amusement.

That made him laugh. "No, but I do stand some chance of understanding should an engineer try to explain one to me. And I certainly have a good deal more mathematical knowledge than I did a year ago."

"Will it be useful?"

"That remains to be seen," he said more soberly. "I suspect the army will have little more use for me, so it depends on what occupation I take up."

"Knowledge is seldom wasted," Mr Stretton put in.

"Indeed. It helps to keep the mind occupied, if nothing else." He shifted in his seat and picked up a package from the table beside his chair. "Miss Stretton, I hope you will accept this gift as a token of my thanks." He handed it to her, and Miss Stretton looked at her father for permission.

"Open it, Jo."

"I have to admit to asking Madame Daniau's advice," Rob said, watching uncertainly as she undid the narrow ribbon and unfolded the silver paper. She gazed at the fine lace of the shawl, her fingers stroking the fabric. "It's Chantilly lace, of a sort," he explained. "Possibly somewhat unpatriotic, as Napoleon encouraged its manufacture."

"It's lovely, thank you," she said softly, holding it up to admire it.

"A fine piece, Captain," Mr Stretton added.

Rob let out a soft breath of relief—he had not been entirely sure if a shawl, as an item of clothing, was a proper gift. She smiled down at it, still stroking it, then turned the full force of her smile on him. Rob swallowed hard and managed a smile in return. "I'm pleased you like it."

. . .

She did like it, very much. Not only the gift itself, but that he had thought about what to give her. "Thanks were not necessary, Captain, not after what you did for Mama, and your letters helped me through the time when we thought she would not recover."

He nodded, his face becoming serious again. His glance flicked briefly towards her father, but he said nothing, and one hand reached for his stick.

No, surely he was not about to leave?

"It must have been frustrating, being confined in Verdun?" Papa asked.

Thank you, Papa!

The captain moved his hand back to the arm of his chair. "It was. But I would have felt that way wherever I was—my leg would have kept me from my regiment even had I not been taken captive."

"How did your injury happen?" Papa asked. "But don't answer if you'd rather not."

"An encounter with a horse coming fast the other way. I don't recall much after it hit me, but I suspect the horse came out best."

Jo had to smile at that; it sounded so much like his letters. "A runaway horse?" she asked, not understanding the circumstances.

"No, French cavalry." He looked uncertainly at Papa, who just waved a hand in a 'carry on' gesture. "We were retreating towards Portugal after failing to take Burgos. We... That is, my company was patrolling to one side of the main column and some dragoons found us." He shrugged. "I was lucky, I suppose, that the French took the few... took us back for medical attention rather than just leaving us there to... rather than leaving us there."

"Rather than leaving you there to die?" Jo asked.

"Well, yes." He seemed surprised at her bluntness, then smiled. "You are unusually direct for a woman, Miss Stretton."

Alfred had called her unusual yesterday, but from Captain Delafield it sounded like a compliment. "What is the point of beating about the bush? I am very glad they did take you back. But you are not fully fit yet?" She felt a blush rising to her cheeks. "I'm sorry—that is a rather personal... I mean, it is not..."

"I'm probably as healed as I'm likely to be." He shrugged. "The army has given me leave for a couple of months, then I'm to be inspected again to see if I am fit for purpose." The words could have sounded bitter, but did not.

"You don't mind?"

"I do, but minding will not change things. At least it happened in contact with the enemy. With our former enemies," he corrected himself. "Too many died on that retreat from the cold or from disease."

"What are your plans now, Captain?" Papa asked.

"I'm staying with Moorven until I have to report to Horse Guards again. He passed on your invitation to dinner, sir. Did you get my note of acceptance?"

Dinner?

"I did indeed. I am pleased you are back in Town in time for it. I look forward to conversing with the three of you tomorrow."

Captain Delafield got to his feet. Papa rose, and the two men shook hands before the captain turned and bowed to Jo. "Miss Stretton, it was a pleasure to meet you in person."

"A pleasure for me, too, Captain." She smiled as she stood. She wondered if it would be appropriate to offer her hand, but then decided to ignore what convention might say and held it out anyway. He hesitated a moment and then shook it, his hand warm on hers, before taking his leave with another of his endearingly wry smiles.

Papa went into the entrance hall to see him off. When he returned, he looked at Jo with a brow raised, waiting for her to make some comment.

"Dinner, Papa? Why didn't you tell me?"

"Oh, did I not?"

"You know you did not." Papa was plotting again, she was sure—the twitch of his lips confirmed it. "Who else is to come?"

"Only Captain Delafield, Lieutenant Moorven, and their friend Lieutenant Chadwick, the engineer. Chadwick might be able to give some advice on that canal proposal that you had doubts over."

"That's a good idea."

"You may join us if you wish, Jo."

"I… Yes, thank you."

"Your mama, too, if she feels up to it, but I suspect the talk would not interest her."

And if Mama did not join them, there was less likelihood that she would find out about Jo's correspondence with Captain Delafield.

Papa had a knowing look in his eye. "What a tangled web we weave, eh, Jo?"

Jo nodded, mutely—but she could not regret any part of their correspondence.

"Don't worry. I doubt the captain will say anything to your mama about you writing to him. You will have to tell her at some point, but not just yet."

"Yes… I mean, no, Papa. If you'll excuse me, I need to tidy my hair."

In her room, she opened the drawer where she kept the letters from Alfred and from Captain Delafield. Her hand hovered over the latter bundle, wanting to re-read them now she could picture the smile that would have accompanied some of his anecdotes.

Then she pushed the drawer shut with far more force than necessary. She was as good as betrothed to Alfred, and she should not *possess* letters from another man, let alone be re-reading them.

Rob went over his meeting with Miss Stretton as he walked back to Grosvenor Street. Her appearance wasn't quite what he had been expecting, in spite of Moorven's description, but now he'd met her he'd be hard pressed to say what it was he *had* thought before. Her manner, though, did reflect the way she'd written to him, and although some of her questions had been quite personal, he hadn't minded. They had already shared thoughts and feelings about many things in their correspondence.

Why she wanted to marry a man like Bengrove was beyond him. Could she really be in search of a connection with the aristocracy, as Bengrove said? He shook his head. It was none of his business—if anyone were to protect her from the kind of life she'd have with Bengrove, it would have to be her father.

He'd been looking forward to tomorrow night's dinner, but now he was not so sure. He'd already liked her from her letters; now, he suspected he was in danger of liking her far too much.

"Tell me again why we're dressing up like this?" John Chadwick lifted his chin as he allowed Moorven's valet to adjust his cravat the following evening.

"Many reasons. Have patience!" Moorven was lounging in a chair watching the final preparations. "I got Father's man of business to look into Stretton's… well, reputation, I suppose. He is known for making shrewd investments in all sorts of things."

"Including canals?" Rob asked, putting the finishing touches to his own cravat.

"I believe so."

"Could be a good contact for you, John," Rob said. "If you want to dig canals, you need to know—"

"I don't want to *dig* them!"

"Don't rise to it, Chadwick," Moorven warned.

"How do you know him, anyway?"

"Rob has been writing to his daughter for more than a year," Moorven said. "She's the one who has been sending the books and newspapers."

Rob winced.

"Rob, you haven't told him?"

Rob tried to hide his irritation. "It's not the kind of thing that comes up in general conversation."

Moorven shrugged. "It's better that he knows." He turned to Chadwick. "Miss Stretton is also the young lady unfortunate enough to be betrothed to Alfred Bengrove."

"I'll just go and see if your man has found a hackney," Rob said, hastening out of the room and leaving Moorven to finish the explanation. Although when he was halfway down the stairs, he did wonder if leaving had been wise. God knew what suppositions Moorven was passing on. But when the other two came downstairs nothing further was said, and they got into the carriage with Chadwick still muttering about having to dress up.

"Regard it as payment for a free dinner," Rob suggested. "Or a job interview."

"Just the thought to help me relax and enjoy the evening!" Chadwick protested. "I'm inept enough at polite conversation without having my future prospects possibly at stake."

"You'll be fine," Rob said. "Just remember to bow deeply when you first meet—"

"No, no, Rob. That's what *Bengrove* would want him to do."

Chadwick ignored them. Rob looked at his friend's legs stretched out before him in the carriage, clad in trousers rather than the standard knee breeches he and Moorven were wearing.

"That new leg is good - you can hardly tell you lost your own," Rob said seriously. Chadwick's wooden leg had a shoe fitted to the bottom, and with his loose trousers the loss of his real leg was scarcely noticeable. "Have you tried riding yet?"

Chadwick nodded. "It works well enough if I don't try to gallop. But it's still obviously a false leg when I walk."

"You weren't so bothered by it in Verdun," Rob said, not quite making it a question.

"It's one thing with other military men, who understand about such things. Not the same with people I don't know. And not with strange young women. Feel like a fish out of water." He ran his fingers around his neck to loosen his cravat.

"Does it help to know that Stretton's house is nowhere near as grand as Moorven's?" Rob asked. "And," he added ruefully, "you won't be the only one limping."

"If you're lucky," Moorven said, "he won't have invited his nephew."

"Nephew?" Rob asked.

"Stretton is related to Lord and Lady Yelden. When we had dinner together, their son was very keen on extracting the details of all the actions I was involved in."

"I'm sure he'd be interested in bridge demolition, then," Rob said.

"Or facing down cavalry," Chadwick put in, getting his own back. "Or the fine art of climbing ladders."

"Cease, children," Moorven said. "We have arrived."

Now it was Rob's turn to feel strangled by his cravat.

It's an evening amongst friends, he told himself. Just friends.

CHAPTER 21

$\mathcal{M}$r Stretton's butler showed the three friends into the library and offered them drinks. Rob took a glass of claret, and sipped it while he browsed the bookshelves. Their host arrived a few minutes later; Moorven introduced Chadwick, and Mr Stretton shook his hand cordially.

"My daughter will be with us in a few moments. I'm afraid my wife is not feeling well enough to join us, so we will be just five to dinner."

Almost as he spoke, Miss Stretton entered. Rob tried not to stare as he took in the way her pale green gown outlined her figure. Her hair was looser this evening, small curls framing her face and falling from a knot on the back of her head.

"Good evening, gentlemen."

She did have a lovely smile.

"Ah, Jo." Mr Stretton waited until she reached him. "This is Lieutenant Chadwick."

"Miss Stretton." Chadwick bowed. "I am pleased to make your acquaintance. The materials you sent us were most gratefully received."

"You are very welcome, Lieutenant."

"Shall we go through, gentlemen?" Mr Stretton said. "As there are so few of us, conversation will be as easy around the table as it is here."

Rob was glad of the suggestion—he would feel more at ease with the serving of food and passing of dishes to break any awkward silences. He wasn't sure what Mr Stretton wanted with him; Chadwick had engineering skills that an investor might find useful, and Moorven had connections. What would he have to say that he hadn't already said in his two previous meetings with his host?

Mr Stretton offered his arm to his daughter and led the way. The dining room held a polished wooden table long enough to seat twenty, but the five places had all been set at one end. Mr Stretton took the head of the table, with Miss Stretton and Moorven in the next places. Rob ended up next to Moorven, across the table from Miss Stretton. As food and wine were served, the conversation started with the usual remarks about hoping everyone was well, and how wet the weather was for the time of year.

Mr Stretton turned to Chadwick once everyone had filled their plates. "I understand you are interested in canals, Lieutenant?"

"That is one possibility I am considering, sir, for when I leave the army. My father wishes me to join his business, but I would prefer a more challenging occupation, if I can get the work."

"What is your father's business?"

"He owns a cotton mill in Lancashire. He concentrates on prices and markets rather than investigating the benefits of more efficient spinning frames or looms. It is those more technical matters that would interest me."

Mr Stretton nodded. "I am considering investing in cotton, although my present focus is a new canal project. However, Jo had some questions about the predicted profits."

As Chadwick's brows rose, Rob quickly spoke. "I think Miss Stretton read some of the books she sent us, John."

"Thank you, Captain." Miss Stretton's smile held amusement. "My query was not based on engineering knowledge, however, but merely on a comparison of this proposal with other, completed, schemes. It appears to be overly optimistic in some respects."

"I am willing to give any advice I can, naturally." Chadwick said, his gaze moving from Miss Stretton to her father.

"What did you do in the army, Lieutenant?" Jo asked, not offended that Chadwick didn't yet take her seriously. "Besides, er, building bridges, I suppose? If you don't mind talking about it, that is."

"Not at all. When it came to bridges, my task was mainly blowing them up. And myself, unfortunately. *Not* a good recommendation for a future employer."

Captain Delafield shook his head with a smile, and Jo guessed it wasn't the first time that comment had been made. "I doubt there is much demand now for people to demolish bridges under battle conditions," he said. "John, tell them what you really did."

"I wouldn't want to bore a lady—"

"You will not," Jo interrupted crisply, and blushed as both Captain Delafield and Lieutenant Moorven grinned. She really must try to control her tongue, even though she felt a little put out at Lieutenant Chadwick's words. But she was being unfair—most men of her acquaintance would have said exactly the same thing.

The lieutenant looked uncomfortable. "My apologies, Miss Stretton. I did not intend to imply you would not understand, although many... my sisters, at least, would not—"

"My sisters would be bored witless," Captain Delafield interrupted.

"It's quite all right, Lieutenant," Jo said. "I took no offence, and you will not bore me."

"Thank you, Miss Stretton." He cast a baleful look at the amused faces of the other two. "A lot of the time is spent surveying ahead of the army, assessing whether roads are suitable for the artillery and supply wagons, for example, or finding where rivers can be forded. And also building temporary bridges."

"To replace the ones you blew up?" Jo asked.

Lieutenant Chadwick laughed. "That was often the case, I'm afraid."

"And one of the first men into the breach at a siege is usually an engineer, showing the rest of us the way," Captain Delafield added.

Lieutenant Chadwick smiled. "Not me, I always happened to be elsewhere at the time. Probably why I'm still alive."

That reminded Jo of the painting she had seen at the exhibition, and she wondered that these men could joke about such death and destruction. She nodded her thanks for the information.

Papa took over, and turned to Lieutenant Moorven. "Do you have ambitions beyond the Navy, Lieutenant?"

"My duty will be with the title and estates when I inherit, although I hope that is some time off. But that does mean the Navy cannot be my permanent occupation. Besides, being incarcerated for three years means I have lost seniority..."

Jo stopped listening properly as Lieutenant Moorven mentioned the resentment that was possible when a superior officer considered himself the social inferior of a subordinate. Across the table from her, Captain Delafield turned his wine glass in his fingers and stared into its red depths with a rather brooding expression. He might be uncertain about his own future, for most of the skills required of an infantry officer would not be of much use in civilian life. Of course, that was why he was interested in the technical books she had sent.

He looked up and saw she was watching him. His expression changed from brooding to politely enquiring, and she blushed. She should be thinking about her own future with Alfred, not what Captain Delafield would do with his time. He *was* a friend, though, so it should not be improper to think about it. Should it?

Rob turned his gaze away. Miss Stretton's blush gave an attractive colour to her cheeks, but he hadn't intended to embarrass her. Moorven's talk about his future moved on to a discussion of art. It was not something Rob had ever taken much interest in, other than appreciating the watercolours done by his sisters, which had adorned the walls of his childhood home. Both Mr Stretton and Moorven sounded knowledgeable about techniques as well as styles of painting, and so did Miss Stretton when she joined in.

"Do you paint, Miss Stretton?" Rob asked.

She shook her head with a rueful smile. "I have had the requisite lessons, but lacked the motivation to develop my skills. It seemed pointless when there are talented artists who can produce much better results than I ever could. I do enjoy looking at paintings, though."

Mr Stretton glanced around the table. "If you have finished eating, gentlemen, would you care to see some of the paintings we have acquired?" He waved a hand to where a decanter of port and glasses awaited them on the sideboard. "Do bring further refreshment with you."

Glasses in hand, they followed Miss Stretton into a parlour, decorated in feminine soft colours. She stopped in front of a moonlit seascape. "This is one of my favourites—I feel I could almost be there in that tiny boat."

Rob inspected the painting. "I should imagine it takes a great deal of skill to make the reflections on water so realistic."

"Indeed. There is so much detail." Miss Stretton leaned closer, and Rob inhaled a faint scent of lavender. He stepped away, thinking that accepting Stretton's dinner invitation might have been a mistake. It was bad enough imagining someone he liked being tied to Bengrove; it would not do to become attracted to her person as well as her mind.

Become attracted? It was too late for that. It was just as well that he was unlikely to be in her company again after this evening.

They left Chadwick inspecting the reflections, and moved on to other landscapes and portraits. Rob kept his distance, listening while the Strettons and Moorven talked. He couldn't help wondering what Bengrove would have made of this evening's conversation. He doubted the man would know much about art, and couldn't imagine him being willing to learn.

How *had* Bengrove persuaded Miss Stretton to marry him?

Rob's belief that he would not see Miss Stretton again was shattered as the three of them took their leave later that evening. Mr

Stretton arranged for Chadwick to call the next morning, then turned to Rob.

"Why don't you come tomorrow with Lieutenant Chadwick, Captain? The queries my daughter has on the canal project may not all be due to technical matters, and two heads are usually better than one."

He shouldn't accept; it would do him no good see more of her. On the other hand, this could help him to work out what he wanted to do next. "I... well..."

"Of course he'll come," Chadwick said, resting one hand on Rob's shoulder. "We'll see you tomorrow, Mr Stretton, Miss Stretton."

Rob could only make his bow and follow Chadwick as he limped off in the direction of the nearest hackney.

Jo was ready long before the appointed time the next morning. Two copies of the canal prospectus lay ready on the desk, together with other papers she had gathered. She was nervous at the prospect of having to explain her concerns to someone other than her father—this would be the first time she'd had any public involvement in Papa's investment decisions.

Well, it wasn't really 'public'. And Captain Delafield understood her interest, at least; she wasn't sure about Lieutenant Chadwick.

The two men arrived promptly at ten, and Chivenor showed them into the library. As they sat in the chairs around Papa's desk, they both looked as uneasy as she felt. Captain Delafield began to read the copy of the prospectus that Papa gave him, but Lieutenant Chadwick sat with the papers in his hand.

"Is something wrong, Lieutenant?" Papa asked.

Jo wondered if he objected to discussing technical matters with a woman, but his hesitation turned out to be a question of his own competence, not hers.

"No, sir," he said. "I just wanted to ensure you are aware that I have no expertise in the construction or operation of canals. I cannot provide you with a professional opinion on this matter."

"I believe you have experience supervising the digging of trenches, Lieutenant. You can give me an *informed* opinion on the digging of a canal, can you not?"

"Yes, I should think so."

Papa nodded. "Very well. Jo, will you explain?"

She took a deep breath. "Firstly, the prospectus does not make a clear case that there will be the amount of traffic necessary to generate the proposed income. I am also concerned about the costs." Jo took some papers from the pile on the desk. "These completed projects are of a similar size, and this is a summary of the costs and distances involved in all three projects. This new prospectus seems rather optimistic."

As they examined her notes and compared them to the prospectus for the new project, Jo felt as if a lesson she had completed was being assessed.

"I see what you mean," Lieutenant Chadwick said, after what seemed an age. "Optimistic indeed, unless there is a local supply of stone and other materials that would reduce the building costs." He addressed his reply to somewhere between her and Papa.

"There is no mention of that in the prospectus," Jo replied. "I would expect such an advantage to be mentioned."

Captain Delafield looked at her. "Miss Stretton, could the costs be explained if the proposers are expecting to have very cheap labour?"

Jo drew her notes closer, pleased that the captain had replied to her directly. Papa respected her opinions on these matters, but this was the first time someone else had. "If the number of men needed per mile is similar to those needed on these completed projects, I think it would almost have to be slave labour, Captain."

He turned to the front of the prospectus again. "This was written before the news of the fall of Paris. Could they have anticipated there being discharged soldiers desperate enough to work for very low wages?"

"It was fairly clear by February that the war would soon end, was it not?" Jo asked. "I remember thinking so at the time.

"Yes, but to assume both victory and a reduction in the number of regiments within a few months is optimistic indeed."

"It is possible that the likely profits have been overstated," Papa said. "It is also possible that there may be some explanation for what seems to be unfounded optimism, and this could be a viable investment. That is why I suggested that both of you investigate, if you are willing. I will, naturally, give you suitable recompense for your trouble."

Captain Delafield looked pleased, but made a protest. "I cannot take a fee, sir. I am wholly unqualified for this task."

"Nor I, sir," Lieutenant Chadwick said.

"Common sense is all I require, gentlemen," Papa replied. "And a certain knowledge of human nature, which I suspect your army careers have given you. Very well, but I will refund all your expenses. Whatever they are," he added with a smile.

The two men looked at each other, then Lieutenant Chadwick nodded. "It will take several days to inspect the proposed route, and some time to make local enquiries."

"In addition to travelling time," Papa said. "Shall we say three weeks? I'd prefer a report in person, rather than merely a written communication, but we will be staying at Yelden Court in Hampshire by then—my brother-in-law's home. It's about six miles north of Winchester."

"We can report to you there," Lieutenant Chadwick agreed.

"Thank you, gentlemen," Papa said. "I look forward to hearing the results of your investigation."

"Thank you, sir. Miss Stretton." Captain Delafield stood and made his bow; his friend did likewise.

"Well, Jo?" Papa said, when they had taken their leave. "What do you think of our new advisors?"

"I will be interested to learn what they find."

But 'interested' didn't describe her feelings. She was pleased—no, happy—that they had taken her seriously, and also relieved that she hadn't made a silly mistake with her figures and reasoning. How embarrassing that would have been, particularly after Captain Delafield had taken his friend to task last night for assuming she would not be interested in technical matters.

"Indeed. And it will be pleasant for Alfred to have his friends at Yelden. He cannot be in your company all the time, no matter how much he might wish it."

That tempered her mood a little; Alfred did not regard Captain Delafield as a friend, so a meeting between them could be awkward. And how much *did* Alfred wish to be in her company? "I have had no word from Alfred since he sent his excuses. And we are setting off for Yelden soon." They would arrive a couple of weeks before the other guests to give Mama plenty of time to rest after the journey.

"Don't fret about it, Jo. There will be time enough for you to get reacquainted in Hampshire."

CHAPTER 22

elden Court, June 1814

Lady Yelden rose from her seat at the end of the dining table, a mixture of pride and irritation on her face as she surveyed the uneaten food remaining on the serving dishes. "Shall we retire to the parlour, ladies? It is just as well we did not wait for the Bengroves to arrive. I hope they have not met with an accident."

"It was a splendid meal, Sarah," Papa said, raising his glass to her. "As usual."

Aunt Sarah smiled. "Thank you, Stretton."

Murmurs of appreciation came from around the table as footmen drew the chairs back for Mama, Jo, and Lydia. Beyond the windows, the sun was dipping towards the horizon, and long shadows crept across the front lawn. Jo paused as she caught a flash of movement where the gravelled drive emerged from the trees. Two coaches.

"I think they might be here now, Aunt Sarah."

"Ah well. Better late than never, I suppose." She turned to the butler. "Stevenson, please ask Cook to provide a meal from what is left in case they have not already dined, and offer them trays in their rooms."

By the time the coaches drew up in front of the house, everyone had assembled in the entrance hall to greet the new arrivals. The nervousness Jo had felt all day intensified—although why she should feel that way, she could not say. She should be looking forward to seeing Alfred again after several weeks apart.

Lord and Lady Bengrove emerged from the first coach, together with another finely dressed woman with sharp features. The servants riding on the roof descended and began unloading luggage.

"Lady Misterton." Aunt Sarah spoke quietly, so that only Mama and Jo, standing just behind her, could hear. "A well-known gossip. What is *she* doing here?" She stepped forward to stand beside Uncle Henry, ready to greet their guests as the Bengroves climbed the front steps. Catherine and Mr Bengrove descended from the second coach, then Alfred, scowling as he said something to his brother. Mr Bengrove nudged him with an elbow, and Alfred's sour expression turned to a smile as he looked towards the door and his gaze settled on Jo. Then her view of him was blocked by his parents.

"Welcome, Lord Bengrove, Lady Bengrove," Uncle Henry said. "I am glad you have arrived safely."

"No thanks to the coachman," Lady Bengrove sniffed. "We had to wait for hours in Winchester while he found a wheelwright. At least the inn provided an acceptable repast."

"Oh dear." Aunt Sarah turned to Lady Misterton. "Did you have a mishap too? How providential that the Bengroves came across you on your journey."

"Lady Misterton is here at my invitation," Lady Bengrove said, either ignoring or oblivious to the note of sarcasm in Aunt Sarah's voice.

"What an impertinence!" Mama said quietly to Jo.

"Who is she?"

"A dowager viscountess, I think. Sarah will know more; I'll ask her later."

"Allow me to present my son George, and daughter Lydia," Uncle Henry said. "And Lady Frances Stretton, and her husband and daughter."

Mama curtsied, seemingly not surprised at Uncle Henry's use of her title. "*So* happy to meet you, Lady Misterton."

The smile, and the almost hidden sarcasm in Mama's tone made Jo happier than she had been in some time; Mama must truly be recovering her health.

"And I, you." Lady Misterton inclined her head, clearly unsure who Mama was, but neither Mama nor Aunt Sarah enlightened her. The housekeeper came to show the new arrivals to their rooms, and Jo followed Mama into the parlour.

"No doubt Lady Bengrove will inform her of my lowly status," Mama said, as they sat down. "She didn't apologise for upsetting Sarah's arrangements, I noticed. And they could easily have sent the second coach on with a message."

"A viscountess apologising to a mere baroness?" Jo said. "Never!"

Mama smiled, but shook her head. "Jo, I'm sorry you'll have to put up with that woman when you're wed. I just hope you and Alfred can buy somewhere to live quickly."

"And at some distance from Bengrove Hall."

"Indeed. I think I will retire, Jo. I am feeling much better now we're settled here for a while, but I don't want to have to spend the rest of the evening in Lady Bengrove's company. And you will want to be with Alfred."

Papa and George entered the parlour not long after Mama had gone upstairs, carrying their glasses of port with them, and Lord Bengrove and his sons soon joined them. Alfred came over to Jo, smiling with his usual charm.

"Joanna, it has been too long." He held out his hands, and she took them, feeling the familiar warmth at his smile.

"Was your business successful?" Jo asked as he sat down beside her.

His smile faded. "What business?"

"You said urgent business had called you out of town. In your note," she added, when he still appeared puzzled. "The day we were supposed to go to the exhibition."

"A family matter, Miss Stretton." Mr Bengrove had come over to them. "We wouldn't want to bore you with the details."

She was soon to *be* family, if the next couple of weeks went well, but this didn't seem the time to point that out. "How is Catherine, Mr Bengrove? Is she coming down for tea?"

"She is rather fatigued from the journey, and decided to rest in our room. Did she tell you she is expecting another happy event in a few months?"

"No, she didn't." Which was odd, as she and Catherine had driven in the park several times before Papa had brought them all to Yelden. "I hope she will feel better in the morning."

"I imagine so. She didn't travel well while she was expecting the first one, either."

"Would she not have been more comfortable remaining at Bengrove Hall?" Jo asked. She was pleased that Catherine had come, particularly now that Lady Bengrove had brought a friend likely to be as unpleasant as she was, but she wouldn't wish days of travel-sickness on her.

Mr Bengrove shook his head, but it was Alfred who spoke. "She will enjoy the grounds here, I think. Jo, will you walk with me tomorrow, as we did when we first met here?"

"I would like that," Jo said. But his brother's presence seemed to have tied Alfred's tongue, for after thanking her he didn't speak. "We could have a game of billiards," Jo suggested, when the silence began to feel uncomfortable. "Cousin George has been teaching me." Her gaze slid sideways to where George was standing with his father and Lord Bengrove, looking bored.

"It's not a suitable game for a woman," Alfred declared, following her gaze.

"Oh? Why?" Jo asked, irritated. Across the room, George must have sensed that they were talking about him, for he turned and came towards them.

"It seems rather… indelicate, Mr Bengrove said, before Alfred could answer. "Leaning over the table as you must."

Alfred cleared his throat again. "If you really wish to play, Joanna, I can teach you."

"Thank you, Alfred, but I need practice, not instruction. As I said, my cousin has been teaching me." Alfred was frowning—perhaps he did not wish to play at all? "If you would rather not, just say so."

"She's not bad, Bengrove," George said, having reached them in time to hear what Jo said. "I'll play, Jo." He jerked his head towards his father. "Anything's better than listening to those two prose on about politics."

"Thank you for the compliment, Cousin, so condescending of you."

He grinned. "Anytime, Coz."

"How about you and me, Yelden?" Mr Bengrove interrupted. "More of a challenge, eh?"

George looked at Jo, who gave a small nod. She had only suggested the idea to break the silence, but Mr Bengrove didn't know that.

"Very well, Bengrove. This way."

As they walked off, Jo turned back to Alfred. "Do you wish me to refrain from playing billiards?"

He reached out and took her hand again. "Not if you really wish to do so, my dear Joanna. But I cannot like the idea of you spending time alone with another man."

Was Alfred jealous? Of *George*?

"George and I have known each other since we were children, Alfred. He is like a brother to me."

"If you say so, my dear." But he was clearly unconvinced, and again an awkward silence fell.

Jo stood. "Excuse me, Alfred. I will go and see if Catherine has everything she needs."

"I'm sure her maid will do all that is necessary."

"I would like to see for myself, however. Goodnight, Alfred."

"Er... Goodnight, my dear."

She left the room, disappointed that their first meeting after several weeks had felt so uncomfortable. Reaching the landing, she paused outside the door of the room that Mr and Mrs Bengrove had been given—Catherine wasn't the cause of her disappointment. Taking a deep breath, she knocked on the door.

Winchester

Rob checked his neckcloth in the mirror, ready to see what the coaching inn could provide in the way of breakfast. Turning, he saw that Chadwick was packing his trunk.

"What are you doing? It's only an hour's journey to Yelden Court, and we'll be back here this afternoon when we've made our report." He would be seeing Miss Stretton again, but only while Chadwick reported what they had found. That was both too much time in her company, and not enough.

"We're not returning—I've already paid the reckoning."

"What?"

"We're invited to the house party as well—didn't Moorven say?"

"*House party*? I thought the Strettons were staying with Mrs Stretton's sister? And what's Moorven got to do with it?"

Chadwick gave him a puzzled look as he dropped his shaving kit into his trunk. "You really didn't know? No, I can see you didn't. You'd better get your own things packed." He nodded towards Rob's trunk, still standing at the foot of his bed.

"Explain."

"Lord and Lady Yelden are having a house party, including the Strettons, Moorven, and our friend Bengrove and his family. Possibly more. The intention is that Miss Stretton can become properly reacquainted with the dear captain before any wedding arrangements are made."

"Moorven told you all this?" Why hadn't Moorven told *him*?

"He wrote, yes. Moorven was invited, and Stretton suggested to him that you and I could also come—be part of the gathering, that is, not just give our report and leave. I believe the reason Stretton gave for inviting Moorven was so that Alfred Bengrove could have a friendly face from Verdun in case he felt out of place."

The two men's eyes met, and Rob shook his head, smiling. "Stretton doesn't really think that, does he?"

"The invitation came via Moorven, so I don't know. But I doubt it. I suspect Moorven knows what he's up to."

"I can't hang around at a house party watching that arse making up to Miss Stretton," Rob protested. "You can deliver the report yourself. I'll take myself back to Gloucestershire."

"Ah, to the lass your sister-in-law wants you to marry."

"Stow it," Rob said, but without heat.

"Look at it another way, Rob. Won't Alfred Bengrove enjoy having three of us there who all heard how he talked about Miss Stretton when he thought no word would get back to her or her father about it?"

"You have a point," Rob had to admit. Perhaps she might finally see Bengrove for what he was. Or her father might come to his senses and forbid the match.

"And if Miss Stretton decides against him, we will be three extra pairs of eyes to make sure our beloved Bengrove doesn't try anything underhand to get his way."

"I suppose, if you put it that way…"

"I do. And Moorven did. To be honest, Rob, if Stretton is pleased with our report, it is possible more work may be forthcoming, and I can't afford to let an opportunity like that pass. If he wants me at the house party—for whatever reason—I'll be there. And you…" Chadwick pointed in emphasis. "You were of material help in coming to our conclusion, so doing as Stretton wishes now may be good for your future, too."

He was right again, curse him. Rob sighed, and opened his trunk.

Rob caught sight of Yelden Court as the chaise turned between massive stone gateposts. The well-proportioned building was built of brick with stone quoins and rows of tall windows. It would have looked intimidating to him only a month ago, but having stayed in Moorven's town house, he had become more accustomed to grand surroundings. The warm red of the bricks gave it a friendly, welcoming appearance, despite the gloomy weather, and Rob began to think that the visit would not be too bad after all.

The chaise drew to a halt on the gravel in front of a shallow flight of steps, and a footman came out to open the door. He looked slightly askance at their plain clothing, rather rumpled and travel-stained from their travels, until a stately butler appeared in the doorway above them and cleared his throat. The footman bowed and went to unstrap their luggage.

"Captain Delafield and Lieutenant Chadwick," Rob said to the butler when they reached the door. "To see Mr Stretton."

The man bowed. "Welcome to Yelden Court, gentlemen. My name is Stevenson." He waved a hand and another footman came to take their hats and coats. "I'm afraid accommodation is in rather short supply at the moment," he went on, a note of apology in his voice. "Lady Yelden hoped that you would not mind sharing a room."

"Not at all," Rob said, and Chadwick nodded.

Stevenson inclined his head. "I will have your trunks taken up."

"The butler doesn't seem too put out about two non-gentlemen," Rob said quietly as they followed a footman up a grand central staircase.

Their room was at the back of the building, overlooking the stables. It was large enough for the two beds, a couple of armchairs, and a small table, as well as a wardrobe and commodious chest of drawers. Rob looked around with interest; they had obviously been given one of the lesser bedrooms, decorated plainly, but there was no sign of fading in the curtains or wear on the carpet.

A footman deposited their luggage in the room, then another man arrived carrying a large jug of hot water. "My name is Parry, sirs. Lord Moorven sent me to assist you during your stay. I have unpacked the trunks that you sent ahead." He crossed the room to the wardrobe and opened the doors. Several sets of clothing hung there, including the one new outfit that Rob had managed to obtain since his return from France. The clothing he had left at Moorven's house on Grosvenor Street.

Parry pulled a letter from a pocket and held it out. "This is for you." It wasn't clear which of them he meant, so Rob took it and broke the seal.

My apologies, gentlemen. I have to be elsewhere on family matters, so I leave you to enjoy Bengrove's company without me. I have sent your clothing on.

M

"Moorven isn't coming." Rob held the note out to Chadwick.

"If you would care to change, sirs," Parry said, "I will lay out your clothing while you wash."

Taking the path of least resistance, Rob allowed himself to be managed without protest, suppressing a grin at Chadwick's grimace when Parry tied a fancy knot in his cravat.

"I'm sure you'll learn to dress yourself one day," Rob said as the door finally shut behind the valet. "Moorven obviously thought you would persuade me to come."

"It seems so," Chadwick muttered. "Bloody managing bastard."

"You didn't know he was going to organise you as well?" Rob said, trying not to laugh. "The biter bit, eh?"

"Bloody liberty, stealing a man's clothes like that," Chadwick said. "Dressed up like a…"

"Gentleman?" Rob suggested.

"But I'm not, am I?"

"You can give a good impression of being one. I'm not either, by many people's standards. Not a title anywhere on my family tree."

"Your family has land; that makes you gentry. Mill owners are not generally considered as such."

"So? Stretton doesn't care, nor does Moorven. They're the two people most likely to be helpful."

Chadwick ran his finger inside his cravat, in a gesture that Rob recognised.

"Don't worry, John. If the other guests don't like us, I'm sure there will be a billiards room or a library we can hide in. Come on, time to go and find Stretton."

And his daughter.

CHAPTER 23

Jo's disappointment with Alfred had faded by the following morning. He and his family had probably all been tired from their journey, and having to wait so long for a wheelwright. If she and Alfred could have some time together without his brother interrupting, she might be able to discuss her involvement in business properly. But that could not happen right away; none of the Bengroves had appeared by the time she finished her breakfast.

"Come for a ride with me?" George suggested, entering the parlour where she stood looking out of the window. It had rained overnight, but now there were patches of blue that hinted at sunshine later.

"Thank you, but no. I agreed to walk with Alfred."

"Probably overslept," George said, glancing at the empty places at the table. "He and his brother were on their third bottle by the time I retired."

Her disappointment of the night before began to return.

George grimaced. "I'm escaping before his brother can challenge me to billiards again."

"Lost to him, did you?"

"No, we were about even. But he proses on about Bengrove Hall and how fashionable it is."

"I hope you were suitably impressed?"

As George shook his head, voices sounded from the entrance hall; the Bengrove sons asking Stevenson something.

"That might be them now." George grinned, then bent to put his mouth close to her ear as footsteps approached. "Enjoy your walk," he whispered, then left, passing the Bengrove brothers with only a nod of greeting.

Mr Bengrove's eyes flicked from Jo to George, and a brief frown crossed his face.

"Good morning," Jo said. "I trust you slept well?"

Alfred stepped forward and took her hand. "Yes, thank you. I'm sorry to have kept you waiting, my dear. My brother's valet failed to wake us on time."

It could be true, Jo supposed. "I will await you in the rose garden, Alfred, if you still wish to walk with me."

"Of course. I will be with you directly."

By the time she had donned her half-boots, spencer, and bonnet, she only had to wait a few minutes before he joined her. He snapped off a pale pink rose and held it towards her with a smile. "I gave you a rose like this when we walked here together two years ago. Ever since then, such blooms have reminded me of your lovely complexion."

She took it, feeling her cheeks flush at his admiring gaze. She didn't recall him doing so, but he *had* sat making daisy chains for her, and gathered bunches of wild flowers from beneath hedges as they walked along nearby lanes. He might well have plucked a rose for her as well.

"The garden is lovely, isn't it?" Jo said, feeling the need to say something. It would look even better in sunshine, but the promising gaps between the clouds had gone and the air had the damp feel of more rain to come.

"It is indeed, but not nearly as pretty as you."

"Mama says the main thing she misses from her childhood is having a flower garden. I would love a garden like this." They passed through an arch in the yew hedge to a lawn surrounded by flowering shrubs and herbaceous plants. "We *would* have a garden, would we not?" she added, when he didn't reply.

"Of course, my dear, if you wish it." He gave her his charming smile again. "It will amuse you in the summer, I think."

"What would you do in the summer, Alfred, if you do not enjoy a garden?"

"I would enjoy walking in it with you, Joanna. And riding about the grounds. That sort of thing."

"Shall we go riding tomorrow, if it is not raining? My seat is much better now than when we first met."

"Do you ride in London, then? I recall you saying that you did not get much practice on horseback."

"No, but I go out with my cousins when we stay here, as we do every summer."

His lips thinned. "Your cousin?"

"My uncle only cares for hunting, and Papa regards horses as mere means of transport. George and Lydia enjoy riding about the countryside."

"I see. What was your cousin saying to you in the parlour this morning?" He said the words lightly, but his expression belied his tone.

"He just hoped we would enjoy our walk." George had done it to tease Alfred, she was sure—and it had worked. She should ask him not to do so again, but how foolish of Alfred to mind what George might have said.

Alfred's expression remained doubtful, and Jo felt annoyed that he didn't trust her not to flirt with another man. Then her cheeks burned again as she recalled her correspondence with Captain Delafield. But they were just friends, too.

She had better change the subject. "Were the business affairs that took you out of London successful, Alfred? Despite what your brother said last night, you would not be boring me if you related a few details."

Another pause. "Oh, they were merely regimental matters, my dear."

She held the rose to her face, breathing its scent. To be fair, she probably wouldn't find details of most army matters interesting, but it did feel like an abrupt dismissal of her question. "But Alfred, if we are to wed, matters such as your postings, or whether you intend to sell out, *will* concern me."

He stopped abruptly and turned to face her. "*If* we are to wed? Is it not settled between us? Joanna, my dear, I have waited so long for you. You cannot turn me down now!"

"I am not doing so, Alfred."

He seemed reassured. "I'm pleased to hear it. Shall we walk on?" He offered his arm again.

He didn't say anything as they wandered along the paths. Jo felt uncomfortable; it didn't feel like a companionable silence. She *did* want to know of his plans for the future, but did not feel she could ask again just yet. "The sweet williams are blooming well this year," she finally said, as they neared the end of the long border, indicating the clumps of pink and white flowers dotted in front of salvias and delphiniums.

Alfred dutifully looked where she was pointing. "Very pretty."

"Aunt Sarah wondered if the cold winter might have killed them. The trees in the orangery had to be wrapped up, you know, it was so cold. We must have an orangery at our new home, as well as a garden."

"Of course, my dear. Whatever you wish."

Jo sighed, and gave up. Mama and Papa talked to each other often, about many things; Alfred had done so, too, when they first met. She would try again later to find some interest they had in common, but this walk had not been a promising start.

"Shall we return to the house, Joanna? It is coming on to rain."

"By all means." They turned and made their way back through the rose garden. As they walked, Jo's attention was caught by a yellow chaise moving down the drive, away from the house.

"Is your aunt expecting other guests?" Alfred asked.

"Papa is expecting some of his business acquaintances; that was probably their hired chaise departing." She looked at his face, wondering how he would react to the news that Captain Delafield was one of them. "Two of your friends from Verdun."

His scowl was fleeting, but she had not imagined it.

"I thought Captain Delafield was your friend, Alfred? You asked him to write to me when you were captured."

"We were billeted together, that is all. He... That is, we hardly saw each other once we reached Verdun."

That didn't explain his hostility, but it was pointless to press him on the matter. And unwise, too; he must not find out about their correspondence.

Alfred stalked off towards the billiards room as soon as they entered the house. Jo pulled on her bonnet ribbons. "Have Papa's guests just arrived, Stevenson?"

"Yes, miss. Your father wishes to see them in the library as soon as they have refreshed themselves."

"Thank you." She had time to tidy her hair first, but she did need to speak to the captain before he was introduced to Mama.

"Mr Stretton is in the library, sirs," Stevenson said, appearing from some hidden corner as Rob and Chadwick descended the main staircase. "If you would follow me?" He led them along a corridor, indicating as he went the doors that led to the dining room, the billiards room, and the breakfast parlour. He announced their names as he showed them into the library.

The room was several times the size of the library in the Strettons' house in London, and felt to Rob more like a parlour with bookshelves than a room solely devoted to books. A sofa and armchairs were grouped around the empty fireplace. It was bright from large windows on two sides, facing both the front and side of the house. One window had a low table beside it, with more armchairs. Mr Stretton was reading, but set his book on the table and rose as they walked in.

"Welcome, gentlemen. Do take a seat." He indicated the other chairs. "I trust you had a successful trip?"

"In a manner of speaking, sir," Chadwick said. "I have definite conclusions, but you—"

"Excellent," Mr Stretton said, but with a smile that removed any rudeness from his interruption. "I apologise, Lieutenant, but Jo should be present when you give your report. We will find a time when we are not likely to be disturbed."

There was a knock on the door, and Rob smiled. "I see what you mean, sir." The three men stood as Miss Stretton entered. She curtseyed; her smile, and the delicate flush on her cheeks, almost made Rob forget to bow in return.

"You timed your walk well, Jo," Mr Stretton said, glancing at the raindrops now running down the window. "I was just saying to these gentlemen that we should set a time to discuss the canal project." He turned to them. "Will tomorrow after breakfast be convenient for your report? That will give you time to settle in. My nephew will be happy to show you around, I'm sure."

Rob recalled Moorven saying something about a military-mad nephew. He'd rather have Miss Stretton showing them around; from what she had written, he gathered she was familiar with this house and its grounds. But such wishes were neither wise nor helpful.

"We will gladly accept your invitation," Chadwick said. "Thank you, sir."

"Come, I will introduce you to some of the other guests."

Before they could move, there was a perfunctory knock, and the door opened. A man of around Mr Stretton's age entered—an older, more rotund version of Bengrove. He stopped just inside the door.

"Ah, Lord Bengrove." Mr Stretton stood and made the introductions. They bowed, Rob hiding his amusement at the clear distaste on Lord Bengrove's face. He must have heard about them from his son.

"I will leave you to peruse the books in peace, Bengrove," Mr Stretton said. "This way, gentlemen."

Miss Stretton fell into step beside Rob as they left the room, and spoke in a low voice. "Captain, my mother does not know about our correspondence." She glanced over her shoulder and frowned.

Rob turned his head to find Lord Bengrove only a couple of paces behind them, and getting closer. "Thank you, Miss Stretton," he said, in his normal voice. "I'm sure we will enjoy our stay."

Her frown persisted for a moment, then she smiled. It was only a gentle curve of the lips, but her eyes showed amusement. She headed up the stairs, and Mr Stretton led them to the billiards room. "I'll introduce you to the menfolk first. You won't want too many new names at once."

Three men stood watching as Bengrove aimed his cue; Mr Stretton waited until he had taken his shot. "Gentlemen, may I introduce my colleagues Captain Delafield and Lieutenant Chadwick? Captain, Lieutenant—this is Mr Edmond Bengrove..."

The older brother who would inherit the title, shorter and more slender than Alfred Bengrove.

"...my nephew, George Yelden, and a family friend, James Newman."

Yelden came forward with a smile and outstretched hand. "Welcome, gentlemen." They shook hands. Behind him, Newman nodded a friendly greeting.

"And you know Captain Bengrove, of course," Mr Stretton finished, addressing Rob.

"Indeed we do, sir." Rob was tempted to refer to Bengrove's trouble with the gendarmes in Verdun, but held his tongue. There was likely to be enough hostility between them without deliberately making things worse.

"Well, I'll leave you to it," Mr Stretton said.

"Billiards?" Yelden asked when Mr Stretton left. "We can play in pairs and have a tournament."

The Bengroves didn't look as if they relished the idea.

"Sounds good to me," Chadwick said before Rob could respond, and limped towards the rack on the wall to choose a cue.

At least if Bengrove was here, he wasn't making up to Miss Stretton.

CHAPTER 24

*R*ob looked around the room as people settled into their places at the long dining table. Lord and Lady Yelden sat at the two ends, with Lord and Lady Bengrove, the sharp-featured Lady Misterton and Mr Stretton in the places next to them. He noticed, with some amusement, that he and Chadwick had been seated across from each other in the middle of the table, as far from the titled guests as possible. Rob wasn't sorry; Lady Bengrove and Lady Misterton had barely been civil when they were introduced, in contrast to Lady Yelden's friendly welcome.

Chadwick, lucky dog, was seated between Miss Stretton and her mama, whereas Rob had Bengrove's older brother and his wife to either side. Conversation was stilted at first, with Mrs Bengrove asking Rob where his family were from and what he'd done in the army. Opposite, Miss Stretton's attention was being monopolised by Bengrove, seated beside her. She nodded and smiled at his words—compliments, probably. Compliments that he did not mean.

Rob did his best to concentrate on the excellent food and what the people beside him were saying, and *not* on watching Bengrove and Miss Stretton. Then Mrs Bengrove turned to George Yelden, on her other side.

"Did you ever think of joining the army, Mr Yelden?"

A natural lull in the conversation meant everyone around the table heard the question and Yelden's reply. "Papa didn't want me to. As I'm the heir, you know. I did fancy myself as a cavalry officer," he went on as quiet conversations restarted. "But even if I had gone against Papa's wishes, I could not afford to buy a commission in a good regiment. It costs a great deal."

"Quite right too," Lord Bengrove said. "Makes sure command is in the hands of those born to it. And the best regiments cost the most, naturally." He looked straight at Rob then. "What regiment were you in, Delafield?" There was a definite note of scorn in his voice, and the other diners fell silent.

"The 30th Foot," Rob replied, forcing himself to speak in a neutral tone.

"A real gentleman buys himself into a decent regiment." Captain Bengrove tapped his glass for a footman to refill it. "And does not need to work his way up through the ranks. I purchased my captaincy as soon as I'd done my time as a lieutenant."

"I'm sure all regiments, and all officers, do their duty," Lady Yelden said, casting an anxious look around the table. Rob was not about to abuse her hospitality by arguing with Bengrove, so he didn't reply.

"There is a school of thought that considers serving more than the minimum time would be beneficial," Mr Stretton said. "Particularly as a lieutenant could have served the whole of his three years in barracks."

Bengrove was beginning to look angry. "Are you saying I'm incompetent, Stretton?"

"By no means," Mr Stretton said calmly. "After all, how could I know?" He glanced in Bengrove's direction, then returned his attention to his plate.

Bengrove could not resist having the last word. "Just a foot regiment," he muttered. "Army couldn't function without the cavalry."

"Didn't notice you at Badajoz, Bengrove," Rob said, finally roused to respond. "Had trouble getting the horses over the walls, did you?"

This drew a crack of laughter from George. Miss Stretton covered her mouth with one hand as she glanced at Bengrove, then looked down at her plate. Bengrove slammed his napkin onto the table and pushed his chair back. A hissed command from his mother made him subside, although his face was still flushed with anger.

"Were you at Badajoz, Captain Delafield?" Yelden asked. "Were you in the breaches? What was it like? I heard—"

Lady Yelden coughed, and George went rather red in the face and stopped.

"The Fifth Division went around the back," Rob said. "We had a much easier time of it than the men in the breaches. If you wish to know more, you may ask me some other time." He gave George a friendly nod, which removed any rebuke from his words. But George's question had successfully deflected the animosity, and conversation returned to general topics.

"That was an uncomfortable dinner, Jo," Mama said quietly as the ladies left the gentlemen to their port and made their way to the drawing room. "Captain Delafield was very restrained in the face of the Bengroves' rudeness; from your Alfred, I'm afraid to say, as well as his father."

"Indeed, Mama." Alfred had chosen to take offence when he could have ignored Papa's comment about experience. Was it wrong of her to be amused by Captain Delafield's riposte? No, she decided. Alfred had set out to denigrate Captain Delafield, and the latter had turned it into a joke instead of becoming angry in return.

When the tea tray arrived, Jo and Lydia poured and passed the cups around. Lady Misterton inspected Jo as she sipped her drink.

"You are a very fortunate young woman to be marrying into the Bengrove family."

"Yes, my lady." Jo did her best to remain polite.

"You appear to have pretty enough manners. I suppose you will manage in the more exalted company you will encounter after your marriage."

"I'm *so* happy you think so," Jo said sweetly, annoyed more at the insult to Aunt Sarah than to herself. "An encomium from a fine lady such as yourself is an honour indeed."

Lady Misterton nodded regally and turned to Lady Bengrove.

"Well, this is cosy," Aunt Sarah said, breaking the following silence. "I do enjoy titled company, don't you, Frances?"

Jo looked at her aunt in surprise, and caught a wink directed at Mama.

"I suppose it is rare for you, Mrs Stretton," Lady Bengrove said. "Joanna will become accustomed to our ways when she marries my son."

"Indeed she will," Mama said. "But it won't take long, I'm sure." She looked towards Aunt Sarah. "Do you remember when Papa took us all to Badminton House the summer we came out?"

"I do, indeed. Her Grace complimented us on our easy manners. I'm sure Jo would be as well received should your family be fortunate enough to receive an invitation, Lady Bengrove."

Jo hid a smile as Lady Bengrove's sour expression deepened.

"And Longleat. Such a magnificent place," Mama went on. "The house as well as the gardens. Fine furnishings, all in the best taste."

"Not as fine as Stowe," Aunt Sarah responded. "The circuit of the lake provides so many different places to admire the view. It was only finished a few years ago, I think."

Lydia, sitting beside Jo, turned to her in bewilderment, but Aunt Sarah addressed her before she could speak. "Lydia, will you please go and check that Stevenson has had the card tables set up in the blue salon?"

Jo, trying hard not to laugh, followed her cousin out of the room.

"Have Mama and Aunt Frances really been invited to all those places?" Lydia asked. "Mama has never talked about it. I think she would have done if she enjoyed it so much."

"They may have been invited to Badminton before they both married. But they didn't actually say they had been invited to the other two places." Or that they had even been there.

"Oh." Lydia grinned. "Mama would scold me if I told fibs like that. But Lady Bengrove is horrid, isn't she?"

Jo took her arm and drew her further away from the door. "She is, and so is her friend, but you must not say so where any of the guests might hear. Now, I don't think we really need to see Stevenson, but it is a good excuse not to return until the gentlemen rejoin us."

It wasn't long until the menfolk appeared, and it took little persuasion for the company to move to the blue salon for cards. Lord and Lady Bengrove sat down with Lord Yelden and Lady Misterton to play whist.

"Poor Uncle Henry," Jo whispered to Mama.

Mama shook her head. "He won't mind, dear. He's so even-tempered." She looked around at the other guests. "I will leave you younger people to find your own amusement and retire for the night." She stopped by Catherine Bengrove on her way to the door and said a few words. Catherine looked tired, so Jo wasn't surprised when she accompanied Mama. Jo moved over to where the rest of the party were standing.

"Whist, Jo?" George asked. "We could make a four with James and Lydia."

James Newman was sitting beside Lydia, their heads close as they looked at a book together. "I wouldn't want to interrupt them."

"You should allow me to get my revenge at billiards," Mr Bengrove said from behind George. George accepted the challenge with a shrug. Papa raised his brows, but said nothing as the two men left.

"Shall we play, Joanna?" Alfred asked.

"If these gentlemen will join us?" Jo gestured to Captain Delafield and his friend. "But I only play for pennies, not pounds, you know."

"There's not much fun in that," Alfred protested.

He hadn't minded two years ago. Jo's irritation must have shown in her expression, for he smiled and nodded towards the other two. "These gentlemen would prefer to play for more interesting stakes, I'm sure."

"I don't m—" Captain Delafield started, but Papa interrupted.

"Do you play piquet, Bengrove? I'll give you a game. Does a guinea a *partie* suit you? And something for *piques* and *repiques?*"

Alfred's eyes shifted from Papa to Jo and then back again. "By all means."

Rob, watching Miss Stretton's face as Bengrove and Mr Stretton sat at the second card table, wasn't sure if she was disappointed or offended by Bengrove accepting her father's invitation instead of playing whist with her. It could not be pleasant to be slighted in favour of a higher stakes game.

"Do you care to play, Miss Stretton? Three-handed whist, perhaps." He hadn't intended to spend any more time than he had to in her company, but the words came out before his caution could stop them.

"Or piquet, if you prefer," Chadwick offered. "I can entertain myself with a book if you two wish to play."

"I know the rules for piquet," Miss Stretton said, "but I have had very little practice."

"I am always willing to assist," Chadwick said, with a bow. "We can play together against Delafield."

Miss Stretton appeared surprised, then smiled. "Thank you, Lieutenant. I will accept your offer." The people at the other tables appeared to be taking their games very seriously, and Lady Misterton sent a glare in her direction. "Should we go elsewhere, though? I would not wish to distract the players here from their games."

Fifteen minutes later, the three of them were settled at a card table set up in a separate parlour. Miss Stretton's maid busied herself with some sewing in one corner. Rob picked up the pack the butler had provided, separated the low denomination cards, and set them to one side. He was glad of Chadwick's suggestion—better to sit opposite her than close beside her.

Rob dealt and quickly sorted his own cards. Miss Stretton frowned in concentration, biting her lower lip as she decided on her discards. He watched her slender fingers sort the replacement cards, and tried to ignore his wish to tuck a loose curl of hair back behind her ear. He'd liked her from her letters, and their meetings since his return had only deepened that liking and added physical attraction to it.

"Rob?" They were waiting for him to exchange his cards. He did so, still feeling disgusted that someone like Bengrove was set to marry such an intelligent and beautiful young woman. The man hadn't even wanted to spend time with her if it meant missing out on some high-stakes gambling.

She won the first *partie* easily and dealt for the next. Rob again went through the process mechanically, and lost again. But when she won the third, Miss Stretton started to look suspicious.

"You're letting me win, Captain!"

"Not deliberately, Miss Stretton. I'm afraid I am just not concentrating well." Her expression changed to one of contrition.

"I'm sorry, Captain. It must be quite tedious for you with me being so slow. And only penny stakes too." The words sounded as if they could have two meanings, but he could detect no sarcasm in her face or voice. She was genuinely apologising for boring him!

Take it lightly, Delafield.

"Why, yes, Miss Stretton. A day is wasted when I haven't won or lost hundreds of pounds. And the pair of us would really prefer to be spending the rest of the evening talking platitudes with people we hardly know."

Jo was momentarily stunned by the captain's first words, but by the time he'd finished speaking, the creases beside his eyes and his compressed lips told her what she should have known. He gave up trying to keep a straight face when she smiled, and the warmth in his gaze made her look away.

"Let us carry on, then." She dealt the cards again, but her concentration now seemed as poor as the captain's, and this time he won by a few points.

"Another game, Miss Stretton?" Lieutenant Chadwick asked. "I could play and—"

All heads turned as the door opened. "What are you doing here, young woman?" Lord Bengrove demanded, his face thunderous. "Alone with *two* men; disgraceful behaviour!"

Jo's shock at the sudden attack rendered her speechless for a moment; before she could reply, Martha coughed loudly from her seat in the corner.

"I am not alone with them, and we were playing cards. As you can see." She managed to sound calmer than she felt. She shot a quick glance at her companions with a small shake of the head. It would be better if she dealt with this herself.

Momentarily disconcerted, Lord Bengrove gathered his anger again. "You are betrothed to my son, Miss Stretton. You should be with him, not consorting with these... these..."

"These *gentlemen*," Jo interrupted. "Alfred preferred to play cards with my father. If you think I am the sort of person to be... improper... with *two* men at once, in my aunt's home with a house full of guests, I wonder that you still wish me to marry your son! Good day, sir." She glared at him. After a few tense moments he turned on his heel and stalked out of the room, banging the door behind him. She leaned back limply in her chair, shaken by the sudden unpleasantness.

Captain Delafield left the table, returning with a glass of claret that he placed beside her. "A drink might help, Miss Stretton."

It did, but her inclination for cards had gone. "Thank you for not speaking, gentlemen, for that was as insulting to you as to me. Although I am loath to end the game just after being commanded to do so by such a man, I think I will retire for the night."

They said their farewells, and Jo went to her room, her mood downcast. She didn't feel any closer to Alfred than she had before this morning's walk—quite the opposite. Papa had not helped, enticing him away with the promise of a high-stakes game, but Alfred had gone willingly.

"That Lord Bengrove's a bit rude, miss," Martha said, as she helped Jo off with her gown.

"That was a very well-timed cough, Martha," Jo said. Although she agreed with the maid, it would not do to say so.

"Them military men are proper gents, though. There, miss. All done."

"Thank you, Martha; you may go."

They certainly acted more like gentlemen than Lord Bengrove did, and she *had* enjoyed that part of the evening. They would discuss the canal project in the morning; she would see him—*them*—again then.

CHAPTER 25

*T*he next morning, Rob was amused to see Chadwick dressing himself with as much care as he had for dinner the night before. "You look as if you are to be interviewed for a position."

"You don't think so?" Chadwick looked surprised.

Rob shrugged. "I suppose it is, in a way, in your case. I'm just the unskilled assistant."

"Skilled enough to take Bengrove down a peg or two last night," Chadwick grinned. "The mental image of him trying to boost his mount up a siege ladder..." He shook his head, then eyed Rob's own dress. "You look pretty smart yourself. It must be to impress your Miss Stretton, if it's not for her father."

"She's not *my* Miss Stretton," Rob said, rather too forcefully. "Come on, let's get some breakfast."

Most of the male members of the house party were in the breakfast room when Rob and Chadwick entered, but the only woman present was Miss Stretton, sitting beside her father, wearing a plain round gown. She looked just as well in it as she had in the more elaborate gown she'd worn last night at dinner.

They chose places at the table as far from the Bengroves as possible, close to George Yelden. "Would you care to ride about the estate this afternoon?" George asked them. Chadwick declined, with thanks, but Rob agreed. He suspected he would be asked to relate tales of army life, but that was a better prospect than having to associate with the Bengrove family.

The Strettons finished their breakfast. Mr Stretton stopped beside Chadwick and Rob on his way out. "I will see you in twenty minutes in the library, gentlemen, if that is convenient?"

"What's going on, Stretton?" Lord Bengrove asked sharply.

"Merely an investment meeting," Stretton said calmly.

"Er, well." Lord Bengrove looked from Stretton to Rob and Chadwick, then cleared his throat. "This is a good time for Alfred to learn a bit about business matters, eh? Mind if he joins you?"

Stretton raised an eyebrow and looked at Bengrove. "If you wish to join us, Captain, please do."

Rob hid a grimace. But perhaps it was only right that Bengrove should take an interest in what would happen to the money Miss Stretton would bring to the marriage. Bengrove himself looked taken aback, but muttered something that sounded like agreement.

"Just what we bloody need," Chadwick complained beneath his breath.

Rob managed a nonchalant shrug. "Can't be helped."

Alfred arrived in the library a few minutes after the others had seated themselves around the table by the window. Jo saw him pause as his gaze fell on her, but he took his place without a word. It might be easier to discuss her wish to continue being involved with investments with him after this meeting.

Papa handed Alfred a copy of the canal prospectus. "We are discussing a scheme in which I might decide to invest. Would you care to look through the details before we begin?"

Alfred started to read, a frown forming as he turned the pages. Jo was disappointed, but not really surprised, when he dropped the document on the desk before getting even half way through. "Don't you have secretaries to deal with this kind of thing?"

"I would not trust an employee to make decisions involving thousands of pounds," Papa said. "Would you?"

"I, er… I suppose not."

"It is rather a lot to take in at once, Bengrove, and clearly you cannot comment on the suitability of this project as an investment. But tell me, how would you go about finding out if this is likely to be a sound prospect?" Papa sounded like a schoolteacher.

Alfred must have thought so, too, for he frowned again as he flicked through the document and found the table of financial projections. "It offers a good return; higher than putting the money in the funds, I think?"

"It does," Papa confirmed. "So would you put money into this based on the information you have?"

"Yes, why not?"

Papa nodded, as if he were pleased with the answer. Jo suspected that Alfred had just fallen into a trap, but she couldn't blame Papa on this occasion. He must be thinking not only of the dowry that he would give her, but the fortune she stood to inherit one day. Jo wanted to be sure the money would not be wasted as much as her father did.

Papa turned to the other two men. "Lieutenant Chadwick, could you summarise what you found out?"

"Certainly, sir." Lieutenant Chadwick had a set of notes with him, but he did not refer to them. "After the queries raised by—"

Papa cleared his throat noisily, and the lieutenant paused, glancing at Jo before looking back at Papa. "After your… er, consultant called into question the estimated costs, I visited the site. The proposed route crosses somewhat marshy ground, poor for agriculture. It is also not ideal for canal construction, but does not pose any insurmountable difficulties. The predicted labour costs assume very low wages, and in my opinion have underestimated the time needed for the work. Both factors lead me to suspect that the costs would be considerably higher than suggested."

"So, not such a good prospect, then?" Papa asked.

"From the engineering side, sir, the costs are not prohibitive. But Delafield took the opportunity to make enquires as well."

"Why Delafield?" Alfred asked. "He has no engineering expertise."

Jo glanced at Captain Delafield's face—strangely, he seemed amused rather than offended by Alfred's rudeness.

"Engineering matters are not the only concern in projects of this nature." Papa said.

Alfred's mouth pursed, but he glanced at Papa and nodded reluctant agreement.

"Will you tell us what you discovered, Captain?" Papa said.

"Thank you, sir." Captain Delafield took a moment to marshal his thoughts. "Through talking to various people, I found two reasons to question the proposal. Firstly, there *are* mines and factories nearby that could use the canal, as the prospectus states, but the volume of goods to be moved does not seem sufficient to generate the income indicated. The report we compiled gives the details. The prospectus suggests that the presence of the canal could encourage the building of more factories, but that is speculative, and any effect would not be seen for some years."

That was one of Jo's questions answered.

"Secondly," Captain Delafield went on, "the man proposing the project is a distant relative of the owner of most of the land across which the canal will run. As Chadwick said, the land in question is not much good for agriculture, and as far as I could ascertain there is little prospect of finding minerals or coal beneath it. The proposer himself does not appear to own any property, so if the scheme failed there is not much likelihood of investors being able to recover their money. It is possible that once funds have been used to buy the required land, the scheme may fail. That would leave the landowner with a tidy sum, out of which he can pay off the bankrupt proposer."

That was interesting. Jo had been suspicious of the predicted profits, but hadn't been able to see any reason for it beyond poor planning.

"Thank you, Captain," Papa said. "It seems the first expert I consulted was correct to be concerned."

Jo was pleased at this public praise. She caught Captain Delafield's eye, and his smile brought a blush to her cheeks.

"So, Bengrove," Papa said, "I hope you can see why it is not wise to take the information in a prospectus such as this at face value."

"Indeed," Alfred agreed stiffly.

"I am considering another scheme," Papa went on. "Would you care to take a look?" He picked up more papers from the table. "I'm afraid I wasn't anticipating quite so many people. Delafield, could you and Chadwick both read the same one?"

"No need." Alfred stood up. "If you will excuse me, my father wished for my company to… to…"

"By all means, Captain," Papa said. Alfred left the room, closing the door rather too hard behind him. Jo looked down at her hands, embarrassed by his abrupt departure, and the fact he'd shown such poor judgement. She dreaded to think of his reaction if he found out that it was her reservations that had set the investigation in motion.

"I imagine your expense account will include a fair quantity of ale, gentlemen?" Papa asked.

Captain Delafield smiled. "I'm afraid so, sir."

"Worth every penny. I *do* have another investment here, but as it is in shipping, it was mainly Lieutenant Moorven's opinion I wished for. It is unfortunate he had to be elsewhere. However, if you are interested, you gentlemen could also give it your consideration. At your leisure, however."

"Thank you, sir." Lieutenant Chadwick picked up the document, and the two men took their leave.

Papa was looking at her, one brow raised, but what excuse could there be for Alfred's behaviour? And why did she feel she needed to excuse it?

"I have arranged to discuss the settlements with Lord Bengrove this afternoon, Jo," he said, when she did not speak.

Not so soon, surely. She needed more time.

"That does not commit either of you to this marriage, of course. I will not sign anything until you have made your decision."

Thank the heavens. That was a relief.

~

George Yelden pulled his horse to a stop as they reached the top of the hill. "Best view for miles around."

Rob reined in next to him. It was good to be out of doors on such a lovely afternoon, even though riding made his ankle ache. "Is this all Yelden land?" Rob asked.

"Not all of it." George turned and pointed, indicating the boundaries of his father's holdings and describing how the different areas were farmed. Rob watched his face rather than looking at where he was pointing, liking the enthusiasm Miss Stretton's cousin was showing for the land he would inherit. Yelden wound down eventually, and glanced apologetically at Rob.

"Hope I didn't bore you, Delafield."

"Not at all. My family has farms in Gloucestershire. The land there is similar, I think."

Yelden nodded, but didn't reply, his gaze on the landscape unfocussed. Rob waited patiently—he obviously had something on his mind.

"Is Bengrove really a friend of yours?" Yelden asked eventually. "I mean, when Uncle Nathan talked about inviting you and Lieutenant Chadwick here, he said you were friends of Bengrove. But Bengrove doesn't like you, does he?"

"The feeling is mutual."

"Oh, good. I mean… er… that's all right, then."

"Why do you ask?"

"It's Jo. She won't be happy married to him." Yelden glanced uncertainly at Rob. "It's not my concern. Or yours, I suppose, but he's such a…"

"An arse?" Rob suggested, as Yelden struggled for a suitable word. "Mutton-headed stiff-rump? Bacon-brained toss pot?"

"All of those," Yelden laughed. "I thought Uncle Nathan had more sense than to allow… Oh, of course. He had no choice."

"No choice?" Rob had wondered how Miss Stretton came to be betrothed to Bengrove. Yelden was correct; it really wasn't anything to do with him, but he wanted to know. After their first exchange of letters, in which she acknowledged that her letter to Bengrove had been sarcastic, her betrothal had not been mentioned in their correspondence, and it was not the kind of thing he could have asked her.

Luckily George didn't notice anything odd in Rob's response. "They met here, when Bengrove was on leave. Jo was with Aunt Frances—Mrs Stretton, that is—but Uncle Nathan wasn't here. Her mama must have given him permission to pay his addresses. He did look very fine in his uniform."

Appearances could be deceptive. "You shouldn't worry. Mr Stretton knows what Bengrove is like, and I suspect he has planned some way of extricating her." He hoped to God he was correct. He must have sounded convincing, for his companion looked happier.

"D'you fancy a pint?" Yelden said, pointing with his whip. "There's an inn down there with good ale."

The sun was still warm, so they sat at a table outside with their mugs of ale.

"I suppose there's no point trying to join the army now," Yelden said. "They won't be needing new officers."

"Do you really want to join up? I thought I'd managed to put you off." Yelden had prompted Rob to relate some of his army experiences while they were riding. The lad had looked rather green at some of Rob's descriptions of sorting out the dead and wounded after a battle.

"You helped stop Bonaparte," Yelden said. "I do realise it can be tedious at times, but you were doing something worthwhile." He took a pull of his ale. "I suppose I'm bored," he admitted. "I can't spend all my time hunting or..."

"Gambling and whoring?" Rob said bluntly, when Yelden shrugged.

Yelden grimaced. "Never been fond of either."

"You'll have the land to manage, one day, and take your seat in the Lords."

"*You* could have done that instead of joining up. Why didn't you?"

"I have two older brothers and four older sisters," Rob explained. "My mother died when I was just a lad, so they all started telling me what to do. I threatened to run away unless they bought me a commission. I don't think your situation is like that?"

"Ha, no, thank goodness. But Papa leaves everything to his steward."

"That doesn't mean you can't take an interest. Find out about new methods, and so on. Visit my brother with me, if you like—he'll bore you to tears with all the latest ideas."

Yelden looked thoughtful and Rob didn't interrupt while he finished his mug of ale. Then he apologised for being so silent. "I might take you up on that offer, if you meant it."

Before Rob could reply, a horse came to a stop in front of their table. Bengrove glowered down at them from the saddle. "Where the hell have you been?" he snarled at Yelden. "I've been all over the countryside looking for you! Where's Joanna?"

"Not here, clearly," Yelden snapped. "What business is it of yours? You are not my keeper, or hers."

"I will be." Bengrove pointed his whip at Rob. "I want a word with you as well."

"You're having one now." Rob replied calmly. A stable boy came running over; Bengrove dismounted and handed over the reins.

"I want to know what you're doing with my betrothed," Bengrove demanded, looming over Rob. Rob sighed, put his mug on the table, and stood up. Bengrove didn't back off, so their faces were close. The smell of brandy was strong; Bengrove must have stopped for refreshment in several inns on his search for them.

Wonderful; just what he needed—an angry and partially drunk lout to deal with.

"I'm not doing anything with your betrothed," Rob said, trying to convey a calmness he did not feel. He longed to hit the man, but that wouldn't solve anything—apart from relieving some of his frustration. He glanced behind him to size up the situation.

"Playing cards alone with her, 'investment' meetings with her." Bengrove poked him in the chest with each point, and Rob backed away.

"We weren't alone, and you preferred to play cards with her father," Rob said calmly. "I was invited to the meeting by Mr Stretton."

"Bengrove, what's—?"

"You stay out of it, Yelden," Bengrove rounded on him. "You're just as bad, trying to poach on my preserves when I was away fighting for the country, not a coward like you, cowering at home—"

"Instead of running up debts in Verdun?" Rob asked, drawing Bengrove's attention back to himself. "Living it up with your whores and gambling away more money than you had?"

Rob heard a grunt of surprise from Yelden.

"And belittling your betrothed in public—"

"Shut your mouth! I'd better not find you've been telling tales to Stretton." He jabbed at Rob again, staggering slightly as Rob moved backwards just fast enough to avoid his finger. "Or I'll... I'll..." He poked once more and Rob took another step away, finishing with his back against the inn wall.

Bengrove smiled in triumph.

"You'll what?" Rob taunted. "Tell tales to your father? Miss Stretton can do far better than someone who'll waste her dowry on—"

With a roar, Bengrove swung a fist straight at Rob's face, only to collapse in agony as his hand smashed into the stone wall where Rob's head had been. Rob picked himself up from the ground; Moorven's manoeuvre worked far more elegantly when both ankles could bend properly.

He dusted his breeches off and looked round. Yelden was laughing, and the serving man was vainly trying to hide a smirk.

Rob turned to Yelden. "It's tempting to kick him while he's down, but he's your guest."

Yelden nodded reluctantly. He called the serving man over and gave him some coins to settle their bill. "And if he absconds without paying," he pointed at Bengrove, still bent over nursing his hand, "send word to me at Yelden Court."

"I thought you were going to run away for a moment there," Yelden commented, once they were mounted and on their way.

"Can't run," Rob replied, straight-faced. "Not with my ankle."

Yelden looked shocked, then laughed.

"I can't claim the credit for the idea though. Moorven used it on him after..." After Bengrove insulted Miss Stretton in a tavern full of people. "Well, it rather relies on your opponent being a bit worse for drink."

"I do hope Jo sees sense," Yelden said.

"Indeed."

"Your ankle up to a bit of a race?" Yelden changed the subject, to Rob's relief. He didn't reply, but kicked the horse into motion. Yelden would probably win on his fine hunter, and it wouldn't do his ankle any good, but a gallop might help ease his frustration that Miss Stretton was still betrothed to that worthless oaf.

CHAPTER 26

*J*o felt at a loose end after the canal discussion. Alfred had not asked her to ride or walk with him. She would have liked to go for a ride with George, but he had gone out with Captain Delafield, Mama was resting, Papa was ensconced with Lord Bengrove, and Catherine had gone with Lady Bengrove and Lady Misterton to look around the shops in Winchester. Or to harass the shopkeepers, Jo thought uncharitably. She was glad not to be with them. Instead, she took the latest newspapers to a back parlour to make her usual notes about interesting business articles. She forced herself to concentrate on that for a couple of hours, but eventually the mixture of feelings she'd experienced during the canal discussion began to occupy her mind. She put her notebook away and fetched her bonnet.

The younger children were playing cricket on the lawn with a couple of grooms and a footman, but Jo didn't feel like joining them. Instead, she went into the flower garden—the scene of yesterday's stilted conversation with Alfred. She had still not managed to discuss where they were to live if they married, nor to raise the issue of her investment interests. After this morning, she was fairly certain he would object to her having any say in investing the funds she would bring to the marriage. Could she really live with a man who had no respect for her opinions or judgement? Particularly when his own judgement appeared to be so poor. And from whom she already had a secret.

She wandered on into the rose garden, spying Lydia in the distance walking arm in arm with James Newman. Jo felt a flash of envy. Lydia and James were in each other's company whenever possible, chatting comfortably and teasing each other, or just enjoying being together. Aunt Sarah was expecting them to announce their betrothal soon.

'Chatting comfortably' didn't describe the time she'd spent with Alfred. There was that enticing smile of his, but she was beginning to think that might be his only good point. Even more telling was the relief she'd felt when Papa said that discussing the settlements didn't mean she was committed to the marriage.

She walked to the edge of the park, still thinking, and when she turned back her decision had been made—there would be no marriage. Papa had wanted her to be sure of her feelings, and now she was. He'd also not wanted Mama to be disappointed, but Mama was so much better now, thanks to Captain Delafield's suggestion and her own determination, that Jo's decision should not set her back. She already shared Jo's opinion of Lord and Lady Bengrove.

However, despite Lord Bengrove having been reminded by Papa that she had only promised to wait for Alfred, the Bengroves appeared to think they were actually betrothed. She must ask Papa about the best way of dealing with that assumption.

Two horsemen on the drive looked like George and Captain Delafield returning from their ride, and before she reached the house George joined her, still in his outdoor clothing. He looked troubled.

"Did you enjoy your ride?"

His brow cleared, and he gave his ready smile. "Indeed. Delafield's a capital fellow. He suggested I ask Papa if I can start learning about the estate and land here. Help the steward, you know."

"I didn't think you were interested in that?"

"I wasn't, but it will be mine one day, and I think I *could* be interested if Papa will let me make improvements. Delafield invited me to go and see his brother's farms, and talk about the newest ideas." George hesitated then, frowning.

"George?"

"I was just thinking it's a pity you're not going to marry someone like Delafield instead of Bengrove. I'm sorry, Jo, but I really cannot like him. *Or his family.*"

Marry someone like Captain Delafield?

Jo put that idea out of her mind for now. "Alfred's parents are… unpleasant, I agree." George looked so concerned that Jo wanted to tell him she had already decided against the match, but she did not. She should tell her parents and Alfred first.

"Jo, do you remember asking me if I'd told him about you being an only child, and your father wealthy?"

She nodded.

"I said I hadn't, and he hadn't asked. Now, I think it's because he already knew. He joined in a card game at my club, won a bit of money off me. He was friendly, and…"

"And a heroic cavalry officer?"

George's face reddened. "Yes—I was more foolish then. The thing is, he more or less invited himself to accompany me when I said Mama was expecting me here. Said it was my chance to win the money back."

"Was it a lot?"

"Not really. It would have used my quarter's allowance to pay him, so I'd have asked Papa for a little more. But I heard that he played deep while he was away, so now, *not* winning a lot from me seems odd."

"Indeed it does. Thank you for telling me, George."

He peered at her face. "I haven't upset you, have I, Jo? I didn't mean to."

"No, *you* haven't. But the thought that he may have only courted me for my money isn't flattering."

"There'll be someone for you, Jo." He gave her a brotherly clap on the shoulder and went into the house.

She found a bench and sat down. It had been plain from the start that Lord Bengrove had wanted some of Papa's money; why had it taken her so long to realise that Alfred almost certainly had the same aim? The charming smile and honeyed words had fooled her, and she had spent much of the time he had been in France making excuses for his poor letters. George was right—she wanted someone who respected her abilities and her wish to use them, someone with a sense of humour, a smile that warmed her inside, and not so inflated with an idea of his own worth that he could not laugh at himself.

Someone like Captain Delafield—or the captain himself? She didn't know, but she would like to find out.

Did he care for her in that way? He had shown no sign of any liking beyond friendship, but how could he when he thought she was betrothed to another?

She had to detach herself from the Bengroves before she could think about that, so she set off back to the house; Papa would be in the library. Papa, who must have known that Alfred was a fortune hunter all this time, and had let her continue to make a fool of herself.

"Is something wrong, Jo?" Papa folded his newspaper and set it aside.

Jo came to a stop in front of the table. "I've been thinking about Alfred."

He nodded. "Have you reached a conclusion?"

"I cannot marry him." But that wasn't all she wanted to say. "Papa, you knew the Bengroves—all of them—were fortune hunters. Why didn't you tell me?" Somehow that hurt more than finding that she'd been mistaken about Alfred.

"I didn't *know*, Jo. I only suspected. Sit down, please."

She sat, rubbing her temples with her fingers. "You investigated the Bengrove finances, didn't you? When that announcement was put into the paper, I mean." Any father would have done.

"Of course. But I dropped my initial enquires when Alfred was reported missing, and we visited Bengrove Hall only a short time after we learned he had been taken prisoner. That didn't give me time to complete my enquiries before we went. However, that visit roused my suspicions. Do you recall Lady Bengrove talking about you living at the Court for some years?"

"Yes."

"Why, when you will have a substantial dowry, would she not be encouraging her son to buy his own estate? Or at least rent a house in the country until the two of you decide where you wish to settle."

"She seemed to think I needed instruction in how to run a large house."

"No. She knew Frances is an earl's daughter, and would have trained you for that. Afterwards, I discovered that Lord Bengrove had put it about—discreetly—that Alfred was betrothed to you. No doubt that was to appease his creditors, as I found that the family is deep in debt. Anything not entailed has been sold, the remaining lands have outstanding mortgages, and their two other estates are let to long-term tenants. I expect they are planning on using your dowry, and your inheritance on my demise, to pay their debts."

So when Lady Bengrove had talked about her eventually running a large house, she'd meant when Papa died. "Why did you allow me to continue thinking we might still wed when Alfred returned?"

"None of this showed that *Alfred* was part of the plan. His parents may have just—"

"No, Papa." Jo repeated what George had told her. "You thought I should get to know him again, but I've seen enough of him now. I had already decided we are not suited before George spoke to me."

Papa smiled. "I am relieved to hear it, Jo. It is best that you made this decision yourself, rather than my just forbidding the match. I don't think your mama will be too upset about your decision if you explain."

"How do we tell the Bengroves?"

"Leave that to me. I discussed the settlements with Lord Bengrove this morning; he was not pleased with my proposals, which will tie up your money so that neither he nor Alfred can use enough of it to solve the family's financial problems. He appears to be under the impression that he can persuade me to change my mind, but I will not. Once he realises that, I think he will be happy for his son to be free to charm some other heiress."

"Poor girl."

Papa chuckled. "Indeed. However it will be quite an uncomfortable situation for everyone once the matter is made plain, and it is rather late in the day now for the Bengroves to depart, so I will avoid any further discussion with them until tomorrow."

"No, Papa." And she must confess to Mama about the letters.

Mama was not in the parlour, although Lady Bengrove and Lady Misterton were. Jo beat a hasty retreat before they could say anything to her, and asked the butler if he knew where Mama was.

"She went into the gardens with Lady Yelden, miss, just as the other ladies returned from Winchester." Stevenson had his usual impassive expression, but she detected a slight twitch of his lips.

She could not confide in Mama with Aunt Sarah present; she would have to wait until they returned to dress for dinner. "Stevenson, should anyone enquire, I have gone for a walk."

"Yes, Miss Stretton."

In her room, Jo took out her two packets of letters and sorted through them. She was not going to marry Alfred, whatever Mama said, but she would prefer to have Mama's blessing for her decision. She left her door open so she would hear Mama returning to her room down the corridor and sat in the window seat to wait. The book she was reading remained closed in her lap, and eventually she fetched some of Captain Delafield's letters. Now she had met him, she could picture his expression as he wrote some of his self-deprecating comments, the way his eyes might have crinkled at the corners if one of her letters amused him. She had not spent much time with him, but she already knew more about him than she did of Alfred.

That wasn't quite true, she realised. Alfred's letters were as good a reflection of his character and disposition as Captain Delafield's; she did know him, but there was not much in him to admire, or even like.

~

Rob changed out of his riding clothes, debating with himself how to pass the time until dinner. He'd seen Miss Stretton walking in the gardens as he and Yelden rode up to the house; the temptation to see if she was still out there walking was strong, but he must not. In fact, for his own future peace of mind, it would be better if he saw as little of her as possible. Nor did he want to encounter any of the other Bengroves, so he settled for trying to read in the bedroom he shared with Chadwick.

"Good ride?" Chadwick asked when he entered the room a couple of hours later.

"Mostly." He related the incident with Bengrove, to Chadwick's amusement. "You?"

Chadwick shrugged. "Practising my aim at billiards. Alone."

"Really? Bengrove's brother seems keen on the game."

"Only when young Yelden's around, hadn't you noticed?"

"What? No." His attention had been too focused on Miss Stretton.

"Keeping the field clear for his brother, I imagine. Can't have her marrying her cousin, can they, not when they need the money she'll bring."

Rob shook his head. "Yelden's a nice enough chap, but he seems to think of her more like a sister."

"That's good." Chadwick winked.

"What do you mean?"

Chadwick raised his brows. "Would you court her if she weren't engaged to that arse?"

"But she is." He'd want to, that was certain, but he'd tried not to think about it. Bengrove wasn't the only obstacle. "And no, I wouldn't."

"Really? Why not?"

"Her father's as rich as Croesus."

"So?"

"I've no income apart from the rent from a small farm. Not enough to support her as she is used to. And not much chance of getting more. Would you want to live off your wife's money?"

"That would probably depend on the wife."

It would still feel like taking advantage. "Forget about it, John, please. You're really not helping. Besides, what you're suggesting would require her to like me as…" *As much as I like her.* Although he was coming to think that 'like' was far too bland a word to describe his feelings.

Chadwick stared at him a moment longer, then turned back to the mirror to finish straightening his cravat. "What say you to excusing ourselves from dinner and spending the evening in the village inn?"

"That's the most sense you've come out with all day!"

At last, Jo heard Mama's voice in the corridor and followed her into her room. "Mama, may I talk to you?"

Mama was unfastening her pelisse; Jo helped her remove it and laid it over the back of a chair. "Of course, dear. Is something wrong?"

"Not wrong, precisely."

Mama sat down and looked at Jo expectantly. But now she had her mother's full attention, Jo didn't know where to start.

"Are you enjoying being with Alfred, dear?"

Jo took a deep breath. "Mama, I hope you are not too disappointed, but I cannot marry him."

Her mother frowned. "Why not? He has not seemed quite the charming young man I remember from when we first met him, but he is probably finding it difficult to adjust to being free again. He wrote you some very good letters, Jo. It might just be that he does not show to advantage with his parents and brother always seeming to keep watch on him."

"It's not that, Mama." His family *had* been keeping watch, but on her, not Alfred. Why else would Mr Bengrove or his father appear every time she talked to George, or to Captain Delafield and his friend? She held out the packet of letters from Alfred. "These are his letters."

Still puzzled, Mama took them and began to read. "Oh, dear—he did find his life in Verdun confining… He wasn't very complimentary about Captain Delafield..." She read on, with no further comment until she had finished, then she looked through them again. "But how is this, Jo? I remember you reading out more than... more than these compliments."

"Those weren't from Alfred. The compliments there..." she pointed to the letters in her mother's hand, "...are the only substance in his letters. Mama, we have nothing to talk about, and I believe he only came to Yelden two years ago to court me for my dowry and inheritance."

"Are you sure about this, Jo?"

"Very sure. It was Alfred's false charm that attracted me, not his father's title. I began to wonder if we would suit after a few months of his letters, but Papa said I should wait until he returned. You were so set on the connection while... while you were unwell, and he didn't want to disappoint you."

Mama sighed, then nodded. "Very well. I only want you to be happy, Jo, and I can see that you would not be if you married into that family. Alfred would have to be a paragon indeed to make up for his parents. Does your father know of your decision?"

"Yes. Mama, I cannot face dinner sitting next to Alfred and pretending all is well. I will ask for a tray in my room. Papa thinks the Bengroves will leave tomorrow once they know." She stood, hoping that was the end of the explanations for now. She could leave her other confession until later.

"But Jo, if Alfred did not write those things about returning soldiers, and the other things you read out, who did?"

CHAPTER 27

o awoke the next morning with a feeling of trepidation. Mama had been shocked when she learned of Jo's correspondence with Captain Delafield, and only partly mollified by learning that she had been given Papa's permission and it was the captain's suggestion that had led to her cure. Jo hoped that sleeping on the matter, and talking to Papa about it, might have made Mama less critical.

But that wasn't the main cause of her reluctance to face the day. She would have to speak to Alfred at some point, but she would rather it were after Papa had told him and his father that there would be no marriage. Most of the menfolk would be going shooting, and the rest of the guests would be driving up onto the downs for a picnic.

Once she was free of Alfred… She shook her head; it would not do to anticipate matters. Still, she felt a great relief at the prospect of being able to please herself rather than wondering what Alfred was thinking, and not having to be polite to the Bengroves.

Intent on avoiding him, she breakfasted in her room, and remained there until she saw the shooting party set off down the drive. Then she looped the train of her riding habit over her wrist and

descended to the entrance hall. She intended to ride to the picnic—
Lydia and the younger girls would fill the space in the carriage with
Mama and Aunt Sarah, and she was not about to go in the Bengroves'
vehicle.

Aunt Sarah was waiting near the front door with Mama, her
mouth pursed and foot tapping. Beyond the open door, Lydia and the
girls waited in the carriage, and George paced up and down beside it.

"I'm sorry if I've kept you waiting, Aunt!" she said, hurrying down
the last few steps.

"Oh, you are not the latest, Jo. Lady Bengrove said she and Lady
Misterton would be here directly, and they are not. I need to make
sure the servants have set out the refreshments properly."

"Why don't you go? If the Bengroves' coachman doesn't know the
way, one of your grooms can go with him."

Aunt Sarah glanced at Mama, then gave a decisive nod, then a
smile. "That's a good idea. We can enjoy the view in peace for a while."

Jo followed them out to where a groom stood with two horses.
George handed the ladies into the carriage, then helped Jo into her
saddle before mounting himself.

"I'm surprised you're not with the shooting party, George," she
said, settling her skirts before taking the reins from the groom.

"Mama insisted," he said with a grimace. "Let's get on with it,
shall we?"

"Miss Stretton!" The call came from the house as the carriage
pulled away. Jo turned her horse to face the door. A maid hurried
down the steps. "Oh, miss, I'm glad I caught you." She paused to
breathe, one hand on her chest.

"What is it?"

"Mrs Bengrove wants to see you before you leave, miss. In her
room, if you would be so good."

George swore as Jo slid down from the saddle.

"I'll see what Catherine wants. You go on, George. The spot Aunt
Sarah has chosen is not far beyond the estate; I'll join you shortly."

He nodded, and trotted after the carriage. Jo turned to the maid.
"What is wrong?"

"I was just told that Mrs Bengrove wants you, miss. She's in her room." She bobbed a curtsey and hurried back into the house. Jo asked the groom to wait with the horse and followed her. There was no sign of the maid in the entrance hall, so she went upstairs.

She knocked on Catherine's door, but got no response. She knocked again, harder, and finally called out, but still there was no response, or even any sound from beyond the door. There must be some mistake, although the maid's request had been clear enough.

Irritated, she strode back along the corridor and ran down the stairs. If she hurried, she might catch up with George.

"Joanna, my dear."

Jo stopped on the bottom step, one hand still on the banister. Alfred stood by the parlour door, with what she used to think of as his enticing smile. Papa must not yet have spoken to him or his father about ending the betrothal.

"Alfred. I thought you had already gone with the picnic party." He was not dressed for the outdoors, and had some kind of bandage on his right hand. What had he been doing?

He approached, holding his left hand towards her. "Why would I do that, when I could spend time alone with you here, instead? I missed you last night when you did not come down to dinner. Are you well?"

She ignored his outstretched hand. "Thank you, I am well. Excuse me, Alfred, but I am supposed to be joining my mother and aunt at their picnic." She walked towards the front door.

"Joanna, please!" Alfred hurried after her and put his hand on her arm. "I need to talk to you."

Conscious of the footman watching them from his post near the front door, Jo stopped and turned to face him.

"Alfred, I am late to the picnic. We can talk later, surely?" He appeared hurt, and she felt a momentary doubt. "Or why don't you ride with me? We can talk on the way."

"It won't take long. Please, my dear."

She suppressed a sigh, and unpinned her hat, leaving it on a table in the hall. "Very well. Let us go into the library."

"This parlour will be better. We wouldn't want to disturb your father's reading." He held the door of the front parlour open for her.

Papa was with the shooting party, but Jo didn't bother to correct him. She left the door open behind her as she entered the front parlour. "What is it, Alfred?"

~

The gig carrying Rob, Chadwick, and Mr Stretton bumped to a halt in a field half a mile from the house, a few yards from the line of pigeon traps. A groom came to hold the horse and they descended, Rob staggering as his bad ankle sent a warning pain up his leg. Walking to the inn last night hadn't been the best of decisions, but it had been a relief to be away from Yelden Court with its unpleasant guests and uncomfortable undercurrents.

The Yelden landau drew up nearby, and Lord Yelden went to speak to his gamekeeper. Lord Bengrove and the elder Bengrove son followed him, leaving Mrs Bengrove still sitting in the vehicle. Rob didn't think it sporting to kill birds released within easy shooting distance, but he'd opted for the informal competition once he found that Alfred Bengrove was to go on the picnic. He didn't want to watch Bengrove dance attendance on Miss Stretton.

Lord Yelden organised his guests into two teams; to Rob's relief, he was teamed with Chadwick and Mr Stretton. As they were to shoot second, Rob and Mr Stretton strolled away from the shooting position, leaving Chadwick to watch.

"Damned waste of time," Mr Stretton muttered, as the first couple of shots sounded.

"I thought you usually spent your time in the library, sir?" Rob said, wishing he'd brought his stick.

"I do. But the house party was my idea, so I should help to entertain the guests. Still, I expect they'll be leaving soon."

"There's an announcement due, then?" Rob asked, a heavy feeling settling in his chest. If Miss Stretton were about to confirm her marriage to Bengrove, he would have to take himself off and try to forget about her.

"No. I'm anticipating that the Bengroves will agree to an amicable end to the arrangement. Publicly, at least." He glanced at Rob. "I hope you and Lieutenant Chadwick will stay a few days longer, though. Young George seems to enjoy your company, and there are one or two other investigations the pair of you may be able to help me with. If you wish to, of course."

Rob hardly heard anything beyond Stretton's first sentence, wondering if his wishes had affected his hearing. "There is to be no wedding?"

"No. Jo has decided against it."

Thank the heavens.

"Ah, my turn." Stretton nodded, and walked back to the shooting line.

But Rob's relief was tempered with caution; the Bengroves still needed money. Would they accept Miss Stretton's refusal without some attempt to make her change her mind?

The question nagged at him as he slowly followed Stretton; something didn't make sense. The only reason he could think of was that Stretton had done something with the marriage settlements to prevent them getting control of the money. Rob was hazy about such things, but an astute investor like Stretton could surely arrange things so Bengrove and the rest of his family couldn't waste Miss Stretton's dowry as they had their own wealth.

Rob closed his eyes, trying to recall that evening in Verdun when Bengrove had been complaining about a possible delay to his marriage. What had he said? Something about taking Miss Stretton to Gretna. And... and having his way with her to force her father to let them marry. Nothing he knew about Bengrove gave him any confidence that Miss Stretton would have had any say in either matter.

Where *was* Bengrove?

He hurried over to where Stretton was preparing to take another shot. "Sir, has Bengrove gone on the picnic with Miss Stretton?"

Stretton lowered the gun, brows rising in surprise. "I believe so. Why?"

"In Verdun, Bengrove was talking... wishing he'd got married before he was sent back to Spain. He said he should have taken her off to Scotland, or seduced her and then you'd have been forced to get a special licence. Moorven warned you, did he not?"

Stretton's eyes widened. "He did, but only in general terms. He said nothing of elopement or seduction—I would have ended things immediately had I known that." He looked towards the carriages, his expression a mixture of anger and anxiety. "George will see she comes to no harm, but I had better return to make sure."

"If Yelden *is* with them." The picnic party hadn't yet set out when Rob left the hall. And the Bengroves had had the best part of yesterday to decide on their next move. Mr Stretton set off towards the vehicles, but Rob thought that by the time he'd got back there and commandeered one, it would be quicker to return to the Court on foot. He set off as fast as his stiff ankle would let him, without waiting to see whether Stretton followed.

⁓

In the parlour, Alfred picked up a folded paper from a table, his expression still hurt. "This document sets out the settlements for our marriage. Do you know what's in it?"

"It doesn't matter, Alfred." She had to tell him now. "We are—"

"It *does* matter." His words were terse—the wheedling tone was fading. "The arrangements your father proposes will not give us enough to live on." He dropped the paper on a nearby chair and came towards her, holding out his hands. "Joanna, my dear, you must persuade your father to change the terms. As it is, it is an insult—no man would agree to it." He smiled, almost managing the charming expression that had fooled her. Now it made her feel queasy, and foolish for ever having succumbed to it.

"Then don't agree!" She ignored his outstretched hands and set off towards the door. "I am late to the picnic. Excuse me."

Alfred was faster, reaching the door before her and closing it. "Damn the picnic! That settlement gives me no money at all."

"We had better not marry, then."

"Not marry! Joanna, my dear, what can you mean?" The inveigling tone was back, but his narrowed eyes belied it. "Don't play games with me, Joanna, please. If you love me, you'll persuade your—"

"I don't," she snapped. "Now get out of my way." She regretted her words as his face reddened and his lips became a thin line. "I do not wish to marry you, Alfred. You should find an heiress with a more persuadable father."

"After all the bloody effort we've put into you?" All pretence was gone now. "No. You'll marry me, and soon, or you'll marry no-one." He pulled a key from his pocket and locked the door, then started towards her, his expression ugly.

Jo's heart began to race, and she backed away. He wasn't just going to wait until they were found together in a locked room; he meant her harm.

She tried one more appeal, even though she knew it would be futile. "Let me out, Alfred, please."

"Oh, no. I'll have you now, and your father *will* pay."

What could she do? A scream might bring the footman in the hall, but would he venture to break the door down without being ordered to? The windows—no, Alfred would catch her before she could open one and shout.

A porcelain vase stood on a nearby table; she flung it at him. It narrowly missed, breaking as it fell to the carpet behind him but not making much noise.

"Bitch!" He came on, seemingly not in a hurry now he had her trapped. She circled around a sofa, praying her legs did not collapse beneath her, but that was little defence. An escritoire stood against the wall. Grabbing the ink bottle, she threw it as Alfred moved towards her; he deflected it with his right hand, wincing, and swore as the top came off and spattered ink on his coat and the carpet.

He moved again, faster this time. Jo tried to scream, but her breath was coming in short gasps and her call wasn't loud enough to be heard beyond the door.

Close enough to grab her now, one hand reached for her hair, but she wrenched herself away. It hurt, but all he gained were a few pins. She fumbled again on the escritoire for something else to use as a weapon.

CHAPTER 28

*R*ob's ankle was on fire by the time he reached the house, but he ignored the pain. A groom stood near the steps holding a horse with a side-saddle on it; Miss Stretton must still be in the house. Was Bengrove here, too?

"Did Captain Bengrove and Miss Stretton go on the picnic?" Rob asked the groom, trying to regain his breath.

"Not that I know of, sir, but…"

The rest of the man's words were lost behind him as Rob ran up the steps and into the open door. "Where is Miss Stretton?" he demanded of the footman on duty.

"Er, in the parlour, sir."

"Alone?"

"Captain Bengrove was with her, sir."

Damn—just what he'd feared. "*Which* parlour?"

The footman pointed to a closed door to one side. Rob hobbled over and tried to open it. As he did, Lady Bengrove and Lady Misterton descended the stairs. "What is happening here? What is all this fuss about?"

"Fetch the key," Rob ordered the footman, ignoring Lady Bengrove. "Now!"

A muffled thump sounded from behind the door, and he forgot the two women. He had to find a way into the room. Getting in through a window was likely to be quicker than attempting to break in through the door.

He hobbled outside as quickly as his ankle would let him, and peered through the window. He couldn't see anyone, but only part of the room was visible. The ground floor of the house was not far above the level of the flowerbeds, but high enough that he couldn't reach the latch.

"Come here," he called to the groom, feeling in his pockets. "Give me a leg up."

The groom cupped his hands with his back against the wall, and Rob stepped up, steadying himself with one hand on the embrasure. The handle of his pocketknife served to break one of the panes, and he reached in to undo the latch. The lack of sound from the room was worrying, but he was nearly inside.

He jumped down. The groom helped him to push the lower sash up as far as it would go, and he swung himself over the windowsill and into the room.

"Captain! Over here."

Miss Stretton's voice, thank God! He stepped into the room to see her in one corner with a poker in her hand. Her hair had come loose, and her face was pale. Bengrove lay unmoving on the floor nearby.

"Are you hurt?"

"No." Her voice wobbled on the word, and she dropped the poker. Rob strode forward and helped her into a chair. "Put your head on your knees if you feel faint."

He waited for her brief nod, then turned back to Bengrove. He wanted to comfort her, but ensuring that her assailant did no further harm was of first importance. Rob rolled him over, noting blood on his temple and a small bronze ornament on the floor nearby. Bengrove groaned, his eyes fluttering.

"I think the key is in his waistcoat pocket," Miss Stretton said. "I didn't want to get too close..." She swallowed hard.

"You did the right thing." Keeping a wary eye on Bengrove, Rob crouched down in front of her. "You're safe now." The urge to take her in his arms was strong, but he resisted.

She nodded, dashing tears from her eyes with a shaking hand.

The door rattled, and someone banged on it. "Open the door, Bengrove!"

"I'd better let them in before they break it down," Rob said, waiting for her to nod before bending to search Bengrove's pockets. "If you move, I'll kill you," he said, quietly enough for only Bengrove to hear him. Bengrove opened his eyes again, but didn't seem able to focus on Rob. He would be no problem for a few moments.

He unlocked the door, and hurried back to Bengrove as George Yelden burst in, followed by Lady Bengrove and her friend and several interested servants. "She's unhurt," Rob said to Yelden. "Get rid of the onlookers, will you? And get a couple of footmen to lock up this piece of scum." He nudged Bengrove with one foot, none too gently.

Yelden ushered the servants out, but Lady Bengrove ignored him and came into the room. Her impression, initially rather smug, changed to consternation as she took in her son lying on the floor.

"Alfred!" She rushed over and knelt on the floor beside him. He groaned again, and Lady Bengrove glared up at Rob. "What have you done to him?"

Jo roused herself at Lady Bengrove's words. Captain Delafield had only just arrived; how could Lady Bengrove think he was responsible?

"Ignore her for now," the captain said quietly. "There'll be time for explanations later. Shall I escort you to your room?"

She saw his gaze move from her face to her hair and then back. "I must look a fright."

"You look…" He broke off and shook his head, an odd expression in his eyes. "Come, before too many interested spectators gather." He offered his arm and she took it, grateful for his assistance. Whatever had given her the strength to throw things at Alfred had deserted her, and her knees nearly gave way when she stood. She swallowed against a feeling of nausea.

"The library, please take me to the library." She wasn't injured; she only needed a few minutes to sit quietly and put herself to rights.

"Are you sure?"

She nodded, hearing the captain send someone for her maid and tell a footman to keep everyone else out, but the voices seemed to come from a long way off. Then a comforting arm went around her waist, and she was held close as he helped her onto the sofa. Gentle pressure on the back of her neck pushed her head down, and she rested it in her hands.

"Just breathe."

She did. Martha arrived, and was sent for tea and biscuits, and when Jo finally raised her head, she found the captain kneeling before her with a glass of wine in one hand.

"No, thank you. The tea will do me more good."

He set the glass on a nearby table and drew up a chair. "Miss Stretton, are you truly unhurt?"

"Truly." She grimaced. "Apart from feeling a complete fool for ever liking him in the first place."

He stood, wincing. "You shouldn't feel that way. You were the subject of a deliberate... campaign, I suppose." His expression held concern, and understanding.

"How did you know? To come back, I mean."

"Your father mentioned that he was expecting Bengrove to agree to breaking your betrothal. I assumed he'd made some watertight financial arrangements that would prevent Bengrove or his family running through your dowry. But from what I overhead Bengrove say in Verdun, it was clear that he'd set out to entice you and would stop at nothing to get his hands on your inheritance. Apart from Chadwick, no-one else here knew Bengrove's true character, and I was afraid he might try something... underhand if he could get you alone. I did warn your father, but I didn't repeat everything Bengrove said. If I had, I suspect he would have shown Bengrove the door before now."

"It is not your fault, Captain. It was unfortunate that Alfred came across me when no-one else was around."

"How came you to be separated from the rest of the picnic party?"

"Catherine Bengrove wanted to see me; she sent a message just as I was setting out."

He frowned. "Mrs Bengrove came to the shooting with her husband and Lord Bengrove."

Jo stared at him. "Her maid came with a message." Which must have been a lie, if Catherine had not even been in the house at the time. "They tricked me!"

"Do not blame yourself, Miss Stretton!" He sounded almost harsh, and she blinked. "I'm sorry. But none of the blame is yours. You could not know what they might do."

"Jo. All my friends call me Jo."

"Jo, then. Will you tell me what happened in the parlour before I arrived? Lady Bengrove is likely to try to absolve her son of any blame."

"He asked to speak to me, so we went into the parlour. He said if he couldn't have me no-one would." She shuddered at the memory. "I hit him with a heavy ornament that was on the escritoire." She thought she'd killed him at first, but when she'd crouched to check, his faint groans and the occasional fluttering of his eyelids had both reassured her and worried her. "I picked up the poker in case he regained consciousness. I was about to call for help when you broke the window."

He smiled, but without real humour, and she thought she detected both sympathy and admiration in his eyes. "You saved yourself, Miss Stretton. Jo."

She shook her head, but Martha hurried in before she could speak, carrying a tray with a pot of tea and a plate with cake and biscuits. She set it on the table beside the sofa. "There's carriages coming up the drive, miss."

Captain Delafield stood and limped over to a window that looked to the front of the house. "The shooting party," he said. "Your father will be wanting to know why I left so precipitously."

Jo put her hand to her hair. Martha pulled a comb from her apron pocket. "Shall I tidy your hair for you, miss?"

"I'll tell your father what happened," the captain said. "That will give you a little time to compose yourself."

"Thank you."

He limped out, and Jo sipped tea while Martha made her look more presentable. She was dismayed to find that her hand shook as she held the cup, but she managed to drink without spilling any, and by the time she had eaten a piece of cake she felt calmer.

George Yelden was in the entrance hall as Rob arrived there, about to go out to meet the carriages. "Is Jo well?" he asked, concern clear in his face and voice.

"She will be," Rob said. "He did no physical harm."

"Thank heavens. I should have waited for her. I would have, if I'd known *he* was still in the house."

"You arrived soon after me—how did you know to come back?"

"I caught up with Mama's carriage, and she said something about Bengrove coming on with his mother. I thought he'd gone with the shooting party."

"It's done now, Yelden. Bengrove was out cold when I arrived; if I hadn't come, you would have taken care of matters."

"Captain!" Stretton hurried up the steps, Lord Bengrove and his elder son not far behind. "What is wrong? Where is Jo?"

"She is well. Shall we go somewhere more private?" Better he recount the tale than make Miss Stretton relive it again by telling her father.

"Breakfast room." Yelden led the way.

Stretton's face paled as Rob summarised what had happened. "She will be well once she has got over her fright," he finished.

"I've sent for Mama and Mrs Stretton to return," Yelden said. "And sent someone for the doctor. Although Bengrove's properly conscious again, with his dear mama pretending to weep over him."

"Pretending?" Rob asked.

"My hearing is better than she thought," Yelden gave a humourless smile. "She told him to agree with what she said, and they might be able to retrieve the situation. It seems the whole family is cut from the same cloth."

"How can they think I would allow my daughter to marry someone who forced himself on her?" Stretton shook his head. "I will go to her now. Captain, I cannot thank you enough for your timely arrival. George, can you see to it that the Bengroves are kept away from Jo—and my wife, when she returns—until we are ready to speak to them? They will not give up easily, I suspect."

"Certainly, Uncle. And, as long as the doctor says it is safe to move Bengrove, the whole family will be leaving as soon as you are finished with them."

When Chadwick arrived back at the house, he and Rob whiled away an hour in the billiards room until the butler came and asked them to join the company in the main parlour. Miss Stretton was sitting on a sofa with her mother; she had changed her gown, and was still pale but looking composed. Mr Stretton stood behind them; he waved Rob and Chadwick towards a couple of nearby chairs. Lord and Lady Yelden and George sat nearby.

"You may summon the Bengroves, Stevenson," Lord Yelden said; the butler bowed and withdrew.

A few minutes later, Lady Bengrove swept into the room, followed by her husband and her younger son. Bengrove's face was pale beneath the bandage wrapped around his head. Playing the wounded hero, Rob thought cynically. Lady Misterton entered behind them.

"There she is." Lady Bengrove pointed an accusatory finger. "The hussy who encouraged my son and then nearly killed him when he wanted nothing more than a kiss from his betrothed!"

Rob got to his feet, not out of respect for the Bengroves, but to remove them from the room if Miss Stretton wished it. Chadwick and Yelden did the same. Rob looked at Miss Stretton, then her father.

"That is a lie," Miss Stretton declared firmly, before her father could speak. "Alfred threatened me when I said I didn't want to marry him. Then he assaulted me."

"A jilt, as well as an encroaching hussy!" Lady Misterton exclaimed.

Rob looked at Mr Stretton again, but he gave a tiny shake of the head. Letting the Bengroves show their hand, Rob guessed.

"I meant you no harm, my dear," Bengrove said, swaying artistically. "I wished only to convince you that we were well suited. But I see how it is." Bengrove looked from Miss Stretton to her cousin. "You prefer to spend your time with Yelden, or these men whom you hardly know." He shot a glance of pure venom at Rob and Chadwick. "Have they sampled your charms as well as—"

Rob started forward, but Yelden beat him to it and slammed a fist into Bengrove's face. He collapsed onto the floor, accompanied by a scream from Lady Bengrove.

"This has gone far enough." Mr Stretton stepped forwards. "Enough, I say!" Lady Bengrove stopped complaining, and Mr Stretton turned to Lord Bengrove. "You and your family have now gone your length, Bengrove. Your son attacked my daughter. There will be no marriage."

"It's more a case of whether my son is prepared to marry your daughter," Lord Bengrove sneered. "Once word spreads about her actions, her reputation will be gone. Who is to say that my son is the first she has been... *alone* with?"

Rob's hands clenched into fists. The father was as vile as his son.

"That won't reflect well on you, either, Stretton," Lord Bengrove went on. "If you refuse to change the settlements to something acceptable to me, your daughter won't be able to show her face in polite society again."

Rob forced himself to stay silent—any intervention on his part now might raise questions that could make Miss Stretton's situation worse. But her cousin took a step forward. "I say, Lord Bengrove, that is—"

"Allow me to deal with this," Mrs Stretton said firmly, to the surprise of both Rob and the Bengroves, from their widened eyes. Mrs Stretton looked at the Bengroves. "You planned this before you arrived, did you not? Hence abusing Lord and Lady Yelden's hospitality by bringing an uninvited guest who is a well-known gossip." She turned her attention to Lady Misterton. "You should think how spreading gossip about your host's family will affect the invitations you receive." She glared at Lady Misterton, who cast her eyes down but made no reply.

"As for your son," she said, turning to Lord Bengrove, "I blame myself for having been taken in by him two years ago, and giving my blessing to his courtship. I was under the mistaken assumption that a connection with the aristocracy would be the best way to ensure my daughter's future happiness. Your family's actions have disabused me of that notion. It would be better for our family to be ostracised than to have your son inflicted on my daughter."

"Well said, Aunt Frances!" Yelden glared at Lord Bengrove. "You are wrong about Jo's marriage prospects. I'd marry her myself if needed to maintain her good name."

No! If she must marry for respectability, let it be me.

Rob just stopped himself speaking. He was relieved to see Miss Stretton frown and give a little shake of her head. "Thank you, George, but that will not be necessary."

"We'll see about that," Lady Bengrove hissed. "I outrank you, Lady Yelden, and you, *Mrs* Stretton. If I say so, the *ton* will readily believe that a cit's daughter toyed with the affections of an honourable man!"

"They will believe the truth," Rob stated. This he *could* say without risking his correspondence with Miss Stretton being discovered. "Your son was extremely disrespectful when speaking about Miss Stretton when we were in Verdun, in private *and* in public. He made it clear that he had courted her only for the money he hoped to gain through the marriage."

Lord Bengrove sneered. "Who will believe a farmer over a viscount?"

"They will believe Viscount Moorven, who also heard him say those things." Most of them, anyway.

"As did a number of other officers," Chadwick put in. "Ones who hardly knew your son, and could not be accused of any bias against him."

"Thank you, Captain. Lieutenant," Mr Stretton said, then addressed Lord Bengrove. "You and I need to have a discussion. One that I think you will not wish to have in front of all these people." His gaze moved to Lady Misterton and back.

"And the rest of you may pack your belongings," Lord Yelden said. "I will order your carriages to be ready in an hour."

"But Alfred isn't—" Lady Bengrove started.

"I neither know nor care about your son's state of health," Lord Yelden interrupted. "He will not die by being taken to the village inn. None of you is welcome in this house at any time."

"Bravo, Papa."

Lord Yelden glared at his son, who merely grinned. Lady Yelden turned to Mrs Stretton. "Come, Frances. And you, Jo. If these people wish to argue, they may do so to an empty room."

Yelden came over to Rob and Chadwick. "Shall we escape to the inn for a while?"

"Sounds like a good plan," Chadwick said. "As long as it's not the one the Bengroves might end up in."

"And if I can go in a carriage," Rob added. A few pints of ale might dull the pain in his leg.

CHAPTER 29

Still feeling shaken, in spite of Mama's routing of the Bengroves, Jo was glad to go to her room with Mama. But to her dismay, Catherine Bengrove was waiting outside her bedroom door.

"What do you want?" Mama snapped as she approached. "Hasn't your family done enough harm?"

Catherine's gaze fell to her clasped hands. "I wanted to apologise. I had no knowledge of what Alfred planned."

"I don't suppose you could have stopped them if you *had* known," Mama said, a little more kindly.

"Bengrove—my husband, I mean—insisted I accompanied him on the shooting party."

"Did your husband also encourage you to befriend me in London?" Jo asked. Catherine must have known the family needed money.

Catherine nodded, miserably. "I did enjoy your company, Miss Stretton. That was not pretence."

That was something, Jo supposed, but wasn't enough to make their friendship survive. "I accept your apology, but you will understand, I hope, that I do not wish our association to continue. Excuse me."

Catherine stood to one side and Jo entered her room. Mama

followed and closed the door as Jo sank into a chair and put her head in her hands. Mama laid a gentle hand on her shoulder.

"It is lowering, I know, to find that someone you thought a friend had an ulterior motive. It may not feel like it at the moment, but you are better off without any of that family. I'm sorry, Jo, that my foolish wishes led us to this."

Jo lifted her head, and grasped her mother's hand. "You certainly gave them a piece of your mind just now!"

"I have to admit that it felt rather good. That such people consider themselves our betters only because your father doesn't have a title..." She shook her head.

"Mama, are you still cross with me about the letters?"

Mama sat down. "I should be, but as your father did not object, and no harm seems to have been done, we will put it behind us."

"And you do not hold it against Captain Delafield that he continued to write to me?" That felt more important than gaining forgiveness for herself.

"He has not taken advantage, has he? He seems a very polite and considerate young man."

Yes, he was. One with a sense of humour, who would listen to her and respect her opinion. Whose smile made her feel warm inside. Who had run to her rescue, in spite of his damaged leg.

"The weather is still fine, Jo. Shall we have the picnic after all?" Mama peered into her face. "We could have the servants bring the food back and picnic in the park. Then we will be out of the house until the Bengroves have gone."

"Yes, let us do that. The children will enjoy it." And now she was free of Alfred she could spend some time trying to work out exactly how well she cared for Captain Delafield. And how much he liked her; she thought—hoped—that he regarded her as more than just a friend.

Rob toyed with his mug of ale as George Yelden quizzed Chadwick about his time in Spain, recalling how Yelden had sprung to the defence of his cousin. Did Yelden think of Miss Stretton as a sister or as something more? He'd been quick enough to offer marriage when confronting Lord Bengrove, and his previous restraint might have been because Miss Stretton was betrothed. A gentleman would not let his own preference show in that case.

That was irrelevant, Rob told himself. Even if Yelden did wish to be more than a cousin to her, Miss Stretton would have to reciprocate his feelings.

He tried to concentrate on what Chadwick was saying, but his thoughts kept returning to Miss Stretton. Jo. The feel of her leaning into him as he helped her into the library, the delicate fragrance of her hair.

Part of him wished that her father were not wealthy, so he could court her without people thinking his motives were mercenary. But he did not wish to deprive her of the advantages that wealth could bring—including, in her case, the interest she took in choosing investments. A man *should* support his wife, and he did not like the idea of living off her wealth. However, being without her was an even less attractive prospect. He could support her in ways beyond the purely financial.

The important thing was that Jo herself did not think that money was his motive for courting her. His friends would not think it, and what other people believed should not be allowed to constrain his future happiness.

Or hers. *If* he were in any way necessary for her happiness.

"Sir?" A man in groom's clothing interrupted his thoughts, but he was addressing Yelden.

"Have they gone, Evans?" Yelden asked.

"Yes, sir. Followed them to the second toll gate. Both carriages."

"Which road?"

"Towards Andover."

"Thank you." Yelden flicked a coin towards the groom, and Evans caught it, touched his cap, and left.

"Good thinking," Rob said. "What's the significance of Andover?"

"If the Bengroves are intent on spreading gossip, I think they would have gone to London. The Andover road means they're probably going back to Staffordshire."

That wouldn't stop them spreading gossip later. And if Alfred Bengrove hadn't been Rob's enemy before, he certainly was now. Although Rob had done little enough, Bengrove could still want revenge for being thwarted.

"Good riddance to the whole family," Chadwick said. He contemplated his empty mug. "Another, or shall we head back now the coast is clear?"

"Back, I think," Yelden decided. "I need some food, and this isn't the best place to get it."

Rob wasn't sorry—the air inside the taproom was thick with pipe smoke and the smell of spilled ale. He limped outside to the gig and Yelden took the reins.

Yelden dropped them off by the front door and drove the gig around to the stables. Chadwick turned to Rob. "Now the Bengroves have gone, I need to go and see my father. I'll take my leave tomorrow. You'll be staying on, though, won't you?"

Rob hesitated. "Does our invitation still stand? You suggested that we were asked to stay on because the Bengroves were here."

"I can't see Yelden asking you to leave," Chadwick said as the butler let them in. "Don't you *want* to stay?"

Of course he did, as long as there was any chance of spending time with Miss Stretton.

"Tell them your ankle is too painful to travel," Chadwick suggested.

"Don't be daft. I'm walking on it, aren't I?"

"A foolish effort to ignore your injury, which will result in a need to rest your foot for the next few days," Chadwick countered, with a grin.

The butler cleared his throat. "Gentlemen, Mr Stretton would like to see you in the library. At your convenience, of course."

Chadwick's hand went to straighten his cravat, and it was Rob's turn to grin. Then he wrinkled his nose—the smell of smoke and ale clung to his coat. "Please let Mr Stretton know we will be with him as soon as we have changed."

Rob had some time to think while he tied a fresh neckcloth and donned his other coat. He wanted nothing more than to court Jo, but was this the time to do it? She had been attacked, and then freed of her betrothal, only this morning. It would be better, perhaps, if she had time to get used to being unattached again before he made any attempt to deepen their relationship.

"Ready?" Chadwick asked, and the two of them descended to the library. Mr Stretton sat in a chair by the window.

"Excellent timing, gentlemen. You have missed the Bengroves departing. Do sit down."

"How can we help you, sir?" Rob asked, when Mr Stretton did not immediately continue.

"It is more the reverse, I'm afraid. After you left us, Captain Bengrove was rather vociferous in his objection to what he called your interference, Captain, although I think he had some ire reserved for you as well, Lieutenant. It is not impossible that he will try to take revenge on one or both of you, but I have done my best to reduce the possibility. However, if any of that family *does* attempt to harm you, in any way, please let me know."

Rob shared a quick glance with Chadwick. "Of course, sir. May we ask what action you have taken?"

Mr Stretton sighed. "Blackmail, I'm afraid. Bengrove—Lord Bengrove, that is—has just discovered that I hold most of the mortgages on his unentailed properties. I informed him that I will foreclose if I find that anything has been said against my family or friends. That includes you."

"Er, thank you, sir."

"In addition, I have useful contacts in the East India Company. Given his financial circumstances, I feel sure Lord Bengrove will readily agree that Captain Bengrove's joining their Bengal Army would be of great benefit to all concerned. That should remove him from the country for several years."

"Poor buggers," Chadwick muttered.

Mr Stretton's lips twitched. "Indeed. Now, I hope you will both stay on for some time? I should say that Lord and Lady Yelden would be delighted for you to do so."

Rob had a moment to think while Chadwick made his excuses, then gave his own. "Thank you for the invitation, sir, but I am not yet sure of my plans."

If he were to absent himself for a while, he should explain his reasons to Jo first.

~

"Thirty hits, that's the best yet!" Jo bent to pick up the shuttlecock, smiling at the flushed faces of the younger Yelden children. "Time to rest in the shade for a while, I think, and have some lemonade." She was as warm as they looked, and a little out of breath.

The children ran off, dropping their battledores. The game had done her good, she reflected as she gathered them up. The exertion of trying to keep the shuttlecock in the air, and the children's chatter, had cleared her mind of this morning's fear and the unpleasant argument afterwards. Now she'd seen the Bengroves' coaches leave, and Papa had told her he would take steps to ensure they made no more trouble, she was beginning to feel that hoped-for freedom. She was beginning to understand what was meant by taking the weight from one's shoulders.

Taking a chair into the shade near the edge of a belt of trees, she sat and sipped her lemonade. In the middle of the lawn, Mama and Aunt Sarah were talking, with Lydia on the grass beside them helping the younger ones to make daisy chains. All calm and peaceful.

A figure came around the corner of the distant house, identifiable only by his limp and stick. Was it telling that she knew, even at this distance, that it was Captain Delafield and not his friend?

But his limp was more pronounced than before; had he damaged his leg further this morning? Papa had said the captain had set off at a run when he'd learned that she might be in danger. Before he got close enough for her manoeuvring to be obvious, Jo brought another chair close to her own.

Unfortunately, the captain's way took him past Mama, who beckoned him towards her. Jo was too distant to hear what was said, but she did detect a fleeting grimace on the captain's face before Mama let him go.

He turned his head in her direction. She gestured towards the empty chair, feeling suddenly shy.

"I think your mother knows about our correspondence," he said as he sat down beside her. "She wishes to talk to me later."

"I told her last night," Jo admitted.

"I hope she was not too displeased."

"She was shocked when I first told her, but Papa's approval and your suggestion about the laudanum helped. After this morning's events, I think I am forgiven."

"That is good. I never intended to land you in trouble."

"I made my own decision," she said, crisply, then wished she could take the words back. To her relief, he was amused rather than offended.

"I know. It is one of the things…" He broke off, then leaned forwards, his smile giving way to concern. "Miss Stretton, are you truly well?"

Very well indeed, sitting here with him. She almost said so, but that would seem too forward. "Will you not use my name, Captain?"

"If you wish. If you will call me Rob."

She nodded.

"But my question still stands… Jo." He frowned. "You are not obliged to answer, of course. But as a friend, I am naturally concerned."

A friend? He was that, of course. But she could still recall the feel of his arm around her this morning, when he had helped her into the library. She had felt safe, protected.

"Yes, I am well. In fact, I feel better now than I have for some time. I have been happier since your suggestion led to Mama's recovery. However, I must have known within myself that marriage to Alfred was not what I really wanted, and it is such a relief to be rid of him. I have not felt so light and free since Mama's illness began. It is unfortunate that it had to happen in such a way, but it is done."

"What will you do now?" He shook his head. "I'm sorry—you will have had no time to think about it."

"I suppose I will go on much as before. There will be a few assemblies in Winchester we might attend while we remain here. Mama has given up the idea of my marrying into the aristocracy, but she still wants me to find a husband."

"I suppose that is the case for most mothers. Or sisters-in-law," he added, with his attractive wry smile. "When I visited my brother, his wife had all but arranged a marriage for me with the daughter of a neighbouring landowner. Your father's invitation to dinner arrived at a most opportune moment."

The irrational stab of jealousy told Jo a great deal about her feelings.

"But it did cut short my visit before I had time to see my sisters, who live near Gloucester, and I have yet to visit my brother in Herefordshire."

That sounded ominous. "Are you planning to visit them soon?"

"I thought to leave tomorrow."

Her reply came out without thought. "Don't go."

CHAPTER 30

"I will stay longer if you wish it." Rob made an effort to keep his tone calm in spite of the hope Jo's words had raised.

Her face reddened, and she looked away, as if embarrassed by what she had said. "I'm sorry. That was rather... abrupt."

"I am yours to command." He gave her a little bow from his chair, hoping she did not think he was making fun of her. His resolve to leave her time to settle to her new circumstances was fast disappearing.

"I... It will be good to have a friend to talk to, without..." She took a deep breath. "Without the vile Alfred and his horrible family around."

"A very mild description."

She smiled at that, but shook her head. "I was such a fool. Before I met Alfred, several young men had courted me, but it was apparent that my chief attraction was Papa's money. I thought Alfred was different, but I was mistaken."

Could she really think she was not attractive in herself? He had never felt such a strong need to reach out and touch someone as he did now—a touch to comfort her. He did, resting his hand on her arm for a brief moment, but they were in full view of the rest of the party and he could do no more. That might be just as well—she had already been mauled once today. "You will find someone who suits you, Jo, and who wants you for your own sake, not your father's money."

He'd meant it as a compliment, but rather than looking pleased she made a brief pout and looked away. Could it be that she was disappointed? That she'd wanted more from him?

Say something now—at least you'll know if it will be possible. And if you make a total fool of yourself, you can leave this evening.

"I suppose I just need to meet more men." She was still not looking at him. "And to know them for long enough to be sure we will suit. Longer than the week I was acquainted with Alfred."

"That sounds sensible." But to hell with sensible—not if it meant she might find someone else. He should wish only for her happiness, he knew, but he wanted to be the one who could provide that.

He drew a deep breath, releasing it slowly. "Jo, would someone you have known for over a year do, even if you have only met him a few times in person?"

She met his gaze, a smile growing, then she looked beyond him. He turned to see Mrs Stretton and Lady Yelden looking in their direction. If this conversation went as he hoped, he didn't wish to be in full view of Jo's relatives.

"Will you walk with me, Jo?" They could be partially out of sight in the dappled shade of the trees without risking impropriety.

She nodded and stood. He offered his arm even though his current halting gait made walking close to her rather awkward, but she didn't seem to mind.

Jo's heart was racing far too fast for the gentle pace of their walk, and didn't ease when they stopped a few yards inside the stand of trees. "Yes." Flustered, she wondered if he would take that as an answer to his last question, not to the *important* one. "Yes, such a man might do. Might do very well indeed."

Rob leaned his stick against a tree and took her hands; neither of them wore gloves, and his skin felt warm on hers. A warmth that spread through her.

"Jo, I do not know what lies in my future, how I will earn a living. But in the few times we have been together since my return I have come to realise that I want you to be part of my life."

Was that a proposal? She looked into his eyes and his expression removed any doubts about his meaning. Her gaze fell to his lips; would he kiss her?

But he did not, to her disappointment. He gave a gentle squeeze to her hands, then released them. "I think it is too soon for you to give me a definite answer. I have had you in my thoughts even before we met in person, but you have only just released yourself from your betrothal. But may I speak to your father? I wish to do this in proper form, and his consent means we can spend more time together until you are sure of your feelings."

"Certainly! I am sure he will allow it." She would not accept 'no' from Papa on this matter.

"Thank you." Simple words, but he put a wealth of feeling in them.

"Shall we walk to the rose garden? There are benches there where we can sit for a while." Nicely out of sight of Mama and away from possible interruptions from the children.

Rob reached for his stick and they walked out onto the sunlit lawn. Jo led the way, and they found a bench in the shade, surrounded by the colours and scents of the blooms. He stretched his bad leg out in front of him, and must have noticed her looking at it. "It will mend, Jo, if I do not walk on it too much for the next few days. I fear I will never show to advantage in a dance, though."

"Do you mind?"

He shrugged, although there was some regret in his voice when he answered. "I was never much of a dancer anyway, so it is but a small loss." He turned his gaze to the rose beds. "This is a lovely place to sit. Peaceful, too. I missed such things in Verdun."

"Are there no gardens there?"

"There were some areas with grass and trees, but it is a walled city, so everything is close together. Madame's house did not have a garden, and there was always noise from the streets. Similar to many English cities, I suppose."

"Would you not want to live in a city, then?" Once the words were out, she wished she had not said them. It reminded her too much of one of her unsatisfactory conversations with Alfred about where they would live.

His smile banished any such thoughts. "I have been sent to various places at His Majesty's whim for more than ten years; it will make a pleasant change to have some choice in the matter. And one can always ride out to the countryside, which was not the case in Verdun. Which do you prefer?"

"Both." That wasn't a very informative answer, but she was distracted; conscious of his closeness, even though they were not touching. "I enjoy the theatre and concerts when we are in Town, and bookshops. I suppose you have not had much opportunity for those things in recent years?"

His lips quirked upwards. "The last play I recall was a production of *Romeo and Juliet*, while we were in winter quarters in Portugal." He half-turned on the bench so he faced her, and smiled in amusement. It deepened the creases at the corners of his eyes. Rich, brown eyes. "With the youngest ensign in the battalion wearing a gown," he went on, "and declaring his love for Romeo in a falsetto squeak."

Jo realised she hadn't heard a word he'd said.

"Is there something on your mind, Jo?" His expression was quizzical.

You.

This would never do. They were spending time together, as he had suggested, but she didn't think he'd wanted her to just gawp at him like some bird-witted ninny. "I... um... have you had any more thoughts about what you want to do? An occupation, I mean." She must make an effort to *listen* this time.

"That would depend on what you decide. And what occupation *you* want if you do accept my hand. What you wish to do with your time, I mean."

She had never thought of it in precisely those terms. Women of her class did not have occupations beyond running a home.

"That is," he went on, looking rather uncertain now, "I assumed you would wish to continue your investment activities. You said you enjoyed seeing if the money invested could help to improve a business."

"Did I? I mean, I *do* enjoy that, but I don't recall saying it."

"It was in one of your early letters."

She shouldn't be surprised that he remembered her words from so long ago; she knew many of his letters by heart. And how refreshing—he didn't intend to merely allow her to continue with her interests, he was encouraging her to do so. She looked away, trying to concentrate on something other than his closeness. "Papa often relies on others to report on his various investments now, particularly since Mama became ill. And even before then, she did not care to travel and Papa did not want to take me without her. I *would* like to visit some of the factories Papa has shares in."

"Or even investigate potentially fraudulent investment proposals yourself?"

Jo glanced at him sharply, wondering if he was mocking her—for not even Papa would have suggested that. But he wasn't—of course he wasn't. He never would. She had long wished to take a more active part in Papa's affairs, and now she would be able to.

Until they had a family… She felt her face flaming as she imagined what would come before that family.

Rob stood abruptly, and reached for his stick. If she were going to look at him in that way, he'd be hard put to keep his hands off her.

"Is something wrong?" she asked.

Far from it—that look had held a great deal of promise for the future. "I think I should see your father, Jo. In case he has any objections."

"I don't think he will." She smiled, with a hint of mischief. "He will have a fight on his hands if he does!"

"Hmm. You could find yourself living in a farmhouse with only enough money for the occasional trip to London."

"It won't come to that. But if it did, I'd soon have the farm running far more efficiently."

"You would indeed!" He bowed and set off for the house before he changed his mind. He looked back as he approached the building; Jo still sat where he had left her, gazing out over the roses. A beautiful scene—because she was part of it.

Mr Stretton was still in the library, sitting in the same chair as he had been earlier—except that now he had a book in his hand and a glass of claret by his side.

"Captain." He inclined his head in greeting, placed a marker in his book, and set it on the table. "Help yourself to a drink—Yelden keeps an excellent cellar."

"No, thank you, sir." He sat down, and wondered where to start. Through the window, the sun brightened the colours of the rose garden.

Ah—Mr Stretton probably already knew what he wanted.

"Have you decided whether you can stay for a while?" Mr Stretton asked.

"That depends on you, sir." His mouth felt dry. Jo's father had allowed her to correspond with him—surely he could have no great objection to his courtship, at least? "I would like your permission to pay my addresses to your daughter."

"It looked to me as if you had already started, Captain." He appeared amused, not disapproving—to Rob's relief, although he didn't think it was a laughing matter.

"I was going to take my leave for a while, to give Jo a chance to forget about this morning's unpleasantness, but she asked me to stay."

"Did she, indeed! Tell me about your financial situation, Captain."

It was better than Bengrove's, but that was little help. "I have some land left to me by my father. A tenant farms it at the moment."

"That does not sound as if it would bring in sufficient income to support a family in the manner to which my daughter is accustomed."

"No, sir, it does not. Nor do I yet have a career that will allow me to do so." He should probably have discussed this with Jo first; but she knew his situation, probably far better than her father did.

"You wish to live on my daughter's dowry, in effect."

Rob kept his resentment concealed. It was a reasonable question, especially from someone who had narrowly escaped becoming the source of funds for the entire Bengrove family. "No, sir, I do not *wish* to. But nor do I wish to deprive Jo—Miss Stretton—of the chance to choose what *she* wishes to do. Whatever settlement you proposed to Bengrove will be perfectly acceptable to me."

Mr Stretton regarded him thoughtfully. "Are you sure you want to marry my daughter, Captain? It is not long since you first met her."

"It is a year since we started to correspond," Rob countered. "*I* am sure. I cannot answer for Jo, which is why I have not asked her to give me an answer now."

Mr Stretton finally nodded. "Very well, Captain, you have my permission to court her. I wish to be sure that she has chosen well before going any further." He smiled. "I am not anticipating that I will refuse, but you will understand my caution, I am sure."

Rob finally relaxed. "Yes, sir."

"Do get yourself a glass of something, Captain. I'm interested to hear more details about how you went about investigating that canal scheme. When I said that you and Lieutenant Chadwick could be useful to me, those were not empty words."

This time Rob accepted the invitation and poured himself a glass of wine. Then he tried to put Jo out of his mind and concentrate on a discussion that might help him to contribute to their future together.

CHAPTER 31

*C*hadwick departed late that afternoon, and Rob didn't see Jo again until the company assembled in the parlour before dinner. When he arrived, she was already deep in conversation with George Yelden. She saw him, and her smile stopped his breath.

"Jo says you're staying on for a while," Yelden said, as he approached. "Pleased to hear it." Yelden inclined his head to where his sister was talking to her young man. "James is no company these days; spends all his time with Lydia."

"Er, George…" Jo started, colour rising to her cheeks. Rob hoped he wasn't going red himself.

Yelden looked from Jo to Rob and back again, and rolled his eyes. "Don't tell me you two are going to do the same?"

"Possibly," Rob said. Certainly, if he had his way.

A broad grin spread over Yelden's face. "Really? That's excellent news."

"Thank you."

"Come for a ride tomorrow, Delafield?"

"Willingly. *If* Jo is also invited and you talk about something other than farming!"

Yelden laughed. "Very well, I promise."

Lady Yelden approached. "Dinner is ready, everyone. Captain, you will sit by me, if you please. George, you may take your cousin in."

Jo gave a rueful smile as Rob offered his arm to Lady Yelden, but he didn't mind being separated from Jo. Not too much. There would be time enough later this evening, and in the coming days, for them to be together.

"Now, young man," Lady Yelden said, once plates were full and conversation started properly. "I think it's time I learned more about the guest Stretton has foisted on me." The smile in her eyes belied her words and Rob resigned himself to providing the basic details of his life. No doubt he would have to do the same with Mrs Stretton at some point.

In spite of what felt, at times, like an interrogation, Rob enjoyed the meal. With the Bengroves gone, there were no tense undercurrents or snide remarks. Apart from the grandeur of the surroundings, it reminded him of family dinners at his brother's house—people were easy in each other's company talking about the inconsequential matters of daily life with smiles and laughter.

"Well, Jo, you seem to have attracted a very pleasant young man," Aunt Sarah said, when the ladies retired to the parlour.

"I'm glad you think so," Jo said, feeling her face get hot—again. She hadn't said anything to her aunt, but before dinner she had opened her heart to Mama, who might have dropped a hint. Or Aunt Sarah had noticed her setting off for the rose garden with Rob this afternoon and drawn the obvious conclusion. "Thank you for allowing him to stay. I should take some time to make sure of my feelings." She *was* sure, but she could not say so without explaining about the letters.

Aunt Sarah nodded, then she and Mama began to discuss plans for the coming days until the gentlemen joined them. George sat down with Mama and his parents for a game of whist, while Papa, as was often the case, opened a book. His brief look in Jo's direction made her suspect he'd deliberately left only Rob to talk to her.

"Would you like to choose a book?" Jo asked, looking at James and

Lydia with their heads together over yet another illustrated volume. "I can show you the most interesting ones in the library."

"That would be helpful, thank you." He followed her to the library and left the door ajar behind them, as propriety demanded. "Shall we investigate the principles of navigation? Or steam engines, perhaps."

For a moment she thought he was serious, but she caught the quirk of his lips and the creases beside his eyes. "That wasn't what I had in mind."

He looked puzzled, but followed her to a corner of the room out of sight of the doorway. "Farming?"

She took a step towards him, standing close but not quite touching. "I wasn't thinking of looking at books at all."

"Ah." He put up one hand to tuck a curl behind her ear. "Something like this?"

"Yes." Her voice sounded breathy, strange to her ears.

"Are you sure, Jo?"

She stepped closer still, lifting her face to his and resting one hand on his chest. That touch did strange things to her insides, even through all the layers of his clothing. "I have to find out at some point what a kiss is like."

His muscles tensed beneath her hand. "You've never been kissed?"

She shook her head.

"I can't say I'm sorry—but Bengrove is even more of a fool than I thought him."

"Forget about him, Rob. Please."

"Your wish is my command." The words sounded flippant, but his tone was not. He drew her even closer with one hand in the small of her back, and her arms crept around his waist as his other hand cupped the back of her head. His lips were soft on hers at first, then firmer, and her mouth opened as her breaths became shorter. Then something else—his tongue? Then surprise turned to not thinking at all as he deepened the kiss and there were only feelings.

. . .

Rob pulled back before he got carried away, moving only a little way so she remained in the circle of his arms. Even in the dim light, he could see the blush on her cheeks and her happy smile.

"That was lovely," she said. "Can we do it again?"

Her eagerness almost tempted him to do so, but caution won. "I would certainly like to, but we have been absent from the parlour long enough."

She sighed, but had to agree. "I don't think Uncle Henry *has* any books on steam engines, but there is one somewhere with drawings of scenery. Shall we find some places that interest both of us?"

Which they would see together? He certainly hoped so, but it was still too soon to presume that his suit would be accepted, no matter how promising her words and actions felt.

"By all means."

So they returned to the parlour and sat close together, poring over the book—to a shake of the head from Yelden, and a knowing smile from Jo's father.

Yelden Court, five weeks later

Jo stood at her bedroom window, ready for the short journey to the village church. Not even the grey clouds and drizzle could dampen her mood; today, she and Rob would finally be together properly. She and Rob had spent a lot of time just walking and talking together, but also with her parents and the Yeldens. It felt to her as though he had already become part of her family, and today he really would be.

During that time, Rob had left for a week to visit his family. If any confirmation of her wish to marry him had been needed, the way she missed him during his absence and the joy at his return would have given it.

And now the place was full of his family, too. All six of his brothers and sisters were here, most with their spouses and children. With a last, happy smile at how different the atmosphere was from when the

Bengrove family had been here, she put them out of her mind. She need think about the Bengroves no longer.

Or not much longer. There was a knock on the door and Papa entered, an opened letter in one hand. "You look lovely, Jo. Are you ready?"

"Yes, Papa." Then asked, in sudden anxiety, "Is something wrong?"

"Quite the opposite." He waved the letter. "This is from the man I sent to Portsmouth. Bengrove sailed for Calcutta last week."

"That's good."

"Indeed—we can forget about the Bengroves now. Are you ready?"

Jo nodded, and picked up the posy of red, pink, and white roses, and Papa gave her his arm to escort her to the waiting carriage. Footmen with umbrellas awaited them at the lych gate for the short distance to the shelter of the porch, where Lydia and Rob's oldest niece, Eliza, straightened her gown. The two girls fell in behind Jo as she took Papa's arm for her last walk as a single woman.

"She's not coming," Chadwick said into Rob's ear, as they waited by the altar rail. Neither he nor Moorven would give way to the other, and as a result Rob had both his friends as groomsmen.

"Don't be an ass, John," Moorven said. "If she'd wanted to escape, she could have done it long ago."

"You do know what to do tonight, don't you, Rob?" Chadwick asked, then chuckled as Rob shook his head. "Better annoyed with me than nervous, eh?"

He might have a point, Rob thought. When he'd first contemplated marrying Jo, he'd pictured a quiet ceremony with only her parents and a few members of his family present, not the whole Yelden clan and *all* his brothers and sisters. Not to mention several of the servants from the house and a few curious villagers who had crept in at the back.

"I'll withdraw my invitation, John, if you can't behave," Moorven threatened.

Chadwick laughed. "And miss the chance of another grand house party? Not a chance. Ironic, though, don't you think?"

"What is?" Rob had to ask, when Chadwick didn't explain.

"Why, Mrs Stretton wanting her daughter to marry Bengrove so she could mingle with the nobs."

Moorven rolled his eyes.

"Yet here she is," Chadwick went on, "marrying a mere farm boy, and she promptly gets invited to Moorven's future seat. A much nicer set of nobs, I hope," he added, glancing sideways at Moorven.

"Most of them," Moorven said, turning his head at a sound from the door. "Your doom approaches, Rob."

"You're as bad as Chadwick," Rob said, then forgot his friends' teasing as Jo walked towards him on her father's arm. She was beautiful, as always, not only because of the tiny rosebuds in her hair or the rich burgundy gown that showed her figure to advantage, but because of the look in her eyes and her lovely smile.

Now there was the service to attend to and the wedding breakfast back at the Court, then the journey to a comfortable inn near Salisbury where they would spend their first night on the way to see the cliffs and moors of Cornwall.

The glance they shared as she came to a halt beside him promised much for tonight.

"Dearly beloved…"

EPILOGUE

*E*dinburgh, *four years later*

     The address was on the edge of Edinburgh's Old Town. From what Jo had seen of the city so far, it wasn't the worst of areas, but not the best, either. Rob helped her out of the hackney, and they mounted the steps to the door. The several brass nameplates indicated that the premises were shared by a number of medical practitioners and men of law, with Mr Campbell's name among them. Jo felt the usual tension inside her before meeting a new business acquaintance —even though this wasn't really a business meeting.

A youth of no more than fifteen let them in. "Second door on the right on the next floor," he said in response to Rob's query, in a strong accent that Jo struggled to understand. Campbell's door was opened by the man himself, and he stood back to allow them to enter.

"Welcome, laddie! And Mrs Delafield." He made his bow, then closed the door behind them. The small anteroom was sparsely furnished and the floor bare, but the chairs looked comfortable, and a table held a few books and periodicals. "Come on through to my office. Shall I send for tea? Coffee?"

"Tea, if you please," Jo said. She'd known she was expecting their third child when the smell of coffee started to make her feel nauseous again; she still had five months to go, but this would be her last business trip for some time. Campbell went to the door and called down to the lad on duty below, then ushered them into his office. This room was more spacious, with several chairs and a desk in one corner. A screen concealed what Jo assumed was an examination couch at one side.

"You appear to have thrived since we were released from Verdun, Captain. How is the leg?"

"It's plain 'mister' now. And the leg is as mended as it will ever be, I think. It's good for most things, as long as I don't overuse it."

"Verra good." Campbell turned his gaze to Jo and gave an unexpectedly charming smile. "I see Delafield has done well for himself. Now, how can I help? You said you had a proposition."

"We do," Rob said. "But first, my wife will tell you a story. Jo?"

A clattering on the stairs announced the arrival of the tea tray, so Jo collected her thoughts while the maid served them.

"A few years ago, my mother miscarried..." She outlined Mama's gradual decline, and how it had been reversed, including an admission of her improper correspondence with Rob before they met. Campbell's eyebrows rose a little at that, but he made no comment. "I did not witness the period when Mama was first trying to reduce her dependency," Jo finished. "However, I believe it was a most unpleasant, not to say painful, experience for both her and my father supporting her."

"It usually is, unfortunately." Campbell nodded. "Your mother is to be congratulated on her determination to remain free of it."

"She did have one lapse," Jo admitted. "She worried a great deal when I was about to be delivered of my first child, and resorted to her tonic for a while. I don't know what would have happened had I or the baby not come through in full health, but we did, which helped her to reduce her use of laudanum to negligible amounts again."

"That is more than many achieve," Campbell said.

"So I understand. Mr Campbell, I am interested in discovering if there are ways of reducing opium use that cause less distress than my mother suffered." Jo picked up her cup of tea and sipped it.

Campbell frowned slightly. "In case your mother lapses again?"

"That is not my main motive." Jo paused as Campbell looked from her to Rob, but Rob just made his usual 'carry on' gesture to her. "Such knowledge would be useful should that situation recur, but there is another, more significant reason. You told my husband that many military men find themselves in similar straits due to battle injuries. We have asked several medical men to take part in our investigations."

"Experimenting on patients?" Campbell's brows rose.

"No." Jo wasn't surprised at his reaction; he wasn't the first who had responded in that way. "Merely keeping detailed notes of those you help in this way, and sharing methods and knowledge with others helping with the project. We have approached a number of physicians in places such as Bath and other spa towns, but their patients are often elderly, and many suffer from other complaints that are likely to complicate any conclusions. We wondered if your practice might include more former soldiers."

He shook his head. "Some, but no more than can be found in any physician's practice. And I am a surgeon, not a physician."

"You are likely to see patients suffering from pain, though, are you not?"

Campbell nodded.

"We are not referring only to officers, but to any former military men—or others, come to that—using laudanum to deal with the pain of injuries. Including those who would not normally be able to pay for treatment."

Campbell's brows rose. "Are you proposing to invest money in the study you describe?"

"Indeed we are. Writing detailed reports and posting them will take time that you would otherwise be using to see patients. You deserve recompense for that, and for seeing patients who cannot pay. I will do the initial collation of findings, and in due course we hope to invite all the participants in the study to meet and discuss their methods and conclusions."

Jo watched Dr Campbell's face as she spoke. One physician they had approached had objected that it would take a man to make sense of such varied data; they had left when he refused to even consider revising his opinion. Campbell merely looked thoughtful, then nodded. Good.

Rob placed a folder of papers on Campbell's desk. "If you think you might be interested, there are more details in there for you to peruse at your leisure. And we would like to invite you to dine with us this evening at our hotel, whether or not you wish to participate."

"And Mrs Campbell, of course," Jo added.

"Thank you, Mrs Delafield, I will be happy to discuss this further this evening. But I am not married."

"I can recommend the state, Campbell," Rob said, as the two men shook hands.

"That went well," Rob said as they stepped out onto the steep street and he gave Jo his arm. He looked in concern as she stretched her back. "Shall I find a hackney?"

"No, thank you. The walk will do me good." She took a few deep breaths, and Rob could see her gradually relax. Since their marriage, Rob had undertaken several investment investigations for Mr Stretton—sometimes alone, more often with Jo. When he and Jo first started seeing investors and factory managers together, she had often been subjected to dismissive comments on her business knowledge purely because she was female. Even when her contributions to a discussion were accepted, too many of the men had an unfortunate tendency to address their responses to Rob. That had happened less often recently, but he knew that the prospect of encountering such attitudes still made her uncomfortable before meeting new business acquaintances.

"We can look into some shops on the way," Jo added. "I'd like to buy Martha and Betty something for looking after the children so well."

"They deserve it," Rob said, resolving to give them some money as well when they reached home again. And some extra time off. "I know we miss the children terribly when we are away, but I cannot say bringing them with us this time has been a complete success, either." Although they hadn't had much choice—after living in a rented town-house in London for several years, they had finally decided to buy a house just outside Town, in a village not far from the turnpike to Winchester. They had moved in before discovering exactly how much work was needed to bring it into good repair, and as a result the house was currently full of builders and decorators.

She sighed, but didn't disagree. "Poor Martha didn't expect to have to help Betty with the children as well as attending me. We have achieved a great deal, though."

They had: visiting the Yorkshire woollen mills and a coal mine in Durham that he and Jo had chosen to invest in, using some of the money her father had given to them on their marriage. They were proving to have been good choices. Then they had travelled on across the border to Edinburgh to see Campbell.

"We must come to Scotland again when the children are older," she went on. "I'd love to see the Highlands."

"You've been reading too many novels by that Scott fellow," Rob accused with a laugh. "But we could return home by way of the Lake District, if you wish? It might take a little longer overall, but we could stay somewhere for a few days for a proper rest."

"That would be lovely!" She leaned into him for a few steps in thanks.

"Are you sure you want to look for gifts today?" he asked. "I think you should rest before Campbell comes."

"Just rest?" She fluttered her eyelashes at him, and he laughed.

"Yes, just rest. This time." He would lie beside her with a book, enjoying their closeness. The project they had asked Campbell to join was one close to her heart, and he hoped they could discuss details when Campbell joined them for dinner. It would take them two or three days to get to Cumberland, where they would have time to spend long, leisurely hours in bed. And again when they finally reached their newly refurbished home, and in the years to come.

HISTORICAL NOTES

PRISONERS OF WAR

During the Napoleonic Wars, prisoners of the officer class were treated very differently than they were during the two World Wars of the last century.

Some captives were exchanged after a battle, mostly because guarding, feeding, and housing prisoners took resources that both armies would prefer to use for their own men. The British were willing to exchange prisoners even after they had been taken to Britain, as had been the case throughout the previous century, but negotiations on an exchange mechanism failed repeatedly. One reason for this was that there were nearly three times as many French prisoners held in Britain as there were British prisoners in France.

Captured officers gave their parole (in this sense, parole means they gave their word that they would not try to escape). They were then sent to one of a number of parole towns where they lived as ordinary citizens, except that they were not allowed to go more than a certain distance from the town. The details of the parole conditions were different in France and Britain, but the principles were the same. The other ranks were not treated so well, living in prison camps or prison hulks (the hulls of retired ships moored in rivers, usually over-crowded and insanitary).

The extract below is taken from *The Depot for Prisoners of War at Norman Cross, Huntingdonshire,* by Thomas James Walker (available via gutenberg.org). Norman Cross was used to incarcerate other ranks, but the book includes a chapter on officers, and also discusses the experience of British POWs in France. This quotes part of a letter from a Lieutenant Tucker, about his time in Verdun.

Lieutenants were allowed 56 francs a month from the French Government, which just paid their lodging. No cause to complain of indulgence, allowed to walk or ride 6 miles in every direction, provided they were in before the shutting of the town gates at 9 o'clock at night. Captains were obliged to sign their names every 5 days, Lieutenants once a day, all other prisoners twice a day. No other restrictions, could lodge where they pleased, and as they liked. There was a first class of society, very good, but very extravagant; they are chiefly people of fortune, who were detained when travelling at the commencement of the war. [...]

There were 2 clubs, where there were all the French, and sometimes the English newspapers: in short, if a prisoner has health, he may spend his time pleasantly enough.

There is no society between the English and French; the latter are a few Military, and tradesmen, who had made their fortunes by the extravagance of Englishmen since the war.

Prisoners were released when Napoleon abdicated in 1814. Some had been held since the resumption of hostilities after the Peace of Amiens broke down in 1803, and included civilians who had been travelling in France at the time (as referred to in the extract).

BANKING

Many POWs received money from home during their incarceration, via connections between banking houses in Britain, France, and Holland. These connections were not strictly legal, but tolerated as long as only private money between civilians was being transferred.

Having the banks transfer books and other documents is an invention on my part, but may have been possible.

THE WAR

Coalitions

The war was not a simple matter of Britain against France, but was a shifting sequence of different alliances. The countries opposing the French and their allies formed a series of Coalitions (seven in all). Britain was the only country involved in all of them. Each Coalition ended when one or more of the participants signed peace treaties with France, and a new Coalition was negotiated and agreed when a treaty was broken.

Trenches

Mr Stretton mentions Chadwick's experience of digging trenches. The Napoleonic Wars did not have static lines of defence protected by trenches as during WW1. However, short systems of trenches were dug to get men to and from artillery positions when a fortified town was besieged.

BOOKS

The Steam Engine by Thomas Tredgold (referred to in Chapter 11) is a real book, but was not published until 1827, so I have taken a liberty with the date there. The *Philosophical Transactions of the Royal Society of London* is the oldest and longest-running scientific journal, and the volume published at the beginning of 1813 (Volume 103) did have articles on new detonating compounds and air pumps.

ROYAL ACADEMY

The exhibition in 1814 *did* have a painting depicting the 'Storming of San Sebastian' by Denis Dighton. You can find the image in the Wikipedia article about the siege. Today the exhibitions are usually in June and July; I cannot find the dates for the 1814 exhibition, but I have taken the liberty of having it end in late May to suit my story.

TRAP SHOOTING

Rob briefly attends a trap-shooting session near the end of the book. Trap shooting allowed for competition, as a consistent supply of flying objects could be produced. Pigeons (or birds such as starlings for the lower classes) were captured and put into small boxes with lids that could be lifted by strings when a shooter was ready to fire. This sport changed to clay target shooting in the early 20th century.

INDUSTRIALISATION

Luddites

The Luddites were a group of textile workers protesting against the introduction of new machinery that resulted in lower wages. Some protests involved destroying the new machinery (hence 'machine-breaking'). The movement lasted from 1811 to about 1816, in parts of the midlands, the north-west, and Yorkshire.

Canals

The 'Golden Age' of building canals in Britain was from the 1770s to the 1830s. Use of the canal network began to decline in the 1840s with the development of the railways.

An Act of Parliament was needed to authorise the construction of a canal. Proposals for canals were put forward both by investors (who would use tolls from the canals as a source of income) and by industrial companies who wanted the canal to move their goods.

FROM THE AUTHOR

Thank you for reading *An Improper Correspondence.* I hope you enjoyed it. If you can spare a few minutes, could you leave a review on Amazon or Goodreads? You only need to write a few words.

My website has more details about my other stories.

www.jaynedavisromance.co.uk

If you want news of special offers or new releases, join my mailing list via the contact page on my website. I won't bombard you with emails, I promise! Alternatively, follow me on Facebook - links are on my website.

ABOUT THE AUTHOR

I wanted to be a writer when I was in my teens, hooked on Jane Austen and Georgette Heyer (and lots of other authors). Real life intervened, and I had several careers, including as a non-fiction author under another name. That wasn't *quite* the writing career I had in mind!

Now I am lucky enough to be able to spend most of my time writing, when I'm not out walking, cycling, or enjoying my garden.

BY THE SAME AUTHOR

THE MARSTONE SERIES

A duelling viscount, a courageous poor relation and an overbearing lord—just a few of the characters you will meet in The Marstone Series. From windswept Devonshire, to Georgian London and revolutionary France, true love is always on the horizon and shady dealings often afoot.

The series is named after Will, who eventually becomes the 9th Earl of Marstone. He appears in all the stories, although often in a minor role.

Each book can be read as a standalone story, but readers of the series will enjoy meeting characters from previous books.

They are all available on Kindle (including Kindle Unlimited) and in paperback. The four full-length novels are also available as an ebook box set.

A duel. An ultimatum. An arranged marriage.

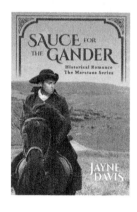

England, 1777

Will, Viscount Wingrave, whiles away his time gambling and bedding married women, thwarted in his wish to serve his country by his controlling father. News that his errant son has fought a duel with a jealous husband is the last straw for the Earl of Marstone. He decrees that Will must marry. The earl's eye lights upon Connie Charters, daughter of a poor but socially ambitious father.

Connie wants a husband who will love and respect her, not a womaniser and a gambler. When her conniving father forces the match, she has no choice but to agree.

Will and Connie meet for the first time at the altar. As they settle into their new home on the wild coast of Devonshire, the young couple find they have more in common than they thought. But there are dangerous secrets that threaten both them and the nation.

Can Will and Connie overcome the dark forces that conspire against them and find happiness together?

Printed in Great Britain
by Amazon